GIVE MY LOVE TO THE SAVAGES

GIVE MY LOVE TO THE SAVAGES

STORIES

CHRIS STUCK

AMISTAD
— 35 —

An Imprint of HarperCollinsPublishers

GIVE MY LOVE TO THE SAVAGES. Copyright © 2021 by Chris Stuck. All rights reserved. Printed in the United States of America. No part of this book may be used or reproduced in any manner whatsoever without written permission except in the case of brief quotations embodied in critical articles and reviews. For information, address HarperCollins Publishers, 195 Broadway, New York, NY 10007.

HarperCollins books may be purchased for educational, business, or sales promotional use. For information, please email the Special Markets Department at SPsales@harpercollins.com.

FIRST EDITION

Designed by Nancy Singer

Library of Congress Cataloging-in-Publication Data is available upon request.

ISBN 978-0-06-302997-2

21 22 23 24 25   LSC   10 9 8 7 6 5 4 3 2 1

For Doris, Jerry, and Lisa

A man does not run among
thorns for no reason;
either he is chasing a snake
or a snake is chasing him.

—*African proverb*

CONTENTS

EVERY TIME
THEY CALL
YOU NIGGER

It happens first in kindergarten. You're five. You and your classmates are playing soccer against the first graders. This is at Saint James Catholic School in Falls Church, Virginia, a school your parents will soon decide is too goddamn expensive. In a year, they will send you to public school, where you will hear the word more often. But this is before all that.

You're on a hot blacktop, in a roiling sea of kids. It seems like there are ten games going at once, multiple balls, multiple goals. You've been alive for only five years. You don't know how the game works. So, you stand near the goal like everyone else. The ball happens to come your way. You try to kick it. You actually connect! And, your luck, the ball gets by the redheaded first grader in goal. Everyone goes crazy except him. He looks back at you with fire in his freckled face. He calls you the word just once. Nigger.

You've never heard it before. The venom in his voice tells you it isn't good. Your friend Jerry jumps on the redhead and drags him to the ground. Jerry is way darker than you and knows the meaning of the word, even at five. The back of the kid's head hits the pavement, sounding like someone cracking open a coconut. There's blood everywhere. Kids scatter. The redhead gets led away by a team of nuns, his white dress shirt now wet and bright red. Everyone watches him leave, before going back to their games. When things settle down, you move away from the goal. You aren't stupid. You let yourself get swallowed by that sea of kids so no one else can call you any other new names.

* * *

The year is 1980, and you're what's called mixed. From that day in kindergarten on, though, the world considers you Black. Not quite all the way Black but Black, Black enough to be called nigger. You even look Black or mixed or like you've got some Black in you. This is what people tell you without you asking. If your mother's Black, they say, you're Black. That's the rule. So, all your bases are covered. You're fucking Black. Your father is white, of German and Irish descent. Your last name in German means "piece." You're a piece of this and a piece of that. You wouldn't want to be anything else.

In your house, the word "nigger" exists but mostly in the abstract. Your three older half brothers from your mother's first marriage, whose father is Black and whom you grow up with, may occasionally say it when your mother isn't around. She doesn't approve of the word. She's lived through segregation. She's been bussed. The word is ugly to her, but at family reunions she still laughs with all her siblings and cousins as they call each other the word as a punch line, with love and affection. You see the word transform from slimy larva into a nimble butterfly. You watch it take flight.

* * *

The second time, one of your white friends says it. Looking back, it's not unexpected. You're in fifth grade and are playing tackle, a form of tag in which you and a gang of your friends tackle the shit out of whoever is holding the football. The game was once called smear the queer, but your PE teacher says you shouldn't call it that anymore. Words and their context haven't quite jelled in your heads yet. You call the game smear the queer anyway when your teacher isn't around.

In the heat of play, you tackle your friend a bit too hard and knock the wind out of him. He's gasping for air. As you get up, he wheezes, "Get off, you fucking nigger." You remember Jerry. You're supposed to do something when a white person calls you this. Naturally, the punches fly. There are bloody lips.

This is in the suburbs, so of course both your parents are called. There's a big meeting with the administration. Your white friend apologizes. He admits that he doesn't know why he used it. He says he's never even thought the word. It just came out. You and your other friends know your white friend's mother is dying of cancer, and his father isn't around. He has a way worse home life than you and your friends of color do. You all still keep hanging out with him, but you never really forgive him. Eventually, his mother dies, and your friend, whose name you'll one day forget, moves away. The only thing you will remember is getting up after your fight, when the two of you are pulled apart. You can see the recognition on your Black and Hispanic friends' faces, even your Arab and Asian friends. They help you up. They take you away. They nurse your wound.

*   *   *

By junior high, you realize the word actually belongs to you. You can say it. Other people can't. But you and your friends don't call each other the word. This isn't the ghetto. Your parents are successful. But you could say it if you wanted. You realize you don't quite understand it, though. It's better to just not say it in public at all. You've said it in the mirror, trying to sound like Richard Pryor or one of your uncles, but you've never had the right cadence. You sound like a child. Maybe you haven't earned it yet.

When a Black kid named Deron moves to your school from Southeast DC, he calls you and your buddies the word in order to make friends. "What's up with y'all niggas? Can I hang with y'all niggas?" He thinks you're just like him. You all feel Blacker, especially your dark-skinned friends who have never seen Southeast like you have, who don't have family there. None of you say the word back to him, and eventually Deron just stops on his own. When you ask him why, he says it's because you and your friends always look at him funny when he says it. So, he just starts calling everyone "bro." It's a good work-around.

"The suburbs," he says. "It's different out here, bro."

*   *   *

At some point, you realize white people know not to use the word now, which is surprising. You have a yearlong grace period when it's not part of your lexicon. All through eighth grade, you're a regular kid. You know it's the fear of an ass-whipping or just looking like a racist asshole that keeps white people in check. But they still find ways to slip up.

In ninth grade, you date a new girl at school named Janelle. She's white and country, horny as all get-out, a little sprite who'll eventually become what your mother calls "fast." She's your first kiss. Your first feel. She teaches you how to navigate her body. It's love at first touch. But then she tells you about life in the country. You can tell she's said the word before. You are in the woods behind your house, smoking a joint of what your friend's older brother said was a twenty sack of Super Killer Skunk but what you will later find out is just oregano. She says her father, a drunk back in the country, often uses the word. Her grand-father, too. She says back home, where the Black people live is called Niggertown. She says her grandmother calls brazil nuts "nigger toes" because they're dark on one side, light on the other. Her uncles, religious folk, often say "mothernigger" instead of "motherfucker." Better to be racist than to curse under God's eyes. She thinks this is kind of funny, the absurdity of it. Who would ever think to combine the word "mother" with "nigger"? She kisses your neck. You agree. You think you're stoned. You think about how all these words are swirling around you, from centuries back, their meanings trailing behind them.

But this is as far as it goes with Janelle. She gets into hard rock music, which you don't understand, but whatever. She still likes to kiss your neck. One day, while you aren't around, she walks down the school hall singing a Guns N' Roses song that says something about "police and niggers" and "immigrants and faggots." This is just as she walks past your queer Black cousin Vanessa, who gladly kicks her ass up and down the hall. That's the end of Janelle. You break up. She moves back to the country. You later hear that she's gotten pregnant at sixteen by some other Black guy. Is he mixed like you? Is he from Niggertown? You and your friends think her pregnancy is sad but sort of funny. You guys wonder what'll happen to that baby. You no longer smoke oregano. You've stepped up to Mexican brick weed that you buy from a senior named Black Dave. You're stoned out of your mind. You start to think, If Janelle is white, does that make her kid white, too?

"Yep," one of your friends says. "The only cracker kid in Niggertown."

Y'all die laughing.

* * *

The word starts coming at you in a variety of ways. For example: hip-hop. Thanks to your older brothers, you've always been into it. Sometimes, when you were a kid, tapes from the early shows floated down to Virginia from New York City. Your brothers listened to them constantly. The Fantastic Romantic 5. The Cold Crush Brothers. The Funky 4+1. The Treacherous Three. Busy Bee versus Kool Moe Dee. Then the movies started coming out and the break dancing movement blew up. Run-DMC ruled MTV. Kurtis Blow advertised for Sprite. But the word didn't figure during these years, not until high school, the early nineties, the golden era.

Just as you stumble into young adulthood, the music starts getting grimy. Every emcee says the word with love and hate. I love my niggas. Fuck you, nigga. You're called the word by cassette tapes and CDs many times over. There's no way to really track it. Millions and billions of times. Nigga. Nigguh. Nicca. Nucca. You love it, but you still don't say it. It's your language, but it's also taboo, for the uneducated. That's the feeling. You and your friends listen to the Geto Boys and NWA, but you know you're not growing up in the same environment that the rappers did. Still, y'all bump that *Niggaz4Life* album, whose title had to be reversed to avoid being censored. It's called *Efil4Zaggin* now. That makes it even better. It's a code that only you and your friends understand. Your parents have no idea what you're talking about anymore, but they look at you suspiciously. They know y'all are up to something.

* * *

Your high school years ramble along. Because you can say a certain word, you and your boys think you have something up on whitey and your teachers. You research all the derogatory names for white people, finding out there are more for you than for them. There's ofay, cracker, peckerwood, blue-eyed devil, but that's it. You can't really use those. They don't have power, and they're old, from your parents' generation. You're Black, and though all your teachers are white, you know if you insult them, the only thing they can come back with is a word they can't say. Or a suspension. It's not much, but it's something. You're becoming a bit of a hardhead now.

You're starting to read your father's books from the sixties and seventies. *Soul on Ice*; *Another Country*; *The Life and Loves of Mr. Jiveass Nigger*; *Die Nigger Die!*; *Nigger: An Autobiography* by Dick Gregory. Your father was a hippie and has all kinds of books. So does your mother. You're reading her Toni Morrison, Alice Walker, Gayl Jones, Buchi Emecheta, and J. California Cooper. You don't understand all of it, but you're absorbing what you can.

Malcolm X directed by Spike Lee has just come out, and you and your boys see it seven times. Coincidentally, you're doing well in school now. Maybe you're smart or maybe your brain is finally working the way it's supposed to. You still get high, but defiance is your new buzz. You're nursing a mild addiction to porn, Black porn. When you understand the notion of exploitation, you stop cold turkey. You're horny as fuck, but you become righteous. Your favorite part of *Malcolm X* is after he's ousted from the Nation of Islam, when he laments that it was the best organization Black people ever had, but niggas ruined it. You like this because you now know the difference between Black people and niggas, the difference between niggers and niggas. You think you're a Jedi in understanding the code. Though you walk through the valley of the shadow of race, you will fear no evil.

Still, you keep a mental Rolodex of when the word is used against you. When those white kids from a less diverse school happen to see you rolling in the black Jetta that you bought yourself, tinted up yourself, bolted new rims on all by yourself, after saving for three of the most boring summers ever, those dumbass white kids shout the word at you. Because they're in eleventh grade and still riding the school bus. Because you have one of your cute Black cousins with you, who they probably think is your girlfriend. Because you have a curly high-top fade like one of your favorite rappers, Special Ed, with your name razored into the back and lines in your eyebrows like one of your other favorite rappers, Big Daddy Kane. You even wear a fat dookie rope that's way out of style and fake as fuck, and, not to mention, starting to turn your neck green. Naturally, you expect to be called this. You almost want to be called it. Sometimes, you're surprised you don't get called the word more often. Cops are starting to look at you funny.

* * *

Once, your manager at the chain bookstore you work at tells you the word's original definition refers to ignorant people, not

Black people. He's wrong, of course. He's an older white man who thinks he's smart and talks to everyone in a you-just-don't-get-it kind of way. He's forty-six and works at a bookstore, which doesn't quite compute. He's kind of sweaty. "So, why can't white people use the word, too?" he says. "It's unfair."

You say, "But isn't life all about context and nuance? If you look up 'asshole' in the dictionary, it says anus. If I call you an asshole, the meaning's different."

He snaps his head at you. He's not sure if you've made a point or just found a funny way to call him an asshole in front of everyone. It's a little of both. This frustrates him. You're only a senior in high school. Why aren't you a bit more stupid given that you're a semipro pothead? That way he could lord it over you. You wouldn't let him, though. Besides, you're taller than he is.

"You know," he says. "There are white niggers, too."

Thank God your father isn't like this. You say, "Why have I never heard a white person call another white person 'nigger,' then?"

It's at this point that your manager decides not to talk to you about this stuff anymore.

You begin to wonder who loves the word more, Black people or white people.

Days later, while shelving books, you hear him on the other side of the stacks, talking to one of your white women co-workers. They're having what you and your friends call a "white moment," white people comparing notes. He asks your co-worker why it's always about race with Black people. Jesus. And then he asks if she knew that you were actually Black.

"Of course," she says. "Isn't it obvious? The hair, the

clothes, the Malcolm X glasses. He's Blacker than most Black people I know."

"Huh," your manager says. "I thought he was just"—he whispers this part—"a wigger."

Your co-worker is even older than him. She doesn't know this term "wigger," but just its similarity to "nigger" makes her cough and say, "I don't approve of that language."

Instead of saying anything, you just come around the corner with your book cart. They look like they'll each shit a brick. You want to be a wise-ass and tell them that "wigger" is a portmanteau, a linguistic blending of two or more words, in this case, "white" and "nigger." Instead of referring to a person of mixed heritage like you, it refers to a white person who is infatuated with Black culture. You could say all that, but then again, you've always known your manager is a chump. He's wrong about everything. It's the end of your time here. You finish out your shift, quietly hurt. You're not coming back ever again. Things are starting to get corny around here anyway.

* * *

You swear off white people for a while. Not your pops, though. He's cool. For whatever reason, you don't have a ton of girls breaking down your door at the moment, but if you did and if they were white, you'd say, "I'm sorry. We're too different." You might mention the phrase "the struggle," which is understandable. You're in college now.

The word still figures pretty prominently in your life, but you got a bunch of other shit going on. You have less time to think about it. You're probably desensitized. White boys don't say it anymore. That's something. Maybe it's finally going away.

They're just happy to be cool with the Black guys now, whom they sort of defer to when it comes to being hip. A few of the white boys are your friends but not tight friends. Acquaintances is more like it. Your real boys are all of color, many different shades. Sometimes, you catch yourself thinking of them as your niggas, even the Chinese and Japanese homies, but that's rare. Black people own the word now. You never forget that.

* * *

When your dry spell ends and the girls start noticing you, you ask out Black girls named Ebony and Mahogany, one named Melody, Latina girls named Carmen and Mary Carmen, a girl from Eritrea named Mariam. To your surprise, some of them actually date you, but most just say "Talk to the hand," and walk away.

During spring semester your sophomore year, you happen to fall in love with an orthodox Muslim girl named Neda. She's olive skinned and cute. She wears a hijab, which frames her face in a perfect oval. Everything else she wears is designer. She drives a brand-new convertible. Her father prints pocket-size Qurans and is a millionaire because of it. She likes that you like Malcolm X, that you're interested in Islam. On the strength of this, she lets you kiss her a few times in her car in the school parking lot. Once, you ask if you can see her hair. You don't realize how big of a deal this is. Reluctantly, she says yes. She removes her hijab. Her hair is shoulder length, colored and highlighted like any other girl's. But now she's scared. She thinks she's going to hell just for kissing you, for showing you her hair. The only way the two of you can do anything more is if you convert.

You're so in love that you actually consider it, but every time you smoke up, jerk off, drink too much, you know all that will go bye-bye if you devote yourself to her and Allah. Being Muslim will bring other words: raghead, sand nigger, dune coon. You realize this is probably as far as the relationship can go. You don't want to live your life that way. It's too complicated. You're Black. She's Algerian. You trade stories of prejudice. You tell her James Baldwin once said Algerians were the niggers of France, and she likes that you know that. She lets you kiss her one more time. You almost think this could work, but you know you'll always feel weird about it. That wouldn't be fair to her. Being mixed and Black is enough for you to handle. The combination of race and religion would totally fuck your mind up.

On the last day of the semester, she gives you a pocket-size Quran gift wrapped with a bow. You can tell she's hoping you'll read it and convert so she can introduce you to her parents. And you do read it. You talk to her on the phone about it during summer break. But then the fall semester starts. She vanishes into her new classes and you into yours. You talk on the phone once or twice, but now she's just a voice. You never see each other again.

Your Ethiopian buddy, whom everyone calls Faheem the Dream and who is technically an orthodox Muslim, too, says you got off easy. You're riding in your Jetta, which is now showing its age. Your tint's got bubbles in it. "Believe me, my dude. Piety does nothing but cramp your style. You almost got hoodwinked, bamboozled, led astray by love." He passes you the Philly and then turns up the Wu-Tang.

You both sing, "Shame on a nigga who try to run game on a nigga."

For some reason, this centers you. You're no longer confused. The word is once again in play. You wipe the sweat from your brow. Phew, that was a close one.

* * *

Your life follows the usual ebbs and flows. College, graduation, career. The word is the thread. You are the tapestry. You realize one day that this one word follows you everywhere you go, like a black cloud or a guardian angel. You're not sure which. The concept of the "real nigga" soon emerges in the collective consciousness. You embody that. On the streets, it means you don't snitch, not even on your enemies. You stand by your people even when they're wrong. But you ain't in the streets. You never were.

You may be a minion in the corporate world now, but you ain't no sellout. You're a double agent working in the belly of the beast. You're like Dan Freeman in *The Spook Who Sat by the Door*. You're around more white people than ever. You may be a nigga, not a nigger, but at least you're a real one. Even white people recognize it. After your supervisor holds you hostage at the water cooler, trying to bond with you over the NBA and the NFL, you go back to your cubicle, thinking you'll burn this motherfucker down if it comes to it. You don't give a fuck. Real ones never do.

Yet, here you are, climbing the corporate organizational chart, snagging a couple of promotions. You realize the word is invisible now. It's a look in the eyes, an unsaid word at the end of a sentence. You imagine you hear it all the time. "Would you like fries with that, nigger?" "Paper or plastic, nigger?" "Where's that feasibility report, nigger? I'm late for my meeting." You're not losing your mind. You think, Get a hold of yourself. You have a career now. You're shining. Don't fuck this up. You just bought a new car and some rims.

* * *

When footage of a famous white actor or politician saying the word comes out, you think, See, I'm not crazy. It is there. It's always been. It's never going away. Both versions: nigger, nigga. On the flip side, you hang with your cousins and you're disappointed to hear them call everyone nigga. "Look at that Chinese nigga over there." "Look at that Eskimo nigga, my nigga." Even squirrels and inanimate objects. You still don't say it. You realize you've actually had it easy in life, all things considered. You probably don't deserve to say it. Does anyone deserve to? You didn't grow up on food stamps. You've never seen a cockroach in your life. You've been harassed by cops only three times and you're still alive to tell the tales. Sure, you've been called nigger by white people what seems like 7,867 times, but that's way fewer than other Black people, fewer than your darker brothers and cousins, fewer times than your mother. You're mixed, biracial, Black enough, but still not what some people consider really Black. How do you reconcile this?

You start dating Black women exclusively. You don't dog them out either. You're special. You date the darkest sisters you can find. Your brothers have shown you the way. When you roll up on a beautiful Black woman at a club, you say what your brothers would say: "What up, dark and lovely? May I have this dance?" Dark and Lovely is the brand of hair relaxer your mother has always used. Only Black women will understand this. It's cheesy and sexist and probably racist, but the fact you pull the phrase out of your ass so easily shows you're down for the cause. They like that you're light skinned. You like that they're dark. Race is a really weird thing, but it's kind of working for you now.

* * *

One day, after a few failed relationships, you meet a woman named Tanisha at the gym. She comes up to you after weeks of you covertly checking her out from across the weight room. Working out, eating right, swearing off alcohol, it's finally paying off. Why didn't you do this long ago? Tanisha's the most beautiful woman you've ever spoken to. And somehow, whatever game you're laying down, she's picking it right up. It's back and forth like tennis. She's not laughing at you. How are you doing this?

You're both in your midthirties. You date for a few months. She surprises you with presents, small ones that are thoughtful but not relationshipy. You take her on affordable weekend trips to Ocean City and Virginia Beach and New York. You're both corporate as fuck and mutually decide to go back to school to get your MBAs. She helps you with data management, which you hate. You help her with strategy execution, which, really, she doesn't need any help with. Eventually, you both become executives at the same company, but you keep your romance under wraps. You fly all over the country for work. Your wardrobe game is off the chain. You have so much money, you have three bank accounts. She has four. Y'all's portfolios are balanced, stacking money every second of the day. You both spoil your nieces and nephews, but you guys don't have time to have your own kids. You're intellectuals. You go to museums. You eat truffles in your pasta and heirloom tomatoes in your salads. You guys haven't eaten chitlins or pig's feet since you were kids.

You take trips everywhere: Bora Bora, Nairobi, Vietnam, Croatia. To stay grounded, you still go on cruises to the Caribbean with your relatives so you don't look stuck-up. You more than willingly get married. Tanisha is black-Black, blue-Black, purple-Black. By extension, you're Blacker now. Standing next to her, you even look a little darker. When DNA tests become popular, you buy the most expensive kits. You both spit into the plastic tubes. You send them off. Six to eight weeks later, you have the results. Genetically, she has way more African ancestry than you, 80 percent, to be exact. Surprisingly, since your mother is pretty dark, you are exactly 45 percent African. What are the odds? You are the most split-in-two, mixed Black person to walk the earth.

Damn, you're so lucky.

*　*　*

But knowing your genetic makeup doesn't stop you from feeling an absence in your life. What do you have to worry about? Two years in and your marriage is showing no cracks. After the wedding, Tanisha stayed at your old company and you moved to a startup so you both could flourish without any conflicts of interest. The people at your new company love you. They love Tanisha, too. You're both known in the industry for doing good work. You play golf with your bosses, and you're kind of good at it but not too good. Oddly, when you hit a nice shot, they never once call you Tiger. You can tell they almost want to.

Since you're the new guy, one of the younger managers, a woman named Brandy, takes a liking to you. She's white and in her late twenties. She constantly tells you how much she admires your work. Rumors are she's had some problems in her love life, so you let it all slide. You think it's innocent. She knows you're married. You're not cocky or anything, but you wonder if she's just living out some fantasy in her head. You don't instigate. You let her flirt and try not to flirt back, though you're pretty sure you're failing.

One day, while none of this is on your mind, you go back to your office after lunch. Brandy is sitting behind your desk, in a skirt, her legs propped up and spread wide for you to see. She isn't wearing panties. You don't want to look, but of course you look. You fucking memorize the image. You don't say anything, though. You just leave and go to your boss's office. You tell him what happened. Brandy, who vanishes and then calls in sick for the rest of the week, is questioned the following Monday. You're surprised she admits to all of it and doesn't play the white girl card or the nigger card, which is sometimes one and the same. You tell Tanisha and the first words out of her mouth are "I'm gonna kill that little bitch." It could've been the end of your career. Brandy has no concept of race. She has no idea how much your life is in her hands. One false word, and you could be in jail. You know all this. Yet you ask Tanisha to chill. You'll work from home until the company decides what to do.

Brandy is transferred to the new office in Boston, where she meets someone and thrives. In a weird way, you're happy for her. It's fucked up, but it's forgotten. You see her once at a conference, and you both act like it never happened. You two sit at the hotel bar, an empty stool between you. She shows you pictures on her phone of her white husband and her new white baby and her little white dog. After, you go back to your hotel room by yourself and jerk off in the shower. You don't even know why.

The truth is you were never worried about Brandy. Not long after you started at this company, when no one was around on a Saturday, you installed a couple of tiny cameras in your office. Since your first job, you've always been paranoid about your white co-workers breaking into your office and stealing your ideas. Now, on a night you can't sleep, you look at the video of her. Because of the angle, you can't see anything X rated. You don't care about that. You wonder what made her do it. Are you that special? In the video, she looks lonely, but maybe you're just imagining that. She waits for you for fifteen minutes, sitting behind your desk, looking in your desk drawers and at your framed pictures of Tanisha. At one point, she almost leaves, but then she hears you coming in. She opens her legs. She tries to look sexy. When you leave, she immediately starts crying and then runs out of there.

She must've had an empty space in her life that she thought you could fill. Maybe she sensed your emptiness. Now you just feel emptier.

Nevertheless, you save the video file. You're not stupid. You make three copies and keep them on separate flash drives in separate places in case you'll ever need them. You're mixed. You're Black. You always keep your bases covered.

* * *

Sad to say, you're getting kind of old now. How unfortunate. You're only forty-three, but you feel ancient. Luckily, your geriatric ass hits the jackpot. Your company is bought by a bigger one from Germany, a multinational monster. You got in early with your firm. You're a partner. You're being swallowed up. After the acquisition, your company will no longer exist. With the stock options and the payout and whatever other shit you're owed, you can not only retire, you have to. There's a noncompete clause.

You have so much free time that you do all the shopping, all the cooking. You vacuum twice a week. You go to the gym and work off that paunch you put on. You go down on Tanisha more than she goes down on you. Once a week, you even take a few bong rips. It's gravy. But then you start to feel like you're retired, which really means you're lonely as hell. At month five, Tanisha starts looking at you like you're just some stranger walking around the house. You make her elaborate weeknight dinners that take hours of prep, yet she still asks what you've been doing all day. Knowing this can't continue, you apply for a nonprofit job that you're way overqualified for. The organization helps relocate African refugees. You become director of development and raise a shit-ton of money in your sleep. You run workshops and get some local news coverage. You become friends with the refugee families. You have some of them over for dinner. They get stomachaches off your lobster mac and cheese.

Feeling like you're starting to fill the hole inside you, you offer to sponsor a young guy from Sudan. He's a former child soldier who's been bouncing from one big brother here in the States to the next. His name is Solomon. His voice is still thick with Sudanese Arabic. He's a recent convert to Christianity, so you wonder if connecting with him will be a problem. You're an atheist of the highest order. Though you flirted with religion in your youth, you've always thought anyone who truly believes in God is not a realist and can't possibly be intelligent. You still think all that, but you're older now. You're fine with people believing what they want. Who cares?

Solomon doesn't proselytize. He doesn't even mention God. Maybe he can see you're an infidel. So, you get along. You take him out for lunch on Saturdays. You call him during the week just to see how he's doing. You give him books to read. You take him to Smitty's, your go-to barbershop, so he can meet the fellas and get edged up by dudes who know how to cut his hair. Sundays, you even take him to church and watch him worship. Every now and then, as you sit on the hard pews, a small part of you feels something, a charge up the spine, but you don't want to admit it.

Solomon's English still isn't the best, so you have to carefully correct him, but you love it. He's learning. He's smart. He asks why the word "knife," when said, starts with an "n" sound, but when written, starts with the letter "k." You tell him about silent letters. He wonders what's more correct: to play the piano or practice the piano. You tell him they're both correct, depending on the situation. This bothers him. He wants black-and-white rules. He wants things to make perfect sense. He's eighteen years old. You teach him about context and nuance, and he slowly starts to get it.

Sometimes, when you're driving, taking him back to his halfway house, you wonder if he's been called his first "nigger," or even his first "nigga." In your most indulgent moments, you want to ask. Or better yet, you want him to ask you, the sage, about it. That way you could tell him all you know. But then your sense and decency come back. Your ego recedes. You watch Solomon look out of the car window with amazement, at all this new scenery, at his new home, and then over at you, his new friend. He's the son you've never had. Admit it, you kind of love him. If you could have it your way, you'd keep him safe forever.

HOW TO BE
A DICK IN THE
TWENTY-FIRST CENTURY

The morning one awakens as a penis doesn't feel that much different from any other morning. Most of my life, I've felt like a giant dick anyway. No matter the season, my entire body was always aroused, itchy, throbbing. That was my mentality, too. The testosterone, it was how I got ahead, my assertiveness, my swagger. As a man, it was expected of me. As a Black man, it was required. Every single morning of my adulthood, as I took a leak, I adjusted my medicine cabinet door so I could get a glimpse of my morning wood in the mirror. Somehow, everything would then seem right, if not in the world then at least in my life.

As with most men, I didn't realize how deep my love for my own ding-dong went. I was vain about it, but how could anyone blame me? I'd known it for so long. When I discovered it in the womb, I'm sure I was instantly smitten. It was my first possession, my own bodily toy. And unless something really weird happened, it would always be there for me, my first friend.

To this day, I still don't know how all this happened, how I magically transformed into a six-foot penis, but I like to think that, in the cocoon of my bed, I somehow dreamed about my-self so intensely that I became the very thing I most desired: me.

* * *

Here's the funny thing: as a man, I wasn't even six foot. I was five foot six. So, transforming into a six-foot-tall penis was quite an accomplishment when you think about it. Then again, that was just how I rolled. I've always been gifted. Before I became a penis, my life had been going exactly as planned. I was loaded. I had businesses, big ones. I owned a skyscraper, where I lived on the top two floors. I had other homes, many others all over the world. Sometimes, I lost track of how many. I was acquainted with a few single women around my age who occasionally al-lowed me in their boudoirs if I threw around enough cash. I'd never been married. I didn't have kids or that many relatives. What more could a billionaire ask for?

As I looked in the mirror that first morning in the fall, though, washing my face, hoping when I dried off and opened my eyes that I'd be me again and not a large penis, it was obvious that washing my face had no effect. I was still a large penis. Per-haps I was finally complete. I'd reached my ultimate form. Was there anything I could do? I didn't look that different, really. Somehow, I still had arms.

I had a head, too, of course, but not my usual head. Unfortu-nately, I had a penis's head. Thank God I was already bald. Hair on a penis might've looked—I don't know—odd. I kind of had a face. If I looked at myself in the mirror long enough, there was something familiar enough there to make me think it looked like me. All things considered, I was just happy I was circumcised.

I could get around just fine, but I didn't have legs in the

traditional sense. That morning, before I even realized I was a penis, I'd risen out of bed and waddled about my home as I usually did, had a cup of tea and read a bit of the newspaper. It wasn't until I was walking past my full-length mirror on the way to the shower, stripping off my pajamas, that I finally saw my new form.

Where my feet usually resided were two watermelon-size testicles sitting cozily in nests of hair. I moved what used to feel like my feet, and the testicles moved. This was, needless to say, fucking freaky. Testicles should never be that big. They really aren't appealing. Yet when I looked up and saw my reflection, almost without meaning to, I elongated and stood taller. Instead of being sickened, I was momentarily impressed at how majestic I looked. I stuck out my chest.

But my spiritual boner lasted only a minute. I was fifty-five. I usually needed pills to keep it up. I vomited. I shriveled. I fell to the floor. Reality set in. I wasn't a man having some weird wet dream. I was a walking, talking reproductive organ. How would I live? How many problems would this pose? Would anyone even notice? I looked back at the mirror and tilted my head like a dumb dog. I bathed in the shock of how sad I looked, how sad a penis looks, even when it's twelve times its normal size.

Naturally, I began to scream.

* * *

Here's the ironic part: my name is Dick. No, really, it is. If it weren't true, it would be too much. In my early twenties, way before all this, people started calling me Dick without my having to ask. My full name is Richard Dickerson, so it was probably going to happen anyway.

I could've insisted on being called Rick or Richie or Rich or the Rickster, if I was white, but Dick always sounded better. It was another irony. A Black guy named Dick. The jokes just wrote themselves. It set me apart, though, which was something I liked. Naturally, one develops a persona to fit one's name. I was with many women, many, many women, and a couple of men, just to try it out. I wasn't that well endowed, though I wasn't exactly little. During a three-month period in my midtwenties, when I was feeling especially inadequate, I used all sorts of ointments and pumps and stretchers to elongate myself. Now, yet another irony, I wasn't just elongated. I was in a penis suit. I could've been a sign waver for a sex shop. Penises R Us. The Penis Pavilion. Get it up and come on in!

Of course, one's first instinct is to blame oneself. I deserved it. I've been bawdy. I've squeezed buttocks without asking. I've been investigated. At one time in my life, I was fine with my reputation. I basked in my wide ray of light no matter how many lawsuits came at me. It was part and parcel of my success. Dick Dickerson, Double D, opinionated OG tech entrepreneur–virile Black man. Yet, that day, when all this was new, I may have thought for the slightest moment that one of my misdeeds had finally popped back up and put a hex on me.

* * *

When one becomes a penis, one's first thought is to consult a doctor. It only makes sense. But what does one wear when one goes out in public as a penis, especially for the first time? I donned some sweatpants, somehow getting my testes through the pant legs. I layered from there, a sweatshirt, a trench coat, and a fedora. I figured a scarf and sunglasses wouldn't hurt either. I thought of a business suit, but a business suit on a six-foot penis would've looked ridiculous. I looked down at my balls, my new feet, and realized I didn't need shoes anymore. None would fit.

I called my driver, Jamison, whom I paid to be at the ready at all times. I descended sixty floors in my private elevator to the garage. As I got in his town car, he said, "Dick, as usual, you look quite erect this morning." I'd given him the name Jamison. He was white. Not that it was related, but he made a lot of dick jokes, I think to please me. That day, unsurprisingly, I wasn't feeling it.

He put the car in gear and was just about to take off, but then he glanced at me through the rearview mirror. He put his arm over the seat, turned around, and looked right at me. "Dick, you okay? You look a little—I don't know—inflamed. You sick or something?"

"Bad shellfish," I said.

"Ooof. So we're going to the doc, then?"

I slapped him on the shoulder, as though spurring a horse. "Yes, my good man. Hurry."

*　*　*

Friends though we were, I didn't have much confidence in Irv Goodenough. I never did. My former college roommate had always been an underachiever and, I suspected, a closeted dope smoker. I visited him for two reasons: (1) to keep the man in business and (2) to prove Mimi, one of my exes, wrong. She seemed to think I didn't have a giving bone in my body, but I had Goodenough. He was my cause, my proof. However, I quickly realized that going to him for answers was probably a mistake.

He sat on a short stool. From the exam table, with that thin paper crinkling under me, I looked down at his bald spot as he seemed to skim my chart instead of actually read it. He had bed-head. He needed a haircut and a shave. I said, "Irv, here is where you look up at me and prescribe a remedy. Now, let's have it."

But all Goodenough could do was yawn. "It's not fatal. At least that's something."

My impatience may have gotten the better of me. I told him to stop fucking around or I'd rescind my monthly stipend. He didn't look like he cared for that. He checked his watch and sighed so deeply he seemed to think of me as a burden. But I was his friend and benefactor. Besides, I thought it was under-stood that he was one of my yes-men. I'd asked him to see me at late notice, sure, but what were friends and benefactors and paid yes-men for?

"Listen," he said. "Dick, I've never seen anything like this, okay? But your health is fine. You have all your organs. Your heart is pumping. Your brain is working the way it's always worked. I mean, Jesus Christ, you have arms! Let's count our blessings here." Goodenough, with his ineffectual, pudgy face, to his credit, tried to soften the blow with a delicately placed aphorism. "Maybe you should just learn to live with this. Be a better Dick."

For some reason, everyone thought I didn't like myself. I loved myself, extremely. How did they think I'd gotten so far? As I left, I realized I'd been misunderstood my entire life.

* * *

When one lives as a penis for a week or so, one quickly real-izes that being a dick is harder than it looks. Let's keep it real. I wasn't just a dick. I was a Black dick. Given this country's history with undermining Black masculinity, I was sure I was being treated even worse because of my skin color. I was certain there was some white dick gallivanting around somewhere, probably in California or Utah, living his life free of scrutiny. Meanwhile, I was in New York. I couldn't go anywhere without being ogled or sneered at or accosted, especially by big burly white women. They often cornered me as I came out of a movie or Jamison's car. They felt me up. They kicked me in the balls, stood on them even. Then they socked me right in the nose and ran away, but not before saying my presence had offended them. "Why don't you just kill yourself?" they said. "You know, this is all karmic retribution," they also said. They started picketing outside my skyscraper.

I know I was a dick and everything, but even I thought that was a bit harsh. I mean, damn, I didn't even know them. I tried to file a police complaint once, but the cop at the precinct desk just said, "Look at you. You were asking for it."

I continued trudging through life. Very few were sympathetic to my situation, but for some reason, a friendly tribe of older Upper West Side lesbians took up my cause for a week or two. To this day, I'm not sure why. They said they understood me, the disembodied penis. I was the symbol of masculinity, Black masculinity no less. It was imperative that I use my station in life for good and not evil. They created Instagram and Facebook accounts on my behalf. I had an illness, they said. Or was it a disfigurement? No one could really say for sure. They were so kind. Though I was already loaded, they set up a Please-FundMe. They cooked me and Jamison dinner once, too. Vegan. I choked down some of their homemade probiotic hooch. On the way home, Jamison and I had to stop at White Castle.

Their message stuck with me, though. I was an anomaly on the gender–sex continuum. "Be out," they said. "Wave your freak flag high. There may be others out there. Stand up for them." On the way out, however, they did say that the gay mafia was very real. They would filet me like a tuna if I abused their trust. So, I took their advice. I stood. I pitched my tent. I did a few TV and print interviews. All the headlines were really punny. "Man Becomes Penis but Doesn't Have the Balls to Hang Out." Stuff like that. I was ridiculed even more. No one took me seriously, not even men. They were actually my worst tormentors. I got death threats from a bunch of hillbillies. Inevitably, the porn industry came a-calling, and I figured it was a good time to hire security and withdraw from public life.

Goodenough referred me to other doctors, good doctors, penis specialists, at my behest. I hoped something as simple as a penis reduction would remedy the situation, but they said, no, that's not how that worked. It would be drastic plastic surgery. I would have to be taken apart and rebuilt. I overheard one of them say they should speak with the federal government about my body, that I should be studied. Naturally, I ran the hell out of the exam room, still in my paper gown. I found my way down a back stairwell and jumped into Jamison's waiting town car, my bare ass kissed by the cold winter air.

* * *

When one encounters a significant life change, such as becoming a penis, one inevitably tries to take shelter in the arms of a lover. Mimi, my old standby, my mean old lady friend, was there for me, at least at first. She pretended to understand and care. We hadn't seen each other in years. She suddenly wanted to reconnect. It was odd, but I went with it. In the past, she'd been terribly vindictive. I thought I was beginning to see her good side again. Yet something just didn't feel right. Whenever I offered to meet in public, she had excuses. Somehow, we always ended up at her place instead. I even had to take the back stairs.

When one becomes a penis, say after the sixth or seventh month, one starts to realize how much we all love penises. They're everywhere in civilization and nature, and we don't even realize it. Cucumbers, bananas, guns, the Leaning Tower of Pisa.

"Tell me those aren't dicks," I said.

"Yes, you"—Mimi pointed at me—"are everywhere, and we"—she pointed at herself—"don't realize it."

She was a lawyer. She was always fucking correcting people. I'd forgotten about that.

"Huh?" I took off my fedora, but she winced so I put it back on. Most people couldn't handle the sight of my head.

"You're a penis now. Us humans don't realize you phallic-shaped beings are everywhere."

"Phallic-shaped beings?" I said. "Do you not regard me as a human being? I'm a human penis, not some donkey dick."

Her hesitance to agree should've been a clue she may have had hidden motives.

After a particularly trying week of death threats and the usual interview requests, Jamison dropped me off at her building. She said she'd make me dinner, kielbasa and sauerkraut. It wasn't until my second glass of wine that I began to feel different, impaired. Mimi sat across her dining table from me, smirking, as though waiting for me to suddenly capsize. Her old varicose-veined legs were crossed elegantly, her ugly, hammertoed foot bobbing up and down like a warning sign. I looked at my wineglass.

"You poisoned me, didn't you, you goddamn weirdo?"

"'Poison' is a harsh word. I prefer 'drugged.' But don't worry. You won't die or anything."

"What'll happen, then?"

She shrugged. "Why ask? You won't remember anyway." She waved. "Nighty night." The room went sideways.

When I awakened, I was tied up on her bed. The fireplace was going. I turned and she was lying next to me, done up in lingerie, smoking a cigarette. She seemed spent. She was panting. I was really dehydrated but at the same time I was covered in nice-smelling oils. Something had been done to me. Though I was all lubed, I was painfully chaffed in other areas, delicate areas.

"You took advantage of me, you witch."

I looked to my left. There was film equipment, tripods and shit, set up across the room, pointing right at us. I could see myself on a flat-screen monitor.

"What the fuck?" I started to scream for help.

But she shushed me. "Remember the night we met?" She sat up and stubbed out her ciggie.

It was at some party twenty years before. "Vaguely," I said.

"What about after? When I went home with you?"

I thought about it. I said, "Oh, is that what this is all about?" I was about to say that men did that kind of thing back then. But even as I thought it, it didn't make me sound very good. "So, you're taking revenge on me now? Why?"

"Because you're a penis now, you asshole. Just the sight of you infuriates me. Don't you have any remorse?"

"For what?" I said. "Slipping you a mickey or for now being a penis?"

"Both, dickhead."

My mind was just beginning to travel back to that night. Had it really been that bad? She took all kinds of pills back then. What was the difference if it was me giving them to her? I hadn't even done anything but spill her onto the bed and pass out next to her. I'd drunk too much. I couldn't get it up anyway.

It was as if she could hear my thoughts. She smacked me across the face. "You just said all that out loud, stupid." It must've been the roofie she'd given me. She mashed the button of a remote with her thumb and stopped filming. She untied me. "Get the hell out. We're through. You're lucky I don't call the cops."

I gathered up my clothes. "I'm lucky?" I was almost out the door when I asked if it wouldn't be too much trouble for me to buy the footage from her and for her to sign an NDA. We could put all this behind us. "What do you think?" Her answer was to pull a hot poker from the fireplace and wave it around like it was a fencing foil. I took that as a no.

*   *   *

When one becomes a penis, one eventually has an existential crisis. It's inevitable. I often overheard people say they wondered what it was like to be me. "Think of the orgasms," they said. "He's probably coming all the time." What everyone failed to remember was that, as a disembodied penis, I was without agency. There were no hips to thrust me. No large hand to manipulate me. I was essentially a loaded gun always waiting to be fired.

My life was a sham. Total success hadn't prepared me for life being a total tease. What was the use of being a large penis if I couldn't at least pleasure myself? I wasn't even connected to a body. What was the point of my life? I was just there, hanging. I fell into a funk. I wanted to be left in my lair.

It took some creative legal web-spinning, but I evicted everyone in my building. I kept it all to myself. I didn't shut myself in. I just didn't go anywhere for a while. I started a garden on the roof. I raised cattle in the underground garage. Other than having Jamison, I became totally self-sufficient. I believed I could find my own cure, so I assembled a large computer that took up one whole floor of my building. I went back to my old programming days. Into one end, I fed it code like branches into a wood chipper. Into the other, I spooned in real-world scenarios and AI protocols so that it could understand our world and perhaps spit out what had exactly happened to me.

While the computer chewed on data for days at a time, I surfed the internet for days on end. I became obsessed. Evidently, there had been more than a thousand ways to refer to the penis since the beginning of records. One of my favorites dated back to 1720. The Love Dart. I read scientific articles about how much men loved their penises. The verdict in every story I read was: a lot.

Jamison often took pity on me. Once a week, he stopped by with some Nathan's hot dogs and a hard drive of movies. They all happened to be those Hollywood special effects films. As we watched, I slowly realized I had the origin story of a superhero. Penis Man. The Incredible Boner. I don't know. I should've been fashioning a caped garment, figuring out whom to save and whom to fight, coming up with a superhero logo, trademarking it. But I realized I didn't really have any superpowers other than making people run away in shock or run at me in anger.

Naturally, I fell off the wagon. I started taking my pills again, just to feel better. It was only one or two at first. After a week, I was swallowing them by the handful. By the time I was grinding them up and snorting them, occasionally injecting them into my eyeballs, I knew I had a problem. I couldn't move without them. I couldn't function. I had no boing-boing anymore.

By the grace of God, I was able to impose my own sort of rehab. Jamison made sure my dealer, Goodenough, would never darken my door again. I fought the withdrawals for a few weeks, but I finally made it out clean and sober on the other side.

* * *

It would've been nice to have emerged from my drug stupor to find my mainframe had finally churned out an answer to my horrendous question. But while I was detoxing, the massive hard drive crashed. Jamison regretfully informed me that my supercomputer would boot up only in safe mode. Otherwise, he said, it was the blue screen of death. He patted my shoulder and told me I should probably give up hope. I moved on.

I disassembled the computer and sold it for parts. Weirdly, I found solace in the art world. Most of my life had been spent finding unequivocal answers to previously unanswered technological questions, which I would then turn into commerce. In art, I discovered, there were no right or wrong answers. Shit, there were no answers at all. There were just questions of humanity, feelings and shit, empathy and commiseration. Artists had no idea what commerce even was. Having the rug of my previous reality pulled out from under me, I could suddenly understand this

form of expression. I went to MoMA and the Whitney and studied sculptures and paintings and installations. I watched perfor-
mance art, which for once didn't totally baffle me. I attended film
festivals, always coming in and finding a seat right as the lights
went down and the curtain went up. Since I had nothing better to do, I started keeping a journal, writing about each play or
exhibition I saw. I started wearing a beret, with the occasional
monocle. I sent my reviews out and eventually became a critic
for a few websites. I can't say which. I reviewed films and books
and plays. I developed a reputation as a hard but fair reviewer.
Though I wasn't too good for a nice hatchet job.

I sold most of my worldly possessions. I found a recipe for a
natural non-habit-forming stimulant on the internet. It was just
a smoothie with veggies and fruits and nuts. I guzzled them by
the glass. I began hanging out with my lesbian friends again. I
took the time to learn their names and not just think of them as
lesbians. I went back to nature. I learned how to ferment things.
I started smoking cannabis, a fair amount of it. It regulated my
moods and gave my life a lustrous merry sheen. I undid my creative legal web-spinning and made my skyscraper into affordable
housing for single and abused mothers. I moved myself into a
small brownstone on the Upper West Side and rented out the
top two floors to Jamison and his family for dirt cheap. I started
calling him by his real name, Cleetus, which he seemed to appreciate. I'd totally forgotten why I'd given him the name Jamison to
begin with.

I wasn't well adjusted, just mildly not as fucked up. I once
saw Mimi getting out of a private car, and I thought she didn't
recognize me. I just happened to be holding a cup of to-go coffee.
She dropped a handful of loose change into it.

I said, "Hey, it's me. Dick."

She said she knew and she didn't care.

I asked if she'd heard of my philanthropic projects. "I'm a changed penis. Sorry I was me for so long."

She made a farting sound with her mouth. She didn't look back, but right before going into her building she did wave. It was her middle finger, but still.

* * *

I left the reviewing business after only a few years, but I still enjoyed seeing the odd play or two. My show of choice was always the Sunday matinee, when no one was around. About a year into my retirement, a new young playwright was debuting his first three-act at a small stage in Brooklyn. The play was based on my life. I was offered a seat up front and the opportunity to do a Q and A with the writer, but I chose to be silent and sit in the shadows in the back, my usual reviewer's sniper spot. While the play wasn't all that good, and its title was much too long (I would've preferred "The Disembodied Penis"), I did appreciate the effort.

Unfortunately, it suffered from a lack of verisimilitude. Without a good amount of recreational drugs, one probably couldn't fully understand what it was like to become a penis if one had never actually become a penis. I was thinking this as I left the theater, as I pulled my beret lower over my face and cinched my trench coat. I wasn't fully understood yet again, but then I thought, how many people are? I was just about to leave the lobby when I heard a woman's voice.

"Excuse me, Dick. Please don't go."

I'd always dreamed a moment like this would happen. It

would be a woman wearing essentially the same thing that I was wearing. She would be about my age. She'd have my same condition but in the female way. We'd be soul mates. She'd say that she'd been trying to find me so that we could talk. We would have coffee and then marry a few weeks later. We'd adopt. It was a fantasy that I never thought would come true.

So, when I turned around and saw it was just a young usher, I wasn't surprised. "Here," she said. "You left your scarf and your monocle."

I thanked her and headed back through the lobby.

The doorman, an older guy, nodded as I approached. He recognized me. In his eyes, I could even see a hint of desire. Perhaps I was what every man really wanted to be. He opened the door as though I were a king, bowing even.

"It's a pity we're not in charge anymore," he said.

I smiled at this poor fool. I thought of the old me. I said, "Is it?" I didn't wait for a response. I just laughed and threw my scarf around my neck. I patted his shoulder and told him to be well. Then I ventured back out into the cold, windy city.

LAKE NO NEGRO

Andre had never been with a white woman, an older woman, a conventionally beautiful woman, much less one he'd just met. But here he was. Her name was Farrah, and they'd stumbled onto each other in the beginner class at the Rock and Rope, a large indoor rock-climbing gym in the southeast part of town. Their instructor randomly paired them up, and for an hour, they scaled a three-story modular wall called the Slab. It was a good partnership. Andre and Farrah picked their way up the climbing holds like spiders up a web. But every time they reached the top, Andre found her giving him a high five or a hug, holding on to him, he noticed, a little longer than she needed to.

She was in her early forties, Andre guessed, and not hurting in the cash department. She possessed the grooming and physique of someone with a salon and trainer at her beck and call. In Portland, so many people were scribbled with tattoos, looking so eccentric and pasty, that Farrah's mainstream glow made her unusual. She didn't look at all like the lead singer of some shaggy folk band. Quite the contrary. She looked like a perky blond aerobics instructor.

As she showered, he lay in bed, sex drunk. He reclined against his wad of pillows and fell into a parade of dreams he never used to have back east. In one, he was an ironclad warrior

atop a powerful white steed. In another, he was the commander
of an army of soldiers. When he opened his eyes after a fourth
little dream, he found she was gone. On the pillow next to him
was a note, though. It said, "Dinner. My place. Saturday. 6pm."
Underneath she'd written the address, some town in the suburbs called Lake Oswego.

* * *

Andre was twenty-six and from DC. He'd journeyed west to
spice up his life. Farrah was from Northern California, but
she hadn't said why she'd relocated or what she did for a living. Andre didn't push. Over his six months in Portland, he'd
learned that this city lacked the irony or speed found in most
American cities. The place was so strange and carefree that
he incorrectly assumed no one there was employed or even
aspired to be. He figured Farrah was, in all likelihood, one
of "those Californians" vilified by Portland's liberals, those
wealthy Californians who bought up the cheap real estate and
spit it back on the market at a profit, something Andre wasn't
that invested in.

That Saturday, he prepared for his dinner date by rent-
ing an electric car and whizzing down to the Pearl District
to buy some dress clothes at a shop called the Social Ladder.
He checked himself out in the store's three-way mirror and
suddenly thought of his old life. Just a year before, he'd been
the definition of metrosexual. He was an up-and-coming yet
bored financial analyst who'd amassed a pretty decent savings.
He got his hair cut weekly. He clipped his fingernails every
Sunday night and often tended to his closet of expensive suits
and coats.

Since he'd come to Portland, however, he'd let himself go. His hair was in naps. He shaved infrequently. And what clothes he had, he lugged down to a Laundromat in a trash bag once every two weeks, washing them without separating the colors from the whites, something his ex, Nina, used to do that drove him nuts. "You're so uptight," she used to always say. "Why do you have to be so weird?"

He missed the tidiness of his old life as well as those designer clothes he'd given to the Goodwill like a dope before he'd moved. Andre imagined a homeless person living on the DC streets, looking like Denzel Washington with all his nice threads, while he was across the country looking like a bohemian. He ran his fingers over his naps, took out his phone, and found one of the few Black barbershops in Portland. He had his head shaved to the scalp, his goatee cut off like a tumor. At home, he dressed and doused himself in cologne, and since he'd recently started smoking weed again, he took a quick bong hit to ease his mind.

* * *

As he traversed the city, fairly zooted, he got introspective. He didn't know why, but memories of Nina had been clamping down on him from out of nowhere. She was partly why he'd moved west, to forget about her even if she'd already forgotten about him. As he neared Lake Oswego, he had a vision of his last night in DC, when he'd made the *Titanic*-size boo-boo of calling her one last time.

When she answered, the endeavor showed promise. Her voice was bubbly, happy, like how it used to be. When she realized it was him, though, she sounded like a bored customer-service rep. He waded through the awkward salutations, which yielded some info: She was well. She was active. And she was living with her parents, a fact he was pleased to hear since it made her sound a little pitiful.

"Are you working?" he said.

"Sure. My writing and pottery are going really well."

"No. I mean actual employment. Something that, you know, makes money."

She simply said yes. She was a barista.

He laughed when she flamboyantly rolled the "r" in "barista." "Isn't that just a pretentious way of saying you pour coffee?"

"If you think Italian is pretentious, then yes," she said. "My boyfriend owns the shop."

That was the first blow. *Boyfriend*. And it was just like her to throw it in when he wasn't expecting it. He didn't say anything for what seemed like minutes and tried to recover by asking the guy's name.

"Alastair."

That was the second blow. The name was so blue blood, so Caucasian, that he didn't know whether to die laughing or curl up in a ball and weep. Andre imagined a towheaded cricket player, someone with an accent, someone related to the British royal family. Instantly, he wanted to murder him, but he thought he did a good job hiding that. "Well, great. I'm glad for you. I guess you've finally made it."

"Why?" she said. "Because he's white?"

"That's not what I meant." He should've stopped there, purely out of embarrassment. This conversation was going to get around to everyone they knew. But he was a little drunk at the time. What honest-to-goodness whiskey drinker would quit now? *Forge on*, the liquor told him. *Break new ground.* "Let me ask you this. Does he call you 'Lovie' when you fuck? Do you guys have cucumber sandwiches afterward?"

She just sighed.

"Tell the truth. When you guys get married, he'll want you to wear a tiara, won't he?" He heard himself squeal in delight.

"You know what? Unlike your weird ass, he's extremely sensitive and caring and loving and brilliant. He's a poet."

"Oh, well, of course he is. Only a poet deserves so many adjectives bestowed upon him." Andre stopped to laugh again. He was astounded she hadn't hung up on him yet. He would've hung up on himself by then. Of course, that was exactly when she did.

* * *

As Andre entered Lake Oswego, he was drenched in that jealousy again. He thought his feelings for Nina had faded. He thought he'd forgotten all about Alastair and his great poetry. He hadn't even had the chance to tell her he was leaving town. Just the idea of them and the snooty kids they'd have made Andre want to go back to his apartment and sulk.

But according to his GPS, he was almost to Farrah's, close enough that it would've been stupid to turn back. Perhaps getting blackout drunk in front of total strangers would take his mind off things. Then he could pack his crap and move to LA or Seattle, or to DC to get his job back.

Remarkably, though, as he escaped the throughways and drove deeper into the woods, Andre found his fog burning off. The avenues turned twisty and lush. Just driving them made his high come back. He'd heard Lake Oswego had been nicknamed Lake No Negro, but no one ever told him if it was because the town, like the rest of Portland, was just really white or if it was really white and anti-Black. Every section of town had a strange nickname anyway. So, who knew? There was no one on the street, white or otherwise. Andre expected to see mansions and topiaries and wrought iron gates everywhere. Instead, the houses were vague structures shrouded in overgrown vegetation, the homes of wealthy people who didn't trim their hedges.

Andre wound over to South Shore Boulevard, gliding until his GPS said he'd arrived. His electric car sat silent as he assessed the residence from the street. It was ultramodern and white, more a structure than a house. It sat below street level on a lakefront property, looking like those Frank Lloyd Wright homes Nina talked about. Andre coasted down the gravel drive and passed a cedar-clad carport with a Jaguar, an SUV, and Farrah's Mercedes parked inside.

He walked up to the door with some carnations and a bottle of Champagne, the real kind, from the Champagne region of France. It was a piece of knowledge Nina had pounded into his brain after he'd once brought home a case of Korbel thinking it was the good shit. He'd picked this bottle, a blanc de noir that set him back a chilly one-fifty, simply to impress but also because he liked the name. The French guy in the wine shop said it meant "white from black grapes," which had a sense of transformation about it, like "water into wine" and "lemons into lemonade."

Andre rang the doorbell, and it produced a classical tune that lasted a minute. Just as it reached its final note, the door was snatched open by a young Asian woman who stood there in a gray sweatshirt with the neck cut out. Andre introduced himself and said he was there for dinner, but she just sized him up, after which she crossed her arms and screamed, "Farrah, your stupid friend's here!"

Andre thought of cracking a joke, but the way she thinned her eyes at him made him decide against it.

The interior of the house was a collection of marble and concrete, stainless steel and wood. Andre felt like he was walking into an issue of *Architectural Digest*. The foyer's ceiling was a huge sheet of glass, a window to the sky. As he stood there, a large chandelier exploded with light, and there was Farrah, gliding down the wooden staircase in a kimono. She greeted him with outstretched arms, the way rich people did on TV.

She said she was glad he'd arrived, surveying him with a smile and evidently approving. "You clean up good." She petted his shaved head and face. "I'm glad you got rid of the goatee. It didn't suit you. You look like a little boy now."

Andre didn't know how to take that. And he was still a little high. "Thanks." He looked at the Asian woman, who was looking back at him like a repulsed teenager.

Farrah then startled him by rubbing her nose against his, and the Asian woman said, "Are you fucking kidding me?" under her breath.

That was when an older white guy emerged atop the staircase, tucking his dress shirt into his slacks. He looked to be in his midsixties, the distinguished air of a politician radiating from every pore. He jogged down the steps obligingly, his knees cracking. "Tanya," he said to the Asian woman. "Shouldn't you be getting dressed?"

Like a chastened child, she said, "All right," stomping down the hallway to the back of the house and blowing through the patio doors.

When Andre turned back to Farrah, he found her and the old guy studying him. The guy was as tan as Farrah. His silver hair swooped back from his forehead in a perfect wave. "I'm Dennis." He reached out his meaty hand. "You must be Andre."

It was at that moment that everything aligned. He looked from Farrah to Dennis, who now stood behind her with his hand on her shoulder, his lips pinched in a half smile, as if to say, "You got it, buddy. I'm the father." Andre thought he could even see a resemblance.

"I didn't know this was a family dinner."

Farrah looked at Dennis and smiled. "Well, that's what we are. One big happy family."

"Come on in." Dennis guided him down the hallway, which dropped them into a recessed great room. To the left was a stainless steel kitchen that looked like a small factory. To the right was a living room, sunken even lower, with numerous African masks on the wall. When Andre first moved to town, some drunk guy in a bar told him, "Tip numero uno, bro. Don't ever go to the suburbs. People are weird out there."

Standing in that sparkling room now, though, Andre couldn't quite believe that.

* * *

Dennis was a real estate developer. According to him, the NorCal market was a sausage fest, overloaded with phonies, blowhards, and racists. He'd moved his business up to Portland to try his hand in the Oregon market. He'd been there for only five months and had already made a killing in condos. Oregon, he said, was truly the last frontier.

Dennis mentioned all this as he ushered Andre into a

large study down the hall. Intricate carved moldings framed the door. Coffered paneling checkered the ceiling. At the center of the room, Dennis sat behind a desk that he said had once been a redwood. He removed two cigars from a humidor and snipped the ends with a guillotine. Andre was on his second scotch. His head felt hot. He wasn't drunk yet, just a little disoriented.

"You've smoked a cigar before, haven't you?" Dennis offered one to Andre and lit it with a wooden match. "Just roll the smoke around in your mouth and then blow it out. Savor it." Dennis demonstrated the maneuver, swirling his hand in the air like a magician. "There you go."

"When I was younger," Andre said, "we used to cut open cheap cigars and roll weed up in them. Does that count?" This was probably too much information, but what did Andre care? He didn't think he'd see these people again.

Dennis let out a bombastic laugh. The scotch urged Andre to elaborate, but Dennis was already walking over to a wall of photos, beckoning Andre to look at the evidence of his travels. There was Dennis and Farrah on safari, Dennis and Farrah riding elephants, Dennis and Farrah with a dead gazelle lying under their smiling faces. He pointed to photos of himself posing in front of vintage sports cars. Andre thought Dennis would show him at least one photo of Farrah's mother, who Andre assumed was deceased, or at least gone. Instead, he pointed to a series of pictures with him and Farrah posing with other couples. Andre noticed each couple was composed of a Black man and an Asian woman. Tanya was in a few of them, too, but she was with different Black guys.

"Who are they?"

"Friends. Acquaintances." Dennis slid back to his desk. "So, do you still get high?"

"A little weed here and there."

"But you've never done any hard stuff. Heroin, amphetamines, that kind of thing?"

"No way."

Dennis sipped his scotch. "Venereal diseases?"

"Um. What?"

"Sorry for the piercing questions, but I'm a piercing kind of guy. You know, syphilis, gonorrhea? The dreaded HIV?"

"Of course not. No."

Dennis considered him. "Is this feeling like an interview yet?"

Andre sucked on his cigar. The nicotine went to his head. "I think we've passed that point."

"It appears we have." Dennis plucked a wisp of smoke from his stogie. "But you understand, don't you? I only have Farrah's interest in mind."

"Sure. She's your daughter. I'd feel the same way."

Dennis's eyes had briefly moved to the window. He looked back at Andre now, as if something was wrong. He smiled and opened his mouth to say something. But Farrah stuck her head in the room and said dinner was ready.

"Shall we eat?" was all he said.

* * *

In the center of the dining table, a roasted goose glistened on a platter. It was surrounded by side dishes in matching bowls. There were vegetables and salads and cheese and fruit and caviar. Andre had never been around food like this. "Damn!" he said way too loud. "You're a cook?" The scotch was coursing through him now like rocket fuel. He was beyond disoriented. He was a little shit-faced.

Tanya was already at the table, dressed in a black blouse and tweed pants. "Don't be stupid. Farrah can't even boil a hot dog. She has caterers."

At that, Farrah gave a huff and looked to Dennis. He placed a hand on Tanya's forearm. "Let's all get along tonight, okay?"

Tanya ignored him and harpooned a goose leg off the platter with her fork.

Andre sat next to Farrah, Dennis next to Tanya. Quite quickly, silence ballooned at the table, and Andre felt he should pop it. "So, Tanya?"

She was dissecting her goose leg without eating any of the pieces.

"How do you know Farrah and Dennis?"

She immediately rolled her eyes.

Confused, Andre looked around the table.

Tanya sipped her Champagne and grinned. "You have no clue what's going on here, do you?"

Andre looked around the table again, and Farrah sighed at Dennis. "You didn't tell him?"

He turned to Andre. "Earlier in the study, you said something about Farrah being my daughter."

This caused Tanya to snicker, and Farrah to say, "Hey," in a parental voice. Dennis waited for them to quiet. "I'm not her father." He waited a beat. "I'm her husband."

Tanya glowed. "Now do you get it?"

Andre slumped back but tried to act normal.

"We're married," Dennis said. "We have been for years."

Andre took in a mouthful of Champagne and swallowed audibly. "Okay. Great."

"We have an arrangement, what some call an open one." Dennis was still eating, speaking between bites. "Polyamory. Are you familiar?"

"I know what it means." Andre looked at the man's hand on Tanya's arm.

"The point of this dinner is to see if you'd fit in our couple-hood. Think of this as an audition of sorts."

Andre set his fork down and polished off his Champagne. "An audition. For couplehood."

Dennis swallowed and now sounded like an encouraging coach. "Yeah, man, my wife likes you a lot. You're growing on me, too. We'd all like you to stay. Am I right?" He turned to Tanya and tried to summon enthusiasm from her, but she just grumbled.

"So, you know that she and I—That we've—"

"That you've what? Fucked?" Tanya said. "Yeah, if you're here having dinner, we can all guess that."

"You really aren't helping." Farrah stood and looked to Dennis. "Honey, control your pet."

Dennis leaned over and whispered in Tanya's ear. Whatever he said compelled her to drop her silverware, push away from the table, and again blow through the patio doors without shutting them.

Farrah walked over and locked the doors. "Just us adults."

"You really don't mind that I've—"

"Had sex with my wife?" Dennis furrowed his brow. "Not at all. Like I said, we have an understanding. She's had relationships with other men. I've had them with other women. Tanya, for example." He wiped his mouth. His plate was clean except for a bare goose bone.

"I like you," Farrah said. "You like me. That's all that matters. You like me, don't you?" She traced the edge of his chest with her finger.

"Yeah," Andre said. "We just met, but you're okay, I guess." He looked at the front door, wondering how weird it would be if he just stood up and ran out.

"Hun," Dennis said. "I think this is too much for Andre with you here. Maybe he and I should talk. Just the two of us. Mano a mano." He scooted his chair back and sucked his teeth. "Let's step out onto the terrace. What do you say, buddy?"

"Actually, I should go." Andre was pretty lit. He already had visions of sleeping in his car. He looked down at his plate and realized he hadn't really eaten.

"Just one more drink." Dennis smiled. "Indulge me."

He poured two scotches, and Andre followed him outside. They stepped onto a flagstone patio and walked past a small Zen garden. They went down some stone stairs and across the manicured lawn to the edge of the lake. The night air smelled of pine and rain. Dennis stopped and kicked off his shoes and walked through the grass barefoot. He suggested Andre do the same, and he did.

They sat across from each other on wooden benches, sipping their scotch.

"Have you had many companions, Andre?"

"Sure."

"I'm not talking sexual experiences. I mean, actual relationships, long-term ones."

Nina had been it on both fronts, but that didn't sound very worldly. "I've had a few."

"Same here. Farrah's my fourth and, hopefully, my last wife. We really connect. I know her soul. She knows mine. You follow? We're not dirty people. Our relationship is just larger than most."

Andre took a sip of scotch, which cooled his nerves. "Whatever creams your Twinkie," he said.

Dennis smiled. "I can't tell you how boring relationships can be. We don't have children so we like to keep it interesting."

"What about Tanya? You wouldn't call her a child?"

Dennis glanced at her guesthouse. Through her window, they could see into her living room, which she'd converted into a dojo. She was still wearing her dinner outfit but was now barefoot and kicking a heavy bag. "She's just precocious. You'll like her once you get to know her." He said she was a black belt in *kara-tay*.

"She's definitely lively."

"That's what I'm talking about. Living life."

Andre laughed. "You sound like my ex-girl. Everyone lives a life."

"True, but I mean life with a capital 'L.' It's a rare thing." Dennis crossed his leg and bobbed his white foot up and down. "Has your life been interesting so far?"

Andre thought about his time with Nina and his time alone, how he'd ventured all the way to Oregon to prove he could be daring, and how so far, he'd failed at it. All he'd really done was start smoking weed again and have sex with Farrah. "My life could be more interesting."

"See, that's the way we look at it. We like companionship, cuisine, travel. You like these things."

"Sure, but I don't think being a kept man is how I want to enjoy them."

Dennis sat forward. "You won't be that. We're not slave owners. You'll be our guest, man. You'll have your own house like Tanya, free of charge."

"I'll be your wife's boy toy."

"C'mon, man," he said. "Don't think like that."

Andre noticed he was calling him "man" a lot now, but for some reason it didn't seem insincere. Dennis's voice took on a fatherly tone Andre wished his long-gone pops had used growing up.

"Consider it friends with benefits." Dennis sat back. "You'll have lunch together. You'll go out together. You'll keep each other company."

Maybe it was the scotch, but Andre found himself asking, "What else?"

Dennis puffed his cheeks and lifted his eyebrows, and Andre realized the options were endless in his life. He could probably charter a spaceship to the moon if he wanted. "You'll go on trips, just the two of you. Sometimes, all four of us. You'll see the world, if you haven't already."

It was that phrase that had the most effect. *See the world.* Andre thought of Nina again. He was ashamed of the bitter feelings he still held for her. She always thought she was smarter than him, more traveled, better read, which she was. For a passing moment, he imagined seeing her later in life, after he'd gone on safari with Dennis, after seeing Paris with a woman like Farrah. It would eat Nina up.

"Would you like to at least see the house?" Dennis pointed at the dark one next to Tanya's.

"If you want to show me."

Dennis unlocked the front door and led him inside the bungalow. He turned on the lights, and the room was suddenly there, like a glimpse of the future. Andre's gaze crawled up a staircase that spiraled to a lofted office. Off the living room was a bed and bath. It was all fresh construction and possessed that uncanny new smell, making his apartment seem like a crack den, which it had probably been at one point.

"It's not much, but I think you'll like it." Dennis walked to the rear of the bungalow and opened a set of french doors that led to a small deck. Across the lake, a flock of kids played on the opposite bank, swinging out on a rope and dropping into the water. Dennis and Andre stood on the deck, watching them as the evening continued to darken.

"So, what do you think? And don't hold back."

"This is nice," Andre said.

"Okay, I'm sensing a 'but,' though."

"But you, Farrah, Tanya, this whole thing? It's weird. You and your wife have a serious race fetish."

Dennis nodded slowly. "Okay, I can appreciate that. This is strange to some. And there is a racial element here. But that's America."

Andre glanced at him, wondering at all his dumb decisions that led to this moment.

"How about this?" Dennis said. "Stay the night. You're too drunk to drive anyway. Try it on like a pair of shoes. If you like it, you stay. If you don't, you go."

"But if I stay the night," Andre said, "will I want to go?"

Dennis shrugged. "Let's find out."

Across the lake, someone called the kids, and they ran up a

lawn, disappearing among the trees. Andre closed his eyes and sipped the last of his scotch, the word "savor" swimming up in his mind. He thought he could still feel Dennis standing next to him, about to say something else, but when he opened his eyes, the man was gone. Andre walked through the bungalow and out the front door, and there was Dennis, strolling up to the patio, where Farrah waited.

They embraced for a moment. They kissed. Then they looked back at him and waved.

Andre thought of Nina. He was about to wave back, purely out of reflex, but Dennis and Farrah had already gone inside. He looked up, tracking a lone bright dot as it drifted across the black sky. Then he happened to turn to his left and find Tanya standing on her porch, watching him. She was wearing a short robe now. Without a word, she was suddenly coming his way.

"What's up?" he said.

But she just blew by him and went into his bungalow.

"What are you doing?"

She lit a joint as he followed her in. "What do you think? You're a pothead, aren't you?" She offered it to him, and he toked.

She was just standing there, being awkward. So, he asked what kind of weed it was.

"I don't know. I can never remember the names. Weed is just weed."

He nodded. She was still being awkward, so he asked if it was him or if everyone around there was strange.

"It's probably a little of both, but yeah, they're oddballs. We all are. You are, too." She looked up and stared at the loft.

"We've been here five months, and this is the first time I've been in this place. It's a mirror image of mine."

Andre looked at the loft, too, and then back at her. "Is that weird?"

She didn't answer. She moved over to the bed and just stood there, looking down at it. "You should sit."

He did, thinking she would, too, but she still just stood. She came over to him and straddled his legs.

"So, is this how it works? They get me drunk, and you seal the deal?"

"Hardly. I'm only ever with him. Men like you are only ever with her."

"Those are the rules, huh?"

She let her robe fall open, exposing her lingerie, her defined abs. "Yep."

"Well, what're you doing now, then, with me?" He looked her up and down. Even with the weed, she smelled like a fragrance Nina would wear.

"I'm saving you, stupid."

"That so." Andre passed the joint. "From what?"

"The trap you just fell in." She pushed him back onto his elbows. She climbed onto his lap. "Believe me, they won't let you leave. They'll seduce you into staying." After a second, she added, "You're not built for this."

"And I suppose you are."

"More than you." She took his hand and put it on her waist.

He squeezed her. "You don't seem very happy here, though."

"Looks can be deceiving." She put his other hand on her breast. Something was briefly happening in his pants, and she pushed herself against it. She took a last puff and set the joint in an ashtray.

"Tell me how you're saving me exactly."

"Farrah hates me. If you and I have sex, she'll lose interest in you. You'll be tainted. Then you can go. See?"

"So, it's a win-win for the both of us."

Tanya smiled.

"Is that what happened with the last Black guy?"

"No," she said. "He got tired of her and left before we even moved here."

"He escaped."

"Pretty much."

Andre nodded. "So, this is your good deed of the day."

"Yep." She leaned over him, nodding, too. "Hug me."

He did. Her body was strong and muscled, powerful. She dragged her chest over his face. "But don't you want to be saved, too?"

"No." She slowly sat up, grinding herself against his lap. She fumbled with his belt buckle.

He watched and then put his hands over hers. "Why? Because they're rich? Because you're comfortable?"

She sighed, looking down at him, shaking her head. She reached over and picked up the joint again. "Saving me won't bring your old lady back, okay? So, don't even try."

"How do you know I have an old lady?"

She smirked. "Everyone has an old something, especially guys." Tanya reached over and was about to stab the joint out in the tray, but he took it from her.

He smoked and propped his arm behind his head. "Well, what about you? Where's your old man?"

"Somewhere," she said.

"The last Black guy, I take it."

She shook her head. "A different one."

Andre thought of Nina again, how she always said he was strange, weird. It was fitting he'd encountered such a weird situation. "Well," he said, putting the joint out, "just so you know, I'm not staying. I never was. I have an electric car sitting out front. I'm leaving first thing, quiet as a mouse."

"Good for you." She watched him, bored now. She yawned and slid off to his side, lying next to him on her back. They both stared at the ceiling.

"I'm tired."

"Of tonight or just everything?" He looked at her, at the tiny bird tattooed behind her ear.

"Both."

"This place can't be good for your head. How long have you been with them?"

"Too long."

"Leave, why don't you."

She turned and looked at him now. "With you, I suppose."

"Maybe. Or just by yourself. I mean, who am I?"

"You're right," she said. "Who are you?"

"Just a guy." He looked at her bird again. "Are you just a girl?"

"No, stupid. I'm a woman."

He laughed. "Well, it's up to you, then, woman." He turned off the light, and the room went black. They settled next to each other. It was so dark that they could've been anywhere, with anyone. He thought of Nina one last time and wondered if Tanya was thinking of her old man. He could almost make her out in the darkness. He could hear her breathing, dreaming maybe. He was about to turn over and drift off, too, but then she took hold of his arm. "This isn't permanent. The two of us."

"I know."

"So let's not make this weird, okay?"

"We won't."

"Are you sure you can even handle someone like me?"

"I think so, but I can't make any promises."

She turned back over. She got quiet again. "Maybe this will actually work, then," she said. "Because I hate promises."

AND THEN
WE WERE
THE NORRISES

In the fall of '85, a few years after my family and I went into witness protection, I started seventh grade at Edward Meany Middle School in Phoenix, Arizona. First period was an art class, which I was late for because I was late for everything back then, even the first day of school. When I walked in, there was only one empty seat left at a two-kid table by the window. Already sitting there was a long-haired white boy who wore a dirty Judas Priest shirt. The outcasts' table. Everyone else in class was white, too, but preppy, like child models in a catalog. So, of course, I took my place with the outcast, like slipping on an old shoe.

As I sat down, I noticed he was drawing even though the class hadn't started yet. I peeked at the picture, and it was some fire-breathing-dragons-and-castle kind of stuff, so detailed with shading and little stars that it looked like it'd been xeroxed from a comic book.

I said, "Wow, you're good," and he barely glanced up at me, flipping his hair out of his face with a quick turn of his head.

He mumbled, "Thanks," as he hunched over his creation even more.

A few minutes later, the teacher came in and took roll. I heard the kind of names I'd heard at all the other schools I'd attended. "Jones, Jeffrey?" Some boy replied, "Here." "Mathis, Jennifer?" Some girl replied, "Here." The teacher then called my name, not my real name, but the one Dwayne, our WITSEC agent, had chosen for me, my new name, "Norris, Charles?" Reluctantly, I replied, "Here." The teacher, who looked like Dustin Hoffman as Tootsie, grinned and asked if I went by Charles or Chuck.

I told her Chuck, since that was what Dwayne said to do.

Predictably, she laughed. "Chuck Norris? Like *the* Chuck Norris? The actor?"

Everyone looked at me and giggled.

"Are you related?"

It was a joke, actually a pretty messed-up one, since I'm clearly Black. Nevertheless, I let Tootsie get her laugh. After Seattle, Dwayne told me, at all costs, not to be conspicuous or I'd be the reason my family got kicked out of the program. Logically, I said, "If you don't want me to be conspicuous, then why'd you name me Chuck Norris?"

Dwayne scratched his cleft chin and looked away. "Because you had it coming."

Tootsie continued roll. Eventually, she called out, "Silver, Sterling?" and the Judas Priest kid looked up from his drawing and said, "Here." He was near six feet tall with the first few sprouts of what I was sure would be a thick mustache by the end of the day. With his long, greasy hair and tiny dagger-shaped earring, he looked like the kind of kid who spent his evenings in a dark room blasting heavy metal and sharpening a switchblade. He slowly looked around the classroom to see if anyone, including Tootsie, would laugh at his name, too.

No one even thought about it.

* * *

By then, my mother was the only one in the family who would speak to me in civil tones. At dinner that night, she asked if I'd met anyone at school. Before I could answer, my older sister, Trudy, muttered, "Highly unlikely, Mother," in her little look-at-me, I-suddenly-have-boobs way. It was obvious she hadn't met anyone yet. She looked a shade more sullen than she usually did. I should've felt sorry for her, but instead I flicked a pea that ricocheted off her forehead and rolled to a stop near my father's plate. He looked up from his food and told us both to can it. Then he kept eating his meat loaf. He still wasn't taking the whole going-into-hiding thing very well.

"Actually," I said, "I did sort of meet someone."

My mother was surprised. She slapped more mashed potatoes onto my plate and dove into her second glass of wine. "What's his name?"

I clammed up for a sec and bulldozed my food with my fork.

My mother looked at me doubtfully. She'd once been a defense attorney. She got bad people out of bad situations, which made me wonder how good a person she really was. She took another long gulp of wine. "Well?"

I said I didn't know if I could tell her.

She looked down. I was at that point considered "difficult," something Trudy relished in.

"He thinks we won't believe him, which I'm sure we won't. Have we ever?" she said.

My mother looked at my father and sister cautiously. She covered my hand with hers. "It's fine. Just tell us his name."

I hesitated at first, as they all watched me. Then I just blurted it out. Even as I said it, it sounded like a lie. "Sterling Silver?" It didn't help that I said it as a question.

Trudy failed to suppress a cackle. My parents rolled their eyes. I'd had troubles in the past, ones I thought I'd outgrown. I was twelve, but to my family, I was still a little boy. I forked a piece of meat loaf and looked down at Rufus, our schnauzer. Even he groaned.

* * *

Phoenix was our fourth city and name change in two years, and it was my fault. Sure, I was good and cagey whenever we moved to a new city or town. I was real spy-like, but eventually I'd let our secret out, and the federales would swoop in and move us under the cover of darkness. It happened first in Seattle, a city I thought was nice and not as rainy as people think. Then there was Denver, which was cold and gave me nosebleeds. After that, there was a place called Boring, Oregon, which was aptly named.

Normally, WITSEC, the Witness Security Program, provides the witness and family with new names and a location far from trouble. Witnesses are encouraged to keep their first names and choose last names with the same initial in order to make it easier to use the new identity instinctively. Once you screw up too many times, though, that idea gets shitcanned, and they just name you any old thing.

I didn't hate my real name, Bernard Black XV. I mean, it would've been nice to keep it. Regrettably, my future, like my father's present, reeked of Financials. We Bernard Blacks, and our family as a whole, went back as far as the 1700s, back to Bernard Black I, a freed slave who was evidently a whiz with figures. With each generation, my ancestral Bernards all put their mark on the financial world, the Black one and a little bit of the white one, with such flair that the *Wall Street Journal* eventually ran a one-paragraph story about our family, calling us the Good Blacks of New York sometime in the twenties. By the time I came along, however, we were on a three-generation skid. Money had jaded us. Whereas my older ancestors rubbed elbows with Booker T., Marcus Garvey, and WEB, my father and grandfather were friends with Roy Cohn, Patrick Buchanan, Michael Milken, and the like. We were rich assholes. There was no other way to say it. We'd sold out. Even on my mother's side (funnily enough, the Whites). My parents both attended prep school and the Ivy League and, like many of their classmates, ultimately became employed by some not-so-nice clients.

However it happened, I wasn't that upset about having that path taken away from me. I became Bernie Brown from Seattle. No more Bernard. Bernie. No more prep. Public. I could be a regular kid, one who, I don't know, actually lived with his family. Unfortunately, things didn't go as planned. In the program, it was said that children have an especially hard time making friends. Unable to share anything honestly, WITSEC kids struggle to connect. In my case, only a few months into our stay, I told someone about my family's predicament. I told them my real name. My sister found out and then my parents. They told

Dwayne. Almost immediately, his cleft chin was in my face. We were out of there.

The same sort of thing happened in every city after that. In Denver, I blabbed. In Boring, Oregon, I blabbed, mostly because it was boring. Anyone would've blabbed. Maybe I just couldn't be someone else. Maybe I kept ruining things because, subconsciously, I wanted everything to be the way it used to be. Or maybe I'd become a saboteur simply because I was a "natural-born shit stain," as Dwayne had started calling me when my parents weren't around.

Whatever the case, now we were the Norrises, my mother, Enid, being Delores, a name she tended to tell people in the manner of James Bond: "Hi, I'm Mrs. Norris, Mrs. Delores Norris." I was pretty sure she'd already dipped into the wine whenever that happened. My sister, Jenny, was now Gertrude, a name I thought for sure she'd slit her wrists over. When Dwayne told us our new identities, I immediately called her Nerdy Gertie, Dirty Gertie, Turdy Gertie. But it was no use. She was going to go by Trudy. She said it sounded rich. My father still told us both to can it.

He wasn't happy about being Chuck Sr. now. Dwayne, in all his wisdom, felt the need to punch up the narrative and give my father the nickname "Big Chuck," even though my father looked nothing like a Big Chuck or even a Medium Chuck. If anything, he was a Diminutive Chuck, a Miniscule Chuck. So was I, but I had a feeling that was Dwayne's lame attempt at irony, a courtesy he didn't grant me. Little Chuck was all I got. When I protested, saying I wanted a more interesting name, Charlie or Carlos or maybe even Carlito, which I thought sounded cool, Dwayne said no. He and his buzz cut wanted to punish me for stepping on his balls. "Little Chuck Norris is it. That's your name. Now shut the hell up."

Obviously, he couldn't foresee my endless ways of adaptation.

*   *   *

It turned out Sterling was in two of my six classes. Our lockers were near each other, our gym lockers, too, and on the way home, we even happened to sit next to each other on the bus. We didn't say a word until the fourth day. He said, "You're that Norris kid."

I nodded. "You're that Silver kid."

When we got off and were walking down a street of brand-new tract homes near Bell Road, he asked if I wanted to see his throwing star collection.

Though I'd never seen one, didn't even know what they were, I said, "Sure. I'm a throwing star aficionado."

He gave me a puzzled look. "Aficionado. That means you like them, right?"

As I was about to say yes, he took out a round, flat piece of metal the size of his palm. It was shiny except for its lethal sharpened edge. He cocked it between his thumb and index finger and hurled it as though trying to maim. It corkscrewed through the air like a fast bird, dipping and diving, until it plunked into a Realtor sign in a freshly landscaped yard twenty feet away. We walked up to it, and the metal was still vibrating. As he yanked it out, as it winked in the sun, I thought it looked like a blade from a pizza cutter. I asked if that was right.

"Yep." Sterling flipped his long hair out of his eyes with a quick turn of his head. "It's not a throwing star, but it'll still fuck something up." He wiped off some of the sign's paint and asked if I wanted a try.

I took it from him, the first time I'd ever held a weapon other than a lacrosse stick. Without hesitation, I chucked the blade, watching it corkscrew through the air till it hit another Realtor sign a few front yards away. The fact that we could've killed someone, or at least scalped them, was quite apparent. Because of that, I thought I should say something like, "Cool."

Sterling said, "Bitchin."

I said, "That means it's good, right?"

He said, "Fuckin' A."

We ran to retrieve it.

* * *

Fortunately, or unfortunately, I'd never developed the talent needed to be the average boy. I wasn't tough or particularly athletic. I didn't care about sports. One of my old gym teachers actually described me as "delicate." So, Sterling and I becoming friends probably seemed odd to others at first. To us, the fact that he was not preppy and I was not white made our friendship inevitable in a very white and preppy school. Luckily, we were only seventh graders, so much wasn't expected of us anyway, especially in public school. I could do my homework and his in fifteen minutes. After that, we were free to spend our afternoons on our knockoff bikes, riding around, having philosophical discussions.

"What's it like to be Black?"

"I don't know. What's it like to be white?"

He thought about it. "I don't know. What's it like to be rich?"

I wanted to tell him it was way better than this, but I thought that would seem elitist. According to Dwayne, we were never supposed to tell people we'd been rich. "Regular," he said. "You're regular people. Average." I put it out of my mind.

I thought of Trudy and my mother. "I wonder what it's like to be a girl."

"It probably sucks. Girls are always sad about something." Sterling hocked a loogy and did a bunny hop up onto a curb. He slowed and then hit the lip of a driveway and did a little jump, spitting as he lifted off into the air. I did the same, surprisingly without wrecking. He turned and looked back at me, flipping his hair out of his eyes. "I wonder what it's like to be a fag."

I waited a second before saying, "How would I know?"

Sterling laughed and put his arm over my shoulder. "Don't be so serious. It was a joke. You're cool." We rode next to each other for a few moments. I looked at him, studying the stubby, coarse hairs over his lip, the tiny moles on his neck. When he finally looked at me and smiled, I felt that same old sensation. I thought, I'll be okay. I can stay here. I have a friend. I can make this work. The sun was shining. If there'd been birds, I was sure they would've been singing.

* * *

Though I'd scored high on the Einstein scale on every IQ test I'd ever taken (160–190), in actuality I was still a little dumb. Even so, it didn't take a genius to see witness protection would put a serious kink in our family groove. Every time we had to relocate, with only a few of our personal possessions, life seemed to lose its meaning. We were whisked away in black vans, sometimes changing vehicles three or four times. We lived in cheap motels for a few months until Dwayne secured a new residence. Each new house was bare, with someone else's ghosts hiding in the corners. All I could think about was my old friends, who were somewhere else, in some other land, where I was sure things still made sense.

In Phoenix, especially for us New Yorkers, nothing made sense. The haboobs, the heat, the lack of decent pizza. Every night before bed, my family and I took turns putting our pillows and bedsheets into the chest freezer so we wouldn't sweat while we slept. We put towels on the car seats so we wouldn't fry our backsides. My mother often drove around in oven mitts. We were on another planet. Before WITSEC, we'd never really left the East Coast, not even for vacation. I'd been at Groton, my sister at Exeter, my parents in Manhattan. But now, with all of us under one roof, we were more messed up than we were letting on. It was a toss-up as to who was worse off.

To combat this, every Saturday, my mother rousted Trudy and me from our beds, where we usually slept till noon, like spoiled rich kids. We'd climb into our Chevy Spectrum to meet my father on his lunch break. Dwayne had found him yet another tax-preparer job, this time at Cactus Taxes out on North Central Avenue. For lunch, we always met at a burger joint called Wimpy's across the street. My mother said we could use some more bonding. She said it was so we would be even keeled, so we wouldn't be so "effed up." I had a feeling she'd already been hitting the wine pretty good by then. She was a dental secretary now. With all her education, I'd probably say screw it and get drunk, too. When I was younger, she seemed so smart and alert, even cunning. Now, having to be low profile just made her seem ordinary.

It bothered me so much that I once asked my father how he'd gotten us into this mess. We were alone, driving through a car wash, our Spectrum engulfed in white suds. The fact that I'd even asked was a huge step for me, since my father always favored my sister. He gave me a sidelong glance and said he may have overextended himself and made deals with the devil. I said I didn't know what that meant, and he said something about his stuck-up white college friends. I waited for him to elaborate, but he just said, "Don't worry about it. Adult stuff," the same thing he said when I told him I'd once seen him holding hands with another woman, a white woman, on a Manhattan street corner.

Maybe the guilt over getting us into our trouble was why he never said much at lunch. He chewed his food really slowly, with an unlit Merit parked behind his ear. He gazed out the window as if somewhere out there was our real life, or maybe just his. Often, as I watched him, I wondered if I was simply looking at myself in the future. Though short in stature, he'd once been a big deal. I'd seen him yell at white people without consequence. At a big Christmas party, I saw my parents, along with all their white friends, snort cocaine off a silver platter. My father even drove a DeLorean for a short time. Now he looked like someone's underpaid guidance counselor. All for what? I didn't even know.

With such a fall from grace, it was no wonder we all ate without talking. We probably looked like the most depressed Black family in the world. Trudy sat next to me, her hair straightened and sprayed with Aqua Net like some girl on MTV. I often slurped on my soda as I watched her glittery fingernails, a different color for each digit, dance across her tray of food. All as she ate ravenously. I had no idea what anyone faced in life. Consequently, I barely noticed when she started ordering more food than the rest of us, two cheeseburgers, two orders of fries, an apple turnover, a Diet Rite, a chocolate sundae. I also didn't notice when she started excusing herself immediately after eating and heading to the bathroom to throw it all up.

I was too busy just trying not to get yelled at. My screwups and the fact that I was the youngest made my mother worry over me. She wiped stuff off my face with a little spit on her thumb. She fixed my shirt collar. She told me to tie my shoes, her sweet, tangy wine breath always in my face. Sometimes, while telling me to do this or that, she'd slip up and call me Bernard. For a moment, we'd be back there in the misty past. I'd feel that crush all children have for their mother. I know she felt it, too. She'd crimp her lips as though swallowing something bitter. Then she'd become my real mother, the defense attorney. She'd say, "I'm sorry. I meant Chuck. Your real name is Chuck." She'd gently press the tip of my nose, like a button, and we were back, in a burger joint called Wimpy's, in North Phoenix, in the dry, hot state of Arizona. Yay.

* * *

Since Sterling and I both lived near Bell Road, the edge of civilization in Phoenix at that time, we were pretty much inseparable by the end of September. My family was in a newer development called Desert Breeze Estates, and his was farther out in an older, loosely developed one called Desert Sands. The first time he came over for dinner, my family just looked at him as he devoured his cube steak and scalloped potatoes and then asked for seconds. We'd never seen anyone eat like that. I think Trudy was especially disgusted. She headed off to the bathroom. My mother, three vinos deep by then, commented on his Judas Priest shirt, which it seemed was the only one he wore. "That shirt sure is—" She paused to come up with the right word, which ultimately escaped her. My father said, "Let's just say it's noteworthy and move on." He slowly slid her glass of wine away from her. She slowly slid it back. Sterling didn't even notice. He shrugged and said thanks and asked for thirds.

I looked at his hair as he flipped it out of his face. I became fixated on a tiny lint ball on the crown of his head. I wanted to pick it off of there, but when Trudy came back and sat down, I found her smiling at me in a weird way. I kicked her under the table. She kicked me back. When dinner was over, my father pushed his plate away and sat in his recliner, chain-smoking, still in his work clothes. Trudy went off to the bathroom again. My mother stayed at the dinner table, drinking. Sterling and I went outside and burned things with a really big magnifying glass he said he'd found.

* * *

The first time I went to his house, he stopped me at the driveway and said, "Wait."

We were both straddling our bikes. I asked what was wrong.

"Nothing." He kicked a rock and looked off. "It's just that you're rich."

I looked up his long, dusty driveway and smirked. "Believe me, we aren't." I started telling him that we used to be rich. I almost mentioned New York, but I thought of Dwayne. I just said my family had fallen on hard times, which after seeing his house made me feel like a fraud.

"No, you're still rich," he said. "Your house is nice. It looks like all the other houses on your street."

I said, "That means it isn't nice and that we aren't rich."

Sterling looked up at his house and said, "Forget it."

The Desert Sands was more of a clump of homes than an actual development. They were dirty and haphazardly terraced on one of the North Hills, all of them surrounded by scrub brush and tumbleweeds, the odd prairie dog poking up out of the dust. When we came up to his house's carport, some guy was inside painting a dented muscle car with a pneumatic spray gun. He was bald on top with shaggy hair around the sides, shirtless, his brawny arms stamped with tattoos. From the looks of it, he seemed to be painting the car the exact same green that it already was. Sterling mumbled, "Rick. My stepdad."

I went to raise my hand to wave, but he stopped me. I looked down at his hand on my wrist. There was an old scar on his thumb. His fingernails were deeply bitten. He let go.

It was then that Rick finally noticed us. He immediately started grumbling as he wielded his paint gun and a lit cigarette in one hand. He called us "little faggots." He told us not to kick up any rocks or dust or else we'd screw up his paint job. We mumbled okay and carefully laid down our bikes and went inside. I looked back at him and thought I heard him call us little faggots again. Then I just heard the hiss of the spray gun.

For dinner, his mother said all they had was cereal. There were no introductions. She just sat on the couch, smoking cigarettes in a wifebeater and pair of bikini bottoms. The room had an odd herbal aroma. A stick of incense smoldered in the ashtray as well as a ceramic pipe shaped like a penis. I looked at it for a second as Sterling made up the bowls of cereal. Then his mother said, "Oh, but fuck a duck. We're out of regular milk. How about chocolate?"

"With Raisin Bran?" Sterling said. "That won't be any fucking good."

I looked at his mother, expecting her to smack him. I'd never heard any of my friends curse in front of their parents, but she didn't seem fazed at all.

"Sure it the fuck will," she said. "It'll be fucking great." As if she thought she'd made our day, she got the gallon jug out of the fridge. She came up behind me, her cigarette dangling out of the side of her mouth. "It's brown like you. You'll like that, won't ya? All you people do." Her gums were severely receded, her teeth the color of butter. She slapped me on the shoulder, let out a phlegmy laugh, and went back to the couch.

I dug in, because I felt I should. I said, "Actually, this is kind of tasty. Sort of."

"No, it isn't. You're just being nice." Sterling got up and poured his bowl into the kitchen sink. He went to his room, and I followed. I looked back at his mother, and she smiled crookedly. "Don't you two be playing any grab-ass in there, you hear?"

I must've furrowed my brow because she laughed so long that I went and caught up with Sterling. Me just turning my back made her laugh even more.

*   *   *

When people sense you're smarter than them, they tend to not like you. Either you ruin the bell curve or you unwittingly make their lives difficult. This is especially true if they're an adult and you're a kid, which was the case with Dwayne. It was unfortunate. A part of me almost wanted to be like him. My life would've been a lot easier. He was white, of average intelligence, broad shouldered and muscular, with a square, symmetrical face. He was married with some children somewhere, I was pretty sure. A gold wedding band usually glinted on his ring finger. Even his cleft chin was somehow appealing, perfectly centered on the tip of his mandible, the mouth of a blossom.

Still, I was sure he despised me. Twice a month, he paid me and my family a visit, showing up in his silver Chrysler K car, sweating in a blue sports coat. He'd check in with my parents, who smiled in his presence but called him a dolt in his absence. He'd go and sit in Trudy's room and talk to her, where I was sure she flirted with him. Then he'd come out, point my way, and say, "You're with me." We'd get in his K car and go somewhere.

He'd ask about school. He'd ask about my family. Then he'd ask if I was maintaining "our cover." I'd give short affirmative answers, and then we'd go to Baskin-Robbins or Farrell's and I'd watch him eat ice cream. This time, though, he turned to me and just said he had me figured out.

"Really?" I said. "And without me even asking. Thanks." The floorboards were littered with copies of *Inside Kung-Fu* with Chuck Norris on the cover.

"You," Dwayne said, "are prone to infatuation. That's what always gets you in trouble." I must've sighed, because he looked at me and asked what was wrong.

I told him I felt bad. I didn't bring any grossly overstated opinions about him.

"Huh?" he said.

"You're psychoanalyzing me."

"Okay."

"In case you didn't know, people don't like that. It makes them feel weird, and it makes you seem condescending."

"That so," he said. "You know what some other people like me don't like? Having some corny-ass kid blow his family's cover every six months, necessitating a new identity and a new home."

I noticed he didn't have his wedding band on anymore. There was just a tan line where the ring used to be. I looked out the window. "Let me guess. You just went back to school. MS in psychology."

My hunch must've been correct, because he told me to zip it. He hated when my comebacks were better than his. I told him I was just processing things. I didn't know if I was still me or if I was slowly becoming someone else.

"See, that's your first mistake. Thinking about it." Dwayne threw on his mirrored aviators. "My dad beat the hell out of me when I was a kid. If I stopped and thought about it, I'd probably kill him and me both." He started to say, "Hell, if my wife knew how to goddamn be one," but then he stopped.

"I guess I should just suppress my feelings and compart-mentalize, then."

"Exactamundo."

I looked out the window as we passed Metso's Cocktail Lounge and then the Paris Adult Theater. Dirty, intoxicated people were swaying out front. "From what I've heard, that leads to more problems."

"Fine." Dwayne destroyed a Chiclet with his incisors. "I can get another psychologist for you to talk to. That sounds like super-duper fun, doesn't it?"

I glanced away and then back at him.

"That's what I thought." We stopped at a red light, and he turned to me intensely, as he sometimes did. As he gathered his thoughts, his face quivering in front of me, I could see my reflection in his sunglasses, two of me staring back. They didn't even look like me.

"Listen, I'm not trying to be a hard-ass. But if we have any more problems, you and your family are on your own. And that ain't no joke."

"Right," I said. "Some mobsters will come and kill us because my father laundered some money."

Dwayne ran his hand over his prickly buzz cut and glanced at me a few times. "That's not what your father did, but hey, things happen. You think they won't, but then they do. That's how life works." He rubbed his ringless ring finger with his thumb and then picked up his hand exerciser and started squeezing it. "I don't think you know how lucky you are. Some of my other cases aren't too pretty. Your family at least had money and education."

"None of which we got to bring with us."

It was a point of contention between him and my parents. All our assets had been liquidated to pay for our relocations. Our pasts were erased. It was something I heard my parents argue about late at night. We didn't exist. We had Social Security numbers but no birth certificates. During some of my mother's drunken fits, she often yelled that she graduated magna cum laude from Yale, with top honors from Harvard. Now, as Delores Norris, she was supposedly only a high school graduate. It had gotten to the point that once we even got in our Spectrum, ready to leave for good. My father backed out of the driveway and wound around the neighborhood for a few minutes. It seemed like all this would be behind us. But he eventually just turned around and we pulled back into our driveway and all went inside like it never happened.

"Sorry," Dwayne said. "But that was the deal. They agreed to it." He looked my way and seemed to soften. Having children probably made him empathize with me. He looked at me over his aviators and shook out a Chiclet, which I took.

We pulled into the Paradise Valley Mall, and he asked if I wanted to see a movie. "Chuck Norris, the greatest action star of all time, has a new film out. Wanna know what it's called?" He gave me a long look. "*Code of Silence.*"

For a moment, I thought he was giving me some sort of subliminal message. It was like him to do that. But then he started telling me that he'd seen the movie six times already, that it was a fine film.

Though I was now named Chuck Norris, I said I didn't know his oeuvre that well.

"Oeuvre?" Dwayne said. "All I know is he kicks mucho ass in it. Good enough?"

I nodded. "*Bellissimo.*"

* * *

Since it was the eighties, Sterling and I were completely unsupervised. We set things on fire on purpose. We set things on fire on accident. We found out that if you put a lit lighter to the nozzle of a can of air freshener and pressed the spray button you'd effectively made a low-powered blowtorch. We singed our eyebrows. When it was really hot outside, we tried to fry eggs on the sidewalk. It never worked.

We listened to Dr. Demento on KZZP. We bought candy

at the Pic 'n Save, which we called the Pick Your Nose. When it rained, we swam in the flooded streets and parking lots. We rode our bikes around half-finished developments that'd been left abandoned. Occasionally, we entered the houses through unlocked sliding glass doors and windows and would fling throwing stars at the new drywall.

We were boys. We called each other fags, fruits, fudge-packers. We watched movies endlessly. At his house, when his mother and Rick were gone, we'd even sneak into their messy bedroom and watch the scrambled Playboy channel on Dimension Cable. A line of static cut the screen in half, naked white bodies wriggling on either side, Sterling and I both getting boners. He'd say, "You're not looking at the guy, right?" And I'd say, "Of course not." Then he'd laugh for a really long time and slap me on the back.

The eighties seemed so bright and neon, so full of commercials, that you could almost forget the feeling of danger that was everywhere. Nukes. Drugs. Stranger danger. Stepdads. The more I got to know Sterling, the more I heard about Rick and his mother. I sensed Sterling didn't like being at home very much. He said sometimes they hit him. When I asked if he wanted me to tell someone, a logical option to me, he said, "No way. Are you crazy? They'll just hit me some more." It was a mode of thinking I slowly came to understand.

A few times, when Rick thought I wasn't at their house, I'd heard him ask Sterling's mother why that "little Black fucker" was always around. He was usually lifting weights in the corner of their living room or punching a speed bag. Sometimes, he stood over a couple of fifty-five-gallon drums in the back of their carport, stirring something that smelled horrible but that he called "primo shit." The first time he called me a name, I looked at Sterling to see if he heard, but he seemed to be in a trance as he played *Asteroids* on his Atari. I sat down next to him, and he did put his arm over my shoulder. But I couldn't tell if it was to comfort me. He pulled his arm back. Our legs were right next to each other. I thought I should move away.

*　*　*

To his credit, Dwayne wasn't completely off with my "infatuations." In Seattle, something had happened. In Denver and Boring, too. There was the word "close." Bernie and Steve are getting too close. Marvin (me) and Peter are too close. Bobby (also me) and Ricky are too close. Their father or uncle or mother would start to think something about me and my family. Some of them were God-fearers. Maybe I was too nice. Maybe I was too different. Wherever we went, we were the only Black family anyway. Maybe that had something to do with it.

With Sterling, I wasn't sure what I felt, but there was a pull. I liked doing boy things, it turned out. Sterling taught me not only how to use nunchucks but how to use them without hitting myself in the balls. He taught me how to open and close his butterfly knife, which he called a balisong, I think to impress me. He said his real father, a former marine, taught him. Sterling's big, blistered hands manipulated my small, soft ones. Hold the safe handle, fling the knife open with a flick of the wrist, let the handle rotate in your grip. The knife was open. Do it in reverse and the knife was closed. There was the vertical open, the horizontal open, the double rollout. The metallic chatter of the knife opening and closing was soothing to both of us. *Flick. Click. Flick.* Open. *Flick. Click. Flick.* Closed.

I became infatuated with the knife. When shut, you would never think there was a blade inside.

I asked where his father was, and he said California and then he scratched his head, as though he wasn't quite sure. "But he's coming for me." He smiled as he flicked the knife. "Real soon." It sounded like an unrealized dream, one that he'd probably been holding on to for some time. I thought it best not to ruin it for him. He said his father moved a lot, was what his mother and Rick called a "dirty hippie." Neither of us really knew what that meant, since his mother and Rick were pretty dirty themselves. The vulgarity of life, as my grandfather used to say. We were in the middle of it. It sent us farther into the world to figure things out for ourselves.

* * *

By the middle of the first semester, we'd gone from innocence to destruction to the taboo, which just meant that we'd sneaked into a few R-rated movies. But we stepped up our game. We cursed around grown-ups. *Fuck. Bitch. Dickhead.* Somehow, when I wasn't paying attention, Sterling had developed the unique ability to show up with things he said he'd "found." His butterfly knife. That big-ass magnifying glass. More throwing stars. The latest issue of a porno magazine called *Black Tail*. We kept a lot of these treasures stashed in Paradise Valley Park, in a huge bush that was hollow in the center. It was so big we could crawl inside and hang out under the canopy, sitting cross-legged as we looked at these illicit things. My heart beat quickly as we played with the butterfly knife, as we flipped the pages of the magazine, me trying to look just at the women. Sterling openly rubbed his crotch, always saying the same thing, "Look at that ass. Look at those tits. Look at that puss." I sort of twisted the waist of my pants to make them tight against my own dick. We got to the back of the magazine and laughed at all the ads for VHS tapes for sale. *Sex Wars. Indiana Bones and the Temple of Womb. Frisky Business.* When it got dark, we put everything but the butterfly knife in a little ammo box we'd buried there inside the bush. We jumped back on our bikes, and Sterling said, "Man, I've really gotta get my hands on one of those tapes, right?"

My privates were still a bit warm. I was almost afraid where this would go. I wondered if we were heading too far into the taboo. I wanted to tell him that he should probably stop "finding" things. We could think of other things to do. But when I looked at him, I thought of his home life and the fact that now he was happy. I said, "Sure. That would be cool. Why not?"

* * *

I didn't see Sterling for a few days after that. I knocked on his door, but there was no answer. I thought maybe he'd gotten in trouble for stealing, that he was locked up somewhere in a juvenile facility, but on the fourth day, his mother slowly answered the door. She was in her usual tank top, a cigarette dangling from the corner of her mouth. She could barely keep her eyes open. "Oh," she said. "Sterling's gone. He's gonna live with his father for a while. He didn't tell you?"

I said no, but I wasn't sure whether to believe her. She said she wanted her kid to live different places. "Not just this hellhole." She said, "You know what I mean?" as though I weren't just a kid. Something in the distance caught her attention, and she watched it for a moment. Then she laughed. I sensed this story was her version of the events. Inside the house, I heard Rick grumble, "Good riddance. I was tired of that little shit anyway." I asked her how long Sterling would be gone, and she seemed to lose her train of thought. Her tired, bloodshot eyes curled up briefly under their lids. I reached out and touched her arm, and she woke up. "Don't worry," she said. "He'll be back." She turned and wandered away from the open door and into the back bedrooms. I saw Sterling's butterfly knife sitting on a table in the foyer. I walked far enough inside to reach in and grab it.

* * *

A week went by and then two. I wrote Sterling a letter and left it at his mother's, hoping she'd send it to him. Three weeks later, I got a letter back. It was written in his chicken scratch. He apologized for not saying goodbye. He said his father, now a truck driver, stopped one night and picked him up. He was living in Los Angeles. He said kids from Arizona were called "zoners" there, but that he'd already earned the respect of some "surfer dudes." The last line said, "See, I told you he was coming for me." He didn't once ask about me. I went to our bush in Paradise Valley Park and read it a few more times. Each misspelled word made me miss him even more. I looked at *Black Tail*. I studied the men and rubbed my crotch. I even ordered one of the tapes from the back, which, with a simple money order, was surprisingly easy to do for a minor. It arrived in only a few days. I popped it in our VCR when no one was home. There were no opening credits. The screen just went from static to a scene with a Black man and a white woman. I thought of Sterling. I watched it a few times, hiding the tape in my bottom dresser drawer like a weapon afterward. Eventually, I just threw it away in a dumpster behind a mall.

I got used to being alone again. I stayed in my room, play-ing with the butterfly knife, as Rufus the dog slept on my bed. I began to feel as though this was how the rest of my life would be. I realized I'd known Sterling for only three months. It'd felt like more than that. I went back to our bush in the park one day and was startled to find some older kids looking at our things. I told them that it was our spot. They laughed and pointed at Rufus. "Who? You and your dog?" I told them it was my stuff. They said, "Not anymore, gay boy. Go home."

I began to wonder if my family and I were now finally set-tled, if this was what was supposed to happen in every other city we'd lived in. Maybe we'd all accepted a certain misery. Maybe we'd adapted. For some reason, I began to hate Sterling for it. He'd gotten out of his purgatory and left me in mine. He'd been rescued. I sometimes dreamed that I'd wake to my family packing all our stuff and leaving in the middle of the night. But in the morning, everything was still the same. My dad was at the dining table slowly smoking a Merit as he read the newspaper. My mother was next to him rubbing last night's wine from her eyes. Trudy was in the bathroom, curling her hair. I was the only one still holding out hope.

* * *

On the day of school pictures, I came outside to wait for the bus and found Dwayne in his K car parked along the curb in front of my house. We were due for a visit, but this seemed unplanned. I looked down in the window, and he was staring toward the North Hills, looking almost directly at Sterling's house. His eyes were pink. His buzz cut was a little long and fluffy. His wedding band still wasn't on his finger, just the tan line. He looked over at me, his head wobbling on his neck. He slid on his aviators and tiredly said, "You and me, buddy." He slapped the passenger seat. "I'm taking you to school."

He'd been drinking. It was obvious. I could smell his musky, stale breath in the car. He shook a pile of Tic Tacs into his palm and threw them in his mouth. When he crunched on them, it sounded like he was eating little rocks. I got in.

"So, what's new?" He gently thumped the wheel with his hand, as though to a song only he could hear.

I said, "Not much. You?"

He touched the base of his ring finger again and cleared his throat a few times. "Same poop. Different toilet."

I looked back out the window.

"Is everything okay with you guys?" He was suddenly keyed up, as though he wanted a task. "Should I be worried about anything?"

I shrugged. "Maybe we'd be okay if you just left us alone."

After a moment, he said, "I can't do that." He glanced at me shyly. "Besides, I don't want to. I like you guys. You're a nice family." His voice cracked in an odd way as we rode past Metso's Cocktail Lounge and the Paris Adult Theater.

I asked if everything was okay with him. "You're acting different."

He immediately said, "Am I?" as though it was a funny thing for me to say. Then he touched his ring finger again. He held it as if it was broken. Suddenly, his smile melted, and he covered his jaw with his hand so I couldn't see. "Fuck," he said a few times and "God, I love that woman." He crouched over the steering wheel and proceeded to bawl.

After a moment, I put my hand on the shoulder pad of his

blazer. I could feel his muscles trembling underneath. I said I was sorry for his loss.

He wiped the tears from his eyes and smiled. "You know, you're a good guy for saying that."

When we pulled up in front of my school, there was a line of kids snaking into the gymnasium, where pictures were being taken. I realized this picture would make my life here official. There was nothing I could do. In the yearbook, my face would be next to my new name. It would be me but not me. I wondered how much of my life would be spent pretending. I turned to Dwayne. "Do you think we're all going to be okay?"

I wasn't sure he understood, but the way he whimpered somehow made me feel better. "One day, I hope."

I got out of the car and left him there. I waited in line. When it was finally my turn, I stood on an X in front of a white background. The photographer held up his hand like a conductor starting a symphony. He smiled. I smiled back. In my mind, I could see Sterling on a California beach. I could see my family living happily in New York. I could even see Dwayne. "Perfect." The photographer lowered his hand and did a countdown. All through that moment of anticipation, I held still. I kept smiling. Even though I knew the flash was coming, I swore I wouldn't blink.

COWBOYS

We were supposed to be unarmed security guards, just a couple fellas watching over things, but Ernie carried a gun anyway. He showed it to me my first night working at the museum. We were about to make our rounds when he said, "Hey, Shelton. I wanna show you something." He hoisted his foot on top of the front desk and drew the gun from a holster strapped to his ankle. He presented it to me on his palm, like it was a mouse he kept in his pocket. The scratched gray revolver was almost as small, the kind corner boys in DC would've called a "better than nothin.'"

"My brother, Ralph," Ernie said, "he's a bail bondsman, by the way. His wife, my sister-in-law, *she's* Black. Myra's her name. Yep." He rocked forward and back on his heels and kept looking at me.

I nodded and said, "Good to know." Then I looked away, hoping he didn't think all us Black folks knew each other.

Ernie was likable enough for a white guy. I mean, I guess I liked him at the time. We had things in common. He was divorced. Sylvie had left me. Like two stray dogs, we could smell how lost and alone the other was.

Five minutes after meeting me, he said he was a retired cop, which made me a little nervous. But he talked so much about "collaring perps" and "walking a beat" that it sounded more like TV lingo than real life. I suspected he hadn't "served on the force" for very long, if at all. The only thing I knew for sure was he was forty-three, just a big white dude who was constantly red-faced and sweating. The sour smell of alcohol seeped from his pores. The damp, curled ends of his hair were always glued to his shiny forehead.

"Here, Shel. Hold it." He gestured at the gun. "See how it feels."

My being from DC had put ideas in his head. Maybe I harbored a dark past that had gotten by the background check. But I didn't, nothing that serious anyway. The worst things I'd ever done were shoplift beer or scrawl graffiti as a young'un.

With Ernie watching me, I took the gun and pointed it. I felt I should comment on it, as if I knew the first thing about them. I moved it up and down and said, "Wow, got a good balance to it," and Ernie beamed like a new father. He was still watching me, waiting for me to do something, so I spun the gun around my trigger finger and handed it back to him like a gunfighter. I didn't even fumble. A new respect sparkled in Ernie's yellow eyes. I'd bought a gun recently and still wasn't sure why. It seemed like a good thing to have, even though I could never hold it for long. A hot second or two, and my hand turned clammy. I'd have to set the gun back in the lockbox in my closet.

As we started our rounds, Ernie walked beside me, watching a wildlife documentary on the cracked screen of his phone. There wasn't much work to do. There never is, guarding a wax museum. We simply sprayed the mannequins with our flashlights and made sure nothing was moving that wasn't supposed to be. It was the weirdest and easiest job I'd ever had, during the weirdest and hardest time in my life. After the first day, I wasn't sure how long I'd last. I wanted to quit after the first hour.

The museum was called the Waxsonian, and it was owned and operated by an older Vietnamese guy who'd reinvented himself when he came to America. He even changed his name to, of all things, Richard Doberman. According to Ernie, he'd been taken in by a white family when he first came to the US and eventually took their last name, even married one of their daughters. "Can you believe that? Dick fucking Doberman. Almost sounds like a porn star, don't it?" Whenever Ernie found something funny, he wheezed out a few chuckles and then exploded in a convulsive fit of coughing. "But you gotta respect the man's hustle. Am I right?"

I said he was right.

Apparently, Doberman had made major bucks in some business or other, enough to make converting an old bank building into the Waxsonian seem like a good idea. Ernie and I could never tell exactly how successful the place was. We didn't think it was important enough to have a security guard, let alone two. All we knew was it somehow stayed open, housing over three hundred mannequins, most of them pretty close to real. There was Obama and all the other famous presidents, celebrities like Babe Ruth, Marilyn Monroe, and Muhammad Ali. When the museum was dimmed to only security lamps, the dummies displayed in the glass cases looked like people frozen in big blocks of ice.

I listened off and on to the British dude narrating the documentary on Ernie's phone. He talked about the "seamless coiling" of a running cheetah. How there's a certain point in its stride when none of its paws touch the ground. I walked alongside Ernie, watching the animal hang in the air. The British dude then started talking about the cheetah hunting a wildebeest, how it swats the back legs, trips the prey, and goes in for the kill.

Ernie stopped midstride and watched. Bored, I wandered over to the cowboy display. Doberman had a thing for westerns and dedicated a whole section of mannequins to those movies. There was Clint Eastwood, squint-eyed, biting down on a cigarillo. Gene Autry, holding a white guitar to his chest. And Roy Rogers, also with a guitar, but standing next to a golden horse. Out of all of them, the John Wayne mannequin looked the most realistic. I caught myself staring at it, half expecting it to wink at me. Then I noticed the mannequin of a Native American behind him like Tonto, set decoration.

That was when Ernie sidled up next to me. "I bet you don't know what happened to cowboys, do you?"

I said I didn't really care all that much, but I guess he didn't hear me.

"It's an easy one. Barbed wire." Ernie selected another video on his phone and waited for it to load. "Cowboys used to keep the cattle together in herds, but when barbed wire fences came along, no one needed cowboys anymore. They lost their families. Some of them became outlaws. There are still some around, like in Wyoming and Texas, but they ain't real cowboys." Ernie tugged at his belt and hitched up his pants. "Now they're just guys on horses."

*   *   *

Around seven in the morning, quitting time, Mr. Doberman walked in the door, happy. He sported a toothy grin, slick black hair parted on the side, and he was threaded in his usual JCPenney's finest: a western shirt, boot-cut slacks, and cowboy boots.

"Everything go all right last night, fellas?" His English was flawless. He sounded more American than we did. If you closed your eyes, you'd swear he was from down south somewhere, Alabama or Georgia maybe.

"Yep," Ernie said. "All was quiet on the home front."

I was the new guy, so I never knew what to say to the dude. I only ever stared at Doberman, unable to reconcile his voice with his ethnicity. Most Asians I'd come across in DC were voiceless people behind corner store glass. They didn't speak a lick of English, much less sound like a country star. "Great," Doberman said. "Why don't y'all get outta here and get some sleep. I'll see you boys tomorrow." He always dismissed us like a sheriff did his deputies, and Ernie and I walked out to our cars.

After my first shift, Ernie invited me to hang out with him in his beat-up minivan for a while, which quickly became our routine, since neither of us liked going home right away. He opened his glove box, and I spotted a bag of weed and a pint of Virginia Gentleman among a wad of old papers and parking tickets. He said, "Ain't too early, is it?" and dug out the bourbon. As he tipped back the bottle and took a few gulps, the brown liquor glugged softly. A string of fat bubbles rose to the top. I'd acquired a bit of a drinking problem growing up. When Ernie passed me the liquor and I felt the bottle in my hand, I couldn't resist. I looked out at those leafy suburban streets and thought of Sylvie. I took a quick swig just to get it over with. The sweet burning liquid swept through my chest in a wave. I licked the warm walls of my mouth. I hadn't taken a drink in three years, a stretch of time when I used to have nightmares about relapsing. During better times, I was so happy to be over all that, but now here I was. I took another swig, and looked out the window again, knowing this was the beginning of a long, ass-ugly binge.

Ernie shook his head and laughed. "Don't be scared. This is the suburbs, brother. No one's gonna arrest us. We own this damn place." I wasn't sure who he meant by "we." He let out a hoot and then rolled down his window and fired a glob of spit into the air like a cannon. He wiped his mouth with his wrist and laid the pint down between us. I lit a cigarette and shook one out for him since he'd killed his whole pack during our shift.

"Menthols?" Ernie grimaced. "What is it with Black guys and menthols?"

"They're stronger," I said. "They taste better, too. They leave your breath minty fresh."

"Well, damn," Ernie said, "you ought to do a commercial."

We passed the bottle a few more times, watching the sun get brighter. The liquor started hitting me. I smiled for no reason at all and watched Ernie squint so hard against the sun that he reminded me of some down-and-out philosopher.

* * *

Even though the town house I'd rented was a damn sight more expensive than I'd counted on, I took the security guard job to forget about Sylvie leaving me more than to pay the bills. I was twenty-six and had my head up my ass. Being a security guard at a wax museum almost made sense with the trajectory my life was taking. The only other job I'd ever had was at a DC hardware store, where I worked since the twelfth grade. I went from cashier to head clerk pretty fast, almost made manager. Then I got the bright idea to move out of the city. We'd lived in DC all our lives. I thought Virginia would be different, even if it was just twelve miles away.

After two months in the suburbs, though, Sylvie wasn't having it. She was a city girl. She wasn't built for the burbs, she kept saying. The girl barely left the house, and when she did, she usually got lost. She spent more and more of her time lounging around in our La-Z-Boy in one of my old football jerseys, one leg draped over the arm of the chair. She looked like she just woke from a nap, her eyes always tired and wet. I'd already run out of comforting things to say. What do you say to someone who can't stop crying? Best I could do was to tell her she needed to get out more. "You're in here hibernating like a bear," I said. "Let me take you out." But she still stared at the TV. *So You're Having a Baby* and *A Baby's Story* on the educational channels were her favorites.

It was our second crack at the whole living-together thing, and the shit wasn't going well. Whenever I went out to look for a job, I'd come home to find all the furniture rearranged back to the way it was in our old place. Every night while Sylvie slept, I'd un-rearrange it, knowing she'd put it right back when I was gone.

Eventually, she moved back in with her mother, and the mail was all I had to come home to after my shift at the museum. It was always just junk mail, but occasionally I'd get a sympathy card, one or two stragglers still being forwarded from our old address. Some of them actually mentioned the pain of losing a child, and I'd wonder when they'd stop coming. I'd heard of people getting twenty-year-old letters that had been lost in the mail. I thought I'd still be getting the things in my fifties. On top of that, once a week I got a bill from the funeral lending company with

PAST DUE stamped on the outside. I had the nerve to open only one of them. I saw the balance, twelve thousand dollars and one cent. That one cent always bothered me. I couldn't open any of the others. I just put them in a box in my closet and crawled into bed with my uniform on, shoes and all.

* * *

At the Waxsonian, Doberman didn't give us much in the way of entertainment, nothing to take our minds off our pitiful lives. There were no security monitors or cameras to mess around with, no high-tech control center with blinking lights. The museum was pretty low budget in that sense. I mean, we weren't guarding plutonium or a nuclear reactor, but the dude could've given us something to tinker with. All we had was our phones and each other's corny stories to keep us company.

By the second week, I had the sneaking suspicion that I'd been hired to keep an eye on Ernie more than guard the museum. Most nights, we shot the shit for a few hours and then dozed off after lunching on microwave burritos and a few beers. Then we'd wake up and shoot the shit some more. On Friday and Saturday nights, car headlights would sweep into the parking lot and rouse us from our naps. Catholic school kids trying to get some booty in their parents' BMWs. We spent those nights chasing them away, Ernie always waiting until the girls had at least a titty out before he tapped on the window.

Occasionally, when he was especially lazy, I'd do rounds by myself. I'd walk the halls of the museum with my flashlight, scanning each mannequin's face. Obama. Frank Sinatra. Richard Nixon. A young Elvis and an old Elvis in dueling poses. I would stroll along, bored out of my mind, and suddenly catch myself in front of the female mannequins. Diana Ross. Dolly Parton. Even Nancy Reagan's old ass.

Though I said I'd never treat the mannequins like people, once or twice I did touch them. The hair on their heads was surprisingly soft and realistic, but their clothes hid broomstick limbs locked into hard, narrow bodies. Even their molded heads were as hollow as pumpkins. I suppose if they'd felt more natural, a less sane man would've planted a kiss on one of them. I wasn't that far gone, but occasionally as I walked around the museum, I did get an eerie sense that the world had stopped, and I was the last person alive.

* * *

I thought working at night would make me feel invincible. I thought I would own the night, but all I really owned was my loneliness. It was the same for Ernie. The way he latched on to me said I was probably the closest thing to a friend he'd had in way too long. He talked a lot about women and what pains in the ass they could be, especially if we broke out the liquor early and caught ourselves staring at Pam Grier.

Even though Ernie had been divorced for a while, he still referred to his ex as "the wife." He'd say how, before she asked for the "big D," which was what he called the divorce, the wife told him that he'd turned into a beast. "She actually used that word, man. Beast! Believe that? Like I got fangs or something and hair all over my body. I mean, goddamn, she didn't even mean it in a good way, like in bed, you know?" Sometimes, he'd lower himself onto the black-tiled floor, his knees popping and cracking, and he'd start doing push-ups, or try to anyway. "She didn't mind me being an animal when a burglar broke into our house. Oh, no, she didn't mind that shit. I had him hog-tied before he knew what hit him." He attempted a push-up, but his arms didn't cooperate.

The one time Ernie asked me about Sylvie, I pretended everything was fine. I never let on that she'd bailed on me before I even took this job. I could tell it made him jealous. I had a woman to go home to, and he didn't. It was one of the only times he ever got shy. He mumbled, "You two engaged?"

I said, "No, we're just living in sin for right now."

He wheezed a laugh that didn't become much more. "No kids then, huh?"

I shook my head, no, but I didn't actually say the word.

* * *

When Sylvie and I first moved, I tried to play up the suburbs as more civilized than the city. I practically bankrupted myself taking her to the best restaurants: all-you-can-eat crab joints, restaurants with cloth napkins, Italian places with real Italian waiters who grated big wedges of cheese over your pasta. Sometimes, I'd let the waiters keep grating and grating just to see how long they'd go. I pointed out forests and fields of grass whenever Sylvie and I passed them. "Like grass is some shit I've never seen," she'd say. I'd reel off facts about the suburbs, like the median income or the price of an acre of land. I ran down crime statistics. I said how there were more potholes in cities, how cities were harder on cars and lowered their re-sale value, and how city people were usually myopic, "which means they can't see far." She said she knew what it meant, even though we both knew she didn't. I barely knew what it meant, and I was the one with a few college courses under

my belt. "More people in cities have to wear glasses than anywhere else," I told her. "Because everything's always up close."
Of course, she turned it around on me, talking about how she
liked things up close, and obviously I didn't.

I just couldn't understand why she wanted to go back
to our old block. It was an okay-looking neighborhood and
everything. There were stately brick houses with clean yards,
some good people. But none of that mattered when you could
still buy weed, rock, and heroin any time of day, a gun, too,
if you wanted. It was a place where it wasn't strange to hear
sirens or pops off in the distance a few times a week. One or
two, and it was probably firecrackers or a car backfiring. More
than that, and it meant somebody was getting clapped. At
least one person in each of our families had been shot, some
of them killed. Men, women, even children.

*   *   *

My third week on the job, Ernie started in about his brother's
bail bond business. "It's booming, partner. There's always gonna
be criminals to bail out." He was tuning a police scanner that
he'd brought in from his van. "It doesn't really get interesting
until they don't show on their court dates, though. That's when
the skiptracing starts. Ralph's skiptraced all over the country.
Geez, all over the world." I'd had to bail out a few hood cousins
so I already knew about bail bonding. Whenever Ernie started
with the cop lingo, I knew not to take him seriously. "It's really
a racket when you get right down to it. Bail bondsmen cater to
the criminal element. They can get away with things cops can't."

We listened to the police scanner, teasing out from the
static a conversation between two cops about a movie one of

them had seen over the weekend. They said something about a blond's nice ass.

Ernie continued. "Ralph's been to West Virginia, Tennessee, Arkansas." He bent his thick fingers back one by one, counting. "He had to fly down to Meh-hee-co one time to get some little chico wanted for a bunch of robberies." Ernie rubbed the stubble on his cheeks. This was another questionable story, but I let it go. I'd learned to enjoy his altered sense of reality. It made me not feel so bad about being drunk.

Ernie and I swigged our beers and gazed out the large museum windows into the night. "I moonlight with him every now and then when I need the money."

I smiled, remembering how he'd made a point of Ralph's marriage to a Black lady.

"You think you'd ever want to help us out?"

I laughed. "I'm not a bounty hunter. I'm not trying to get shot either."

"Believe me, you won't get shot. The most I've ever had to do is tackle somebody and sit on them till Ralph threw on the cuffs. I get paid up to two grand just for doing that."

"Really." My funeral bills were so overdue that a deep-voiced collector was leaving messages on my phone once a week. I would've had to sell a kidney just to partially pay them off.

"I'm telling you," Ernie said, "it's easy. You look like you're in great shape. You play ball in high school? What am I saying? All you guys play ball, don't ya?"

"I did, but I don't know about all of us. I bet you're gonna ask if I like fried chicken next."

"Man, you know I didn't mean it like that. Besides, I love fried chicken."

I draped my arm over his shoulder and pulled him to me. "Of course you do, Grand Wizard. Haven't burned any crosses lately, have you?"

Ernie pushed me away. "I'm telling you. You got nothing to worry about."

My block back in DC flashed through my mind.

"Nothing will happen to you. I'll set it up."

I didn't have one reason to take him seriously.

* * *

During my fourth week, Ernie and I really started getting cockeyed on the job. A twelve-pack of beers one night, a fifth of Wild Irish Rose the next, Thunderbird and Rebel Yell after that. Ernie was shadowboxing with the mannequins by then. He stood in front of Clint Eastwood playing draw, and I stood drunk and antsy by the front desk. He ambled over to me, tossing the gun from hand to hand, around his waist, and under his leg.

"That thing's not loaded, is it?"

He said, "What am I, an amateur?" and set it on the desktop. His hair was curled up more than usual and pasted to his slick forehead. "If Patty could see me now. She'd say I need to get my poop in a group."

Stupidly, I asked why she left him.

You'd think I'd just insulted his mama. He whipped his head around. His eyes blazed, but then they died out. "I don't know, man," he said.

The alcohol made me serious all of a sudden. I put my hand on his back, but I didn't leave it long.

"You know what it was? She started taking these fucking

classes at the community college, psychology and whatnot. Then she started hanging out with one of her teachers. She'd come home wanting to analyze me and shit." He said after she kicked him out, she actually let the teacher move in.

I messed up by asking if he thought the wife was hooked up with the teacher.

"Hell no. Patty ain't gay." He looked at me for a long time. "How you gonna ask me something like that?"

I told him I was sorry.

He spun away. He got down and did one enraged push-up. Then he lowered himself back to the floor. "I told you about the burglar, right? I had him hog-tied before he knew what hit him."

"Yeah, you told me."

"Who's gonna protect Patty now? That teacher?" He rose one creaky joint at a time and plopped down next to me at the front desk. He tipped his chair back against the wall and took a nip from the bottle. "Man, all the big Ern wants is a nice woman to be with. A good meal, some cable TV, maybe a glass of wine. And I don't even drink that much." He swallowed a long hit of Rebel Yell and took a wincing breath. "I'm a Christian. I wear a plastic watch, and I drive a minivan."

I laughed to fill the dead air around us. Ernie chimed in halfheartedly. He handed me the bottle, and I partook of its pleasures. "You ever been shot?" I picked his gun up off the desk.

"Nope."

"You ever seen anyone get shot?"

"Shit yeah. What about you?" He focused on me. His bloodshot eyes brightened. He hoped I had a ghetto story to tell.

I lied and said no, I hadn't.

* * *

Sylvie had been gone for a month and a half, and I was spending a lot of time on the couch. My house still had a landline, an old beige touch-tone phone that I kept next to me, the mismatched black cord coiled up like a snake. When she first left, I took satisfaction in watching all the sports I wanted since she always griped when the channel rolled over to ESPN. Eventually, though, I started watching all her shows. *Bundles of Joy. Babies Do the Darndest Things.* Even *Oprah*. I'd sit there and dial her mother's house, and I'd always hang up after the first ring. On rare occasions, after I'd hung up, I'd call her a bitch in my head and feel like a criminal. I was drinking like a fish, smoking like a chimney. Somehow, I even lost my cell phone and was too messed up to get a new one. I was back on my bullshit.

So, it was never a question of if I'd do something stupid but when. Conveniently, it happened on a Sunday, my night off. I was home, holding down the couch as usual, my fifth beer balanced on my chest. The phone was on my stomach. In the lockbox next to me, the metal plating of my gun reflected lamplight as clear as a mirror. When the phone rang, I thought it was just the bill collector, but then I thought it could've been Sylvie. I was so out of it that I almost expected to hear her voice when I picked up. But it was only Ernie on the other end, saying my name.

"Everything all right?" He'd never called me before. I didn't even remember giving him my number.

"Yeah, all's fine." He inhaled deeply. A long silence passed.

"Well, what's up?"

"Nothing. I'm just calling to see if you want to make some money tonight."

"Tonight? We're supposed to be off, aren't we?"

"It's my brother, Ralph," he said. "He needs some help. I told him you were interested. He needs two guys this time."

I sighed. "I never said I was interested."

"It's not anyone violent. Ralph'll handle everything. He probably won't even need us, and we'll get paid just for showing up. He said we can split the bond collateral three ways. It'll be a little over a grand apiece."

I could hear that collector's bottomless voice echoing in my ear.

"One thousand dollars," Ernie said. "For doing nothing." After a moment, he said, "You'd be doing me a favor, too. Seriously, I could use the money. The wife's got the irons to my ass on the alimony." His voice took on a low, pitiful tone I'd never heard before.

I stood and walked a wide circle in the living room as the long phone cord curled around my feet. I didn't say anything for a time.

"Shel, you there?"

"Yeah."

"Maybe you can just watch this first time. See how it goes down."

"I don't know." I looked at my beer. "I've been drinking. Well, actually, I'm drunk."

Ernie said, "Shit, so am I."

Surprisingly, that was all it took.

* * *

I drove over to the Waxsonian, where Ernie and his brother were already waiting next to a large truck. The fat-tired Ford was as red as a fire engine. All the spotlights and long antennas made it look like a humongous remote-controlled toy. Ralph appeared to be in his late thirties, shorter than Ernie, about my size, and stocky as a silverback. He wore a camouflage baseball hat with military insignias.

"Ralph Zabriski. Nice to meet ya." He removed a hand from the pouch of his sweatshirt. We shook firmly. He had a large holstered revolver perched on his right hip; a flashlight and stun gun were on his left. "Now that we're all here," he said. "Tonight, we're gonna be violating one Josephine Powell. She goes by Phiney."

"Violating," I said.

"It's a law-and-order term. Don't take it literally. Just means we're taking her into custody." Ralph popped a stick of gum into his mouth and continued. "Phiney's staying over at a house somebody rented for her. I'm gonna knock on the door and ask her to step outside. If she's cooperative, I'll cuff her. You guys will be around back just in case."

I asked what crimes she committed.

"Bad checks, in the tens of thousands."

"See, told you, petty larceny. Easy money, buddy." Ernie grinned at me, his eyes glassier than usual.

Ralph hopped up on one of his truck's large rear tires and dug around in a toolbox in the truck bed. I thought again about his wife. I wondered if she was light skinned like Sylvie or dark skinned, if she was heavyset or thin, if she resembled Sylvie at all.

"Ernie, you ride with Shelton. You guys will follow me. Now, I gotta know. Are either of you armed?"

"Always." Ernie removed his gun from his ankle holster and set it on the hood of the truck with a clank. I pulled mine out and set it gently next to his. It was bigger and shinier than his. His face twisted up ever so slightly.

Ralph picked up my gun and looked at it. "Since neither one of you is sober, I should confiscate these till we're done."

I prayed he would. I didn't know why I'd brought it.

"But I'm not gonna," Ralph said. "You might need them. I'm just telling you right now, if anything happens, you're on your own."

Ernie and I looked at each other and nodded.

"Okay. Here." Ralph dumped six pairs of handcuffs onto the hood of the truck. "Take two each," he said. "Phiney hasn't exactly been eating at the salad bar."

* * *

She was staying at a house in East Falls Church. We arrived there around ten thirty, the moon hanging low in the sky. We parked a few houses down from hers and walked up the street, ducking under tree limbs. She lived in a small shotgun bungalow. As we hid in the shadows, Ralph told us to go around back. He'd take the front. "I'm not losing my license because of you two," he whispered. "So, don't do anything stupid." He tapped the revolver on his hip. "Don't pull these out unless she's got a weapon. Hear me?" He pointed to the stun gun hooked to his belt. "If she puts up a fight, I'll just tase her."

Ernie and I split up, and I crept around the right side of the house. It was one of those moments when you don't feel like yourself. I didn't know how I'd ended up there. I was sitting on the couch drinking beer and watching TV a half hour earlier. I sneaked into the backyard through an open gate and heard Ernie climbing noisily over the fence. Finally, he poked his head around the other corner of the house. That was when Ralph knocked on the door.

Someone began stomping around inside the house, a series of thumps that rattled the windows in their frames. I tiptoed up the porch steps and peeked through the back door. I could see straight down a hallway to the front. Without realizing it, I caught a glimpse of her. All the lights were off. Phiney's big body moved slowly across the dark hallway. It was like looking through the observation window at the National Aquarium as a large fish glided into view. She moved in front of the door and turned on the hall light. She was a sister, light skinned like Sylvie. And she wasn't just plump. She was built, muscular. The woman had been working out. She was a head or two taller than Ernie and broad as a barn. She wore a pink tank top and shorts. Her hair was, for some reason, tied up in crooked pigtails.

She opened the door, but as soon as she saw Ralph, she flung it closed. It snapped his head back, dropping him to his knees. Phiney spun around and charged down the hallway. I moved to the side of the door and ducked down by the porch steps. I had no idea what I was gonna do when she exploded through the door. I fumbled with the handcuffs in my back pockets and dropped them. I reached for my gun and dropped that shit, too. What the fuck was I doing there? Ernie shuffled around behind me as the door flew open and slapped the outside of the house. She stopped and stared down at us. My shoulders were level with her knees. The porch light eclipsed her head, a black sphere hovering where her face should've been.

I reached out and clutched one of her legs and prickly hairs brushed the palm of my hand an instant before she kicked me right upside the head. I fell to the ground and tasted dirt and beer, with a chaser of vomit. Her legs blurred by me as she ran to the back fence faster than I expected. She called for help. She screamed that we were killing her. It was so dark I couldn't see her or Ernie anymore. I could only hear their feet swishing through the grass.

I followed the sound and made out Ernie in the darkness. He was pulling at her clothes, trying to get a hold of her. He kept saying, "C'mon. Come with me." At one point, I swore he called her "sweetie." The next thing I knew, Ernie tripped and hit the ground. All his air left him in a painful wheeze. He gasped my name, reaching an arm out. I helped him stand. I looked ahead and could barely make out Phiney swinging a leg over a chain-link fence and disappearing into a neighbor's yard. Ernie threw his good arm over my shoulder, and we made our way back to the front. I almost wanted to go back and find my gun. But then I thought, fuck it, leave it. I didn't want it. Ralph yelled, "I'm going after her," and sped away in his truck, skidding around the corner, but we didn't care. A few moments later, tires screeched. There was some kind of collision. Ralph's horn blared. Then it stopped.

Ernie and I didn't say anything to each other. He slumped on the hood of my car and let his bum arm dangle. After fifteen long minutes, Ralph's truck crawled around the corner like a tank and stopped in the middle of the street, all of its spotlights blazing. Ralph jumped out and hobbled over to us, wiping blood from his upper lip. He blew his nose and spat a wad to the ground. "This is the third broken nose in three years. You guys okay?"

I said I was fine.

"Ernie?" Ralph studied his face.

"Leave me alone, you asshole."

"Where is she?" I peered into the cab, expecting to find her restrained in the passenger seat, but it was empty.

"In the back," Ralph said.

I turned to the truck bed and saw the outline of her big body. Ralph and I walked around to the tailgate. "What the fuck did you do to her?"

He scratched his neck. "I was chasing her, and she ran into my fender. I was only going five miles an hour."

Phiney lay on her stomach, groaning like she was dreaming. Her arms were bent at her sides. Three linked cuffs held her wrists over the small of her back. I followed the length of her body and saw that she had only one slipper on. Her other large foot was bare and callused. I couldn't believe I was standing there with two white dudes I barely knew, over the body of a woman I just helped hunt down, a Black woman.

"We need an ambulance."

"No, we don't," Ralph said. "Calling an ambulance will open a can of worms we can't close. No, she got her clock cleaned, that's all. Seen it a hundred times."

I leaned over the truck bed and watched her. Her face twitched. The rhythmic rising and falling of her body showed she was breathing. Her eyes fluttered, and she mumbled gibberish, something about going to jail. We were just standing there when Ernie lifted her large foot and gazed at it.

Ralph was too busy massaging his nose to notice. "It was hell getting her in here," he said. "She's five hundred pounds if she's an ounce."

Ernie held Phiney's foot loose in his hand, as if it had just fallen into his palm. His head tilted to one side. Her other slipper rested against her leg. It was the biggest terry cloth slipper I'd ever seen. I picked it up and eased it onto her foot. Ernie set her leg down. We didn't dare look at each other.

* * *

Ernie and I didn't talk much on Monday night. We barely drank. His left arm was in a sling, and I had a knot on my forehead. It was around one in the morning, and we were watching a documentary on his phone. It was about African pelicans, how they migrated north, stopping at lakes and rivers for rest and water. About halfway through their trip, though, they ran into a drought. What used to be a lake the size of a football field had dried to dust. The British dude narrated so heartlessly. The ground was cracked, waves of heat wiggling up. The pelicans stopped flying and started walking so their chicks could keep up. After a few days, they had to leave the chicks behind. For their own survival, the British dude said. They showed the pelicans flying away as the chicks on the ground watched them go. Some of the chicks flapped their wings. Some still walked. One simply stopped. It didn't squawk or try to fly. It just sat there and waited.

"That's messed up," I said. "The cameraman's right there, I'm sure he's got some water." I sat forward and wrung my hands.

"They can't," Ernie said, flatly. "It'd mess up the flow of nature." It was about the only thing he said all night.

* * *

When seven rolled around, quitting time, Mr. Doberman strolled in the door, smiling as usual. One look at us, though, and he was confused. "What the hell happened to you two?"

I glanced at Ernie. He didn't want to talk. "Rough weekend," I said. It was probably the most I'd ever said to the dude.

He blinked a few times. I could see his wheels turning. What stupid shit had we been up to while he wasn't there? An empty fifth of Rebel Yell that we'd forgotten about stuck up out of the trash can next to the front desk. He picked it out and held it up by two fingers. He eyed both of us again before dropping the bottle back into the trash. "Fellas?" he said. "Don't come back here. And don't think about asking me for a reference."

He watched us go. I looked over my shoulder and saw Doberman glancing around, inspecting things. It made me want to go back and apologize. *This isn't the real me. I'm not usually like this.* But I turned and jogged up to Ernie. We went out to our cars like any other morning. I began to think on that morning, genius that I was, that maybe I'd attached myself to the wrong person. Ernie was so pitiful with his back hunched, his arm pressed tight to his body by the sling. We'd probably never see each other again, but all I said was, "Later, man." I got in my car and let him leave out of the parking lot first. He didn't give me his usual wave.

I'm still not sure what Ernie and I were to each other. We weren't alike, really. We hadn't picked each other. Life had put us together. I knew almost nothing about him. I didn't know where he grew up, couldn't say if he was left-handed or right-handed. I didn't even know where he lived. I thought I should've known at least one true thing about him. That's probably why I followed him that last day.

I stayed a few car lengths behind, expecting to tail him home to some run-down apartment building or maybe a dingy trailer. To my surprise, he stopped in a cookie-cutter residential neighborhood a few miles from the museum. He parked in front of a ranch house across from a golf course. The house was a dull blue with white shutters and boxy bushes. A sprinkler shot a long jet of water over the lawn. As I parked a half block or so behind him, a middle-aged woman in a yellow robe came out on the front steps to water her plants. When she saw Ernie posted across the street, she paused there, and her face stiffened.

A second later, another woman came outside. She wrapped her arm around the wife's waist. They both glared at Ernie before turning to go back inside, first the wife and then the teacher. He didn't get out or try to talk to them. He just sat there in front of the house, probably tipping his head back to take a drink.

I stayed there for five minutes, realizing this was a funeral. He eventually pulled away, and I turned my car around and went back to my rented house. I sat by the phone, trying to pump myself up to call Sylvie. I rearranged all our furniture, worked up a good sweat, and then stopped. This call wasn't going to be easy. It was my last chance. After some hesitation, I dialed the number. I circled the living room as the line rang. By the tenth ring, I thought no one was there, but I let it keep going. I turned and something made me look back. I could see the long black phone cord trailing behind me just like a tail. And that was when someone finally answered.

CHUCK AND TINA GO ON VACATION

All their friends were doing it: traveling to interesting places, staying in amazing rentals. Mike and Kenya were the first. In December, they went to Bali and rented one of those over-water bungalows. They posted videos of themselves diving into the ocean right from their porch and dog-paddling to a swim-up bar. #balibrunch. In April, Ricky and Sanjay went to the South of France and posted videos of themselves dressed in robes and stocking caps, roaming their rented château like Ebenezer Scrooge. #castlelife.

June wasn't much better. Lisa and Marla went to Iceland and stayed in a modern fortress. They asked Chuck and Tina to go, but unfortunately Chuck and Tina couldn't swing it. "It has a private chef," Marla said. "Are you sure? The food's gonna be cray-cray." No, Chuck and Tina said. They were sure. All of Lisa's and Marla's posts consisted of plates of food, puffin, lamb, walrus, each dish speckled with luscious sauces.

Upon seeing them, Tina sat Chuck down, and they liked each and every post so as not to appear jealous.

"But are we jealous? I don't feel jealous."

"That's because we're not. We're just happy for our friends, the way they'd be happy for us."

After a moment, he said, "Do you think they'd be happy if we went somewhere interesting and amazing, too?"

Without hesitation, she said, "Probably not."

* * *

The right place for them came along in September. Jabari, a friend of a friend, had just finished renovating a small rental in Mexico. He had a weeklong slot open, and Chuck and Tina could have it at a discount. The only problem was Mexico wasn't exactly high on their list. It wasn't that they were prejudiced, classist, or some snobby first-worlders. They were Black. They were conscious. They were woke. It was just that they'd already been to Cabo and now wanted to go somewhere more exotic, Madagascar, Uruguay, somewhere their friends had never been. "So, instead of being snobs," Chuck said, "we're just picky and competitive." He pulled at his soul patch.

"Yeah, but who isn't all those things?" Tina swiped through the pictures on the travel site. "Holy shit. The apartment has a private pool. We've never stayed anywhere with a private anything." They were used to hostels and rooms for rent, scary bathrooms shared with who-knows-how-many mysterious people. This place, though, was a work of art, a modern three-bed, two-bath open concept. It was hard to tell where the apartment ended and the patio began. It was new. It was almost like it was theirs.

Seconds after seeing the last pic, Chuck and Tina whipped

out their Air Miles card that they had no business putting more money on.

"Fuck it," she said. "Why the hell can't we do it?" She clapped like a quarterback ending a huddle.

Chuck hit the Book It Now button and saw the final price. Really, it wasn't that bad. But all he could think of was their next credit card bill, and their student loans. Their balances were up there, a frothy wave of already-spent cash cresting over their heads. Without meaning to, he made a weary face.

"I'm not making you do this, am I?" She was sitting cross-legged on their old love seat, stroking their cat, Kunta.

"Not at all. This place is cheap as hell, but we have to be careful after this. That means no going out."

"It means no going out for you, too."

Chuck nodded. "A little fiscal austerity never hurt anyone."

Tina nodded, too, but slowly, as though her mind had wandered. She twisted one of her dreads. "But debt is part of being an adult, isn't it? Besides, I think it'll be good to have something to look forward to."

Chuck didn't really need much to look forward to except a couple of beers after work. But he agreed. Why start a fight when they were supposed to be happy?

* * *

As their plane reached cruising altitude, Tina said, "Can you believe we haven't been anywhere in five fucking years?" When she was excited, she cursed openly in public. She'd taken full advantage of the weak complimentary coffee before takeoff, stacked it on top of the two cups of real coffee she'd gulped at the gate.

Now she was as wired as a cokehead, talking loudly over the noise of the plane. Chuck hated when she got like this, but he knew she hated when he came home from the bar with one too many beers on his breath, knocking over shit.

"Yeah, this is gonna be great. A real recharge."

"We're gonna recharge our asses off," she sang.

"We're gonna have a pool. We can go skinny-dipping." After fifteen years, he still thought she was the most beautiful, shapely woman in the world. She, on the other hand, didn't consider being shapely a good thing. Just the mention of skinny-dipping made her turn away and look out the window, wrinkling her nose as though she'd picked up the scent of a stray fart.

Her long-lost mother had been shapely. She was six months dead now. Chuck was still kicking himself for calling Tina shapely just last week. They were coming home from a friend's party and were climbing the four flights up to their apartment. He was pretty drunk, and she was really drunk. He was just trying to get some, after so long, but her drinking dysphoria had set in. Too much booze made her morose. "I will never be like my mother. Fuck her drug-addict ass and fuck you, too." She was suddenly screaming.

Chuck cleared his throat and looked at the floor. "Okay. Fine." He put his hands up as if he were being robbed.

She tried to hide her shame, but then she turned to him. She jutted out her bottom lip and said, "Sad emoji." As consolation, she led him into the bedroom, and they lay down. She unzipped his slacks and began to stubbornly jerk his dick. It'd been months. But he'd had too much whiskey at the party. There was a reason they called it whiskey dick. After a few frantic tugs, she just said forget it and dropped his thing like a TV remote with dead batteries. She rolled over in her party clothes. He rolled over in his. They both fell into a long, deep sleep.

* * *

After customs and an hour-long ride with the private driver they booked, they reached the hill town of San Miguel de Allende, in Mexico's central highlands. Chuck and Tina could feel the elevation in their heads and their lungs. For a moment, they felt drugged but in a good way. It was evening, and they looked out from the comfort of the blacked-out SUV. The streets were cobblestone, the architecture baroque.

Jabari's place was in the Centro, near spas and boutique hotels, restaurants and coffee shops. The apartment was on the top floor of a two-story bright-yellow building. They walked into a domed living room, the ceiling's intricate spiral brick pattern making Chuck think of fallen dominoes. To the rear, the lighted pool glowed like an aquarium. It was flanked by a gas grill and a couple of hammocks and teak patio furniture. Just like in the pictures, this place was a work of art. And it actually was hard to tell where the house ended and the patio began. There were six glass patio doors that folded open at the touch of a button. Chuck pressed it, and a small colorful bird flew in, did a quick loop around the living room and then glided out, tweeting as it left. "Oh, hello, little bird," Tina said.

Chuck kept opening and closing the doors, trying to figure out how they worked, until she told him to stop.

"I love everything about this place."

"Yeah," Chuck said. "The smooth concrete just waiting for someone to crack their head open on is really swank."

Tina playfully flipped him off. She opened the bright cabinetry, ran her fingers along the little Day of the Dead tchotchkes and art on the walls. As they walked through the place, she just kept saying, "Holy fuck. Can you believe this? I can't believe this."

Chuck wandered into the kitchen and played with the bank of switches and dimmers for all the different lights. He messed around with the remote-controlled air conditioners and the industrial ceiling fans that spun so fast they looked like they'd fly off and kill you. He opened the gigantic fridge and found Jabari had left it stocked with snacks and beer. "Are you kidding me?" Chuck reached for two cold ones and twisted off their tops. "Okay, babe. I'm convinced. This is gonna be the best trip ever."

* * *

Their last few vacations had been bad. Years ago, when they went to Japan, everyone told them not to go in June, monsoon season. Chuck and Tina didn't listen. They were itching to go somewhere, anywhere. Of course, it rained the entire time. They didn't get to see half of the temples on their itinerary, and most of the restaurants they wanted to try were closed. They'd go back to their tiny Ueno hotel room soaked down to their underwear, their socks blue from the ink bleeding from their jeans. It sounded worse than it actually was, but it seemed to be the beginning of weirdness in their marriage.

All their trips were like that now. Chicago was windy. Miami just wasn't their style. Even Vancouver, BC, probably the most innocuous place in the world, had been a bust. They'd gone for her thirtieth, a risky proposition since her birthday celebrations had become suicidal events. Just being in a new place made them overdo it on the day drinking. Each night, in their budget hotel room, she cried into her box of takeout, lamenting how old she was. What had happened?

In grad school, they'd had so many good trips, Glacier National Park, the Outer Banks, London. After grad school, they had more good trips, Amsterdam, Paris, Stockholm. They prided themselves on two simple facts: they'd never been on a cruise, and they'd never been in a tour group. Their student loans hadn't cramped their style yet. Chuck and Tina were even beginning to think they were cosmopolitan. "We'll live abroad one day. I just know it," Tina said.

Now, who knew? They'd recently developed aches and pains and the need to use reading glasses. They'd rounded the age of thirty-five. Death was just up ahead. So, at this stage in their lives, did they really need to live abroad? They already lived in Brooklyn. What would be the point?

*　*　*

Chuck stumbled through the apartment for some bottled water in the fridge. Evidently, it was morning, and he was hungover. They'd drunk a lot and, it turned out, gone skinny-dipping, too. Yeah, he remembered that now, slightly. Their clothes were strewn all over the patio, along with empties of Jabari's beer. As Chuck awakened further, he felt a familiar crustiness in his boxer briefs. He looked down in there, and the sour funk of intercourse wafted out. He smiled to himself. It was such a lovely smell. He even felt lighter, maybe from finally getting rid of his pent-up sperm. But then he felt terror light through him. He'd had sex with his wife and now didn't remember a second of it. Shit, they really had to stop drinking. He went back to the bedroom and found Tina twirling one of her dreads around her finger and staring at the ceiling, wide awake.

"Everything okay?" he said.

She blinked and didn't answer.

"Hello?" He handed her a bottle of water.

"I nodded yes." She rolled away from him and drank. She did this sometimes. She was thinking about something, and it was best not to ask what it was. "I'm hungover, okay? Leave me alone."

"It's okay. We're good." He thought of asking if she'd found a new therapist. She'd had a minor disagreement with her last one. But he knew she'd just ask if he'd found one, too. After his father passed, he'd gone and talked with a soft-spoken white guy named Bob without telling her. At first, she thought he was having an affair. He eventually admitted he'd been seeing Bob, and then he ended it as though it were an affair. He didn't want people knowing he was in therapy. For him, it was as bad as knowing someone frequented a prostitute.

The last year had been nothing but loss, though, first his pops and then her mom. Chuck and Tina were parentless now. All they had was each other. His head ached. His eyeballs wanted to explode. Bringing any of this up with a calamitous hangover would've been bad. They were supposed to be forgetting things, not remembering them.

"C'mon, let's rally," he said.

They got ready and humped it over to a nearby expat coffee shop. They scrolled their phone screens looking for things to do, realizing they didn't have even one idea. Chuck said he'd gotten so busy with work that he didn't do any research.

Tina stared off and bit her fingernail. "Neither did I." They'd meant to get a guidebook from the library, but they both kept putting it off. This is what their life had become. They used to be prepared and thorough. Now, maybe because they went out too much and occasionally drank too much, they were losing the details of their life. They forgot to pay bills. They spent money just to have something to do. Somehow, the excitement of life had vanished, and they were standing there patting their pockets like it was a set of keys they'd lost.

Chuck found a list of local museums. They were always good vacation fodder, nice, sober experiences that made eating and drinking copiously after seem earned and necessary. "I mean, isn't that what vacationing is about?"

"What?" Tina said. "Going to museums so we have an excuse to drink?"

"No." Chuck shrugged. "I just mean living and being together." He snapped a pic of her and then opened one of his apps and posted it. "See?"

* * *

Chuck and Tina rallied hard and spent the next day or so posting everything: their lunch (a Mexican po'boy with fried oysters), them wearing big straw hats, them wearing little straw hats, their dinner (a table of local dishes, full of beans and beans and more beans). They went on a posting terror, riddling all the apps everyone used.

"It's like a blanket media campaign. Chuck and Tina Go on Vacation."

"We're doing a posting drive-by," Chuck said. "We're dumping on these fools."

As they barhopped the next afternoon, they were startled to see that their social media history mirrored the spiritual ditch they'd been stuck in. Some of their posts had just been sad, pictures of graves and flowers and funeral programs. Why had they posted that?

Chuck took a picture of a fly on the rim of his beer bottle and immediately posted it. "But not anymore. We're correcting our lives. Am I right?"

"We're killing them, baby," Tina said.

They sent off posts like bullets at a gun range. Each time they clicked Share, they felt a jolt of electricity, like the few times they'd done coke or ecstasy. They shared everything, even a really cool slow-motion video of them jumping into the pool, holding hands.

* * *

They rode that feeling into their third night. They ate at an expensive Italian place, posted each dish online with a funny caption. They drank bottled water with no ice, which they also posted. They had two bottles of wine with dinner; a white and a red. It was their perfect amount of alcohol. Yet another post.

As they strolled back to the Centro, Chuck said something about Jabari's apartment, and Tina corrected him. "Our apartment, good sir." They were a little tipsy but definitely not drunk. He forgot what he was saying because she was happy now, walking elegantly in her espadrilles like when they started dating. She looked down, a content shine to her face. Chuck pulled out one of his secret packs of cigarettes, and she didn't even scold him for it. They shared an American Spirit as they tried not to roll their ankles on the bumpy cobblestones. They held hands. At the apartment, they started to change into their swimsuits for one last dip, but once they were naked, they went to each other and then the bed.

"Finally." He moved on top of her.

She sighed. "Why do you always have to say odd things right before you put it in?"

"Do I?" He stopped and thought about it.

She reached down in between their legs and just said, "Let's get this show on the road."

* * *

The vacation was going well enough, but they were shocked to find their thirty-post sharing spree had garnered very little interest. Someone had liked and commented on something, but it was just his aunt Vernell. And the picture wasn't even of Chuck. It was one of the churches in town. All she said was, "Don't eat anything that ain't cooked down there, you hear? You'll get the shits."

Her comment had already gotten ten likes, with a bunch of laughing emojis. Chuck immediately sniffed out the setting to delete the comment and the one to block Aunt Vernell.

"Why can't I get rid of her this easily in real life?"

"Your aunt's been cray-cray. She's probably never even been to Mexico. Has she ever left Yonkers?"

Chuck was pretty sure she hadn't. "Why are my relatives so tiring?"

"You haven't seen her in a long time."

"I know. Now she's popping up, talking shit." They were at a different expat coffee shop, a shabbier one around the corner from the apartment. A knot of flies fought in the middle of the dining room. Chuck and Tina were drinking macchiato and crunching on stale biscotti. They'd already had goat cheese omelets that weren't that good. Tina told him not to eat the parsley and slice of shriveled tomato that still garnished their plates. He asked why, and she said, "That's just what the internet told me." They both looked at their apps and were now realizing their social media lives were complete duds. Tina had a like here or there from distant friends, ones without discerning tastes.

"It's sad," Chuck said. "I was expecting an avalanche of love."

"Maybe we should make our profiles public. Then strangers will like them and boost our numbers." Without telling him, she found her app's privacy setting and undid it.

"You mean be public like Marla?"

"No, not like Marla. She's a social media hoe. We can be subtle."

Chuck's mind wandered back to Aunt Vernell. It brought up that old generational conflict that he'd talked to Bob about. Along with his father, Vernell had raised him. They went to church a lot, yet they cursed and drank a lot. They didn't think much of gays or Asians or Jews or pretty much anybody, even most Black folks. Now she was his last relative. He closed his phone and looked out the window at a gaggle of Mexican women in traditional Guanajuato dress.

"Don't worry," Tina said. "Your aunt's tripping. She should keep the negativity to herself."

"Yeah." Chuck shook his head. "But it's the only thing she's good at." He gazed out the front window again. He looked at Tina and realized she was the only thing he had going for him. Without thinking, he ate the slice of shriveled tomato that garnished his plate.

"Uh-oh," Chuck said.

"You didn't just eat that, did you? I told you not to."

"I know. Shit." He darted his eyes around. He touched his throat. "It didn't taste bad, though."

"Oh." Tina's face loosened, and she looked back at her phone. "I'm sure it'll probably be fine, then."

* * *

Within fifteen minutes, he bloated up and exploded from both ends in Jabari's master bathroom. After his fourth dash to the toilet, he decided to just stay in there for good. He cursed Mexico. He cursed the trip. Why did they come? Aunt Vernell was right, that old prejudiced biddy.

"No, she wasn't right," Tina said. "It's just bacteria. Mexico isn't any filthier than America. We just have different bacteria. It's racism that fuels that narrative. It's like people thinking Chinese food gets them sick because of MSG. MSG is in everything." She looked up "food poisoning and Mexico" and was now reading from her phone. "See? I told you. When people from Mexico go to America, they have the same problem. It's bacteria. I mean, you got sick at a Denny's, remember?"

"We were in Arkansas," Chuck said.

"My point exactly."

"Fuck that. Fuck this place. I'm dying." He puked uncontrollably while she watched from the doorway. He jerked and heaved. His body expanded and contracted. He looked like he'd give birth to a demon.

"When we get back home, I'm getting you on my probiotics," Tina said. "You've always had a bad digestive system."

"Please just leave me. Let me die." He actually began to weep. "When will this end? Oh, God."

As she eased out of the room, she watched him ball up on the tile floor in his underwear like someone in detox. "I'll bring you something to eat, okay? I promise."

"I'll never eat again, you hear me? I think I just cracked a rib." He let loose on the toilet, dry heaving, groaning in agony.

Softly, Tina said, "I love you?"

* * *

She was out on the street, in the sun, by herself. She didn't know what to do, but then she stopped and had a coffee and looked at a map on her phone. She was suddenly determined to have a good time. She hated that he was sick, but now she was relieved to be out of that apartment and away from him. She realized she didn't just want to go on vacation with him. She wanted to go with herself. He could be such a weenie sometimes anyway. He acted like he was the only person to ever get the flu or a sore throat. But she still loved him. It was luck that they were still together. Neither of them had wandering eyes. They were committed without really trying. However, that didn't mean she didn't occasionally dislike or resent him. As her therapist, Erica, had said, it didn't mean she didn't want to be with him.

"Right?"

Tina's exact response was "Sure, I guess." She stopped seeing Erica right after that. She had a vague sense that the woman just wasn't on her side.

Now that Tina thought about it, her stomach wasn't feeling the best either. As she wandered the streets, she slipped down an alley to spit up a morsel, which she deposited into a hole in the sidewalk that had rebar and wires sticking out of it. When she emerged and was back in the sun, she was fine. She was hopped up on caffeine. She was speed-walking around the square. He could never walk as fast as her, and now she didn't feel that pull to slow down. She happened upon a huge food and craft market and felt like a young traveler again. She tried fresh juices and a lamb soup. She discovered a stand that sold deep-fried grasshoppers in different flavors.

She saw Mexican people and white people and Black people and Asian people. She struck up a conversation with an older Mexican man about bread and how Americans don't think bread exists in Mexico. "We make better bread than the French," he said. Tina told him the bodega under their apartment back home baked fresh bread and always made their building smell sweet and yeasty. But that was more when she and Chuck were first married. Their building didn't quite smell like that anymore.

She sucked down another coffee and called Marla. "Hey, girl. I'm so glad I'm not in New York right now."

"Well, good for you. I gotta go feed that damn cat, don't I?"

"Yes, you have to feed him. If that cat dies, I will kill everyone. He's all I have."

"Well," Marla said. "There's Chuck, too."

"Of course. Girl, what're you doing?"

"It's one o'clock. I'm working."

Tina hadn't heard her. She'd just sat down at a bar and was telling the bartender she wanted a Corona.

"You're bored, aren't you?" Marla said. "You always want to go on vacation but don't want to be away from your life."

"Bitch, I just got rid of one therapist. Don't make me get rid of you, too."

Marla laughed. "You convince yourself that you don't like the place you're in, even though it's just fine."

Tina fluttered her eyes. "Girl, whatever. Chuck's sick. He ate a bad tomato. He's puking all over everything."

"He's probably being a real crybaby about it, isn't he?"

"Kind of, but it's pretty bad. I've never seen him this sick."

Marla wasn't listening. She was yelling at someone about deliveries coming through the back. She called them "fucko."

"Hey, have you ever had grasshoppers? They're really good."

"Chapulines? Did you have the mango ones with the spicy seasoning?"

"Girl, I'm eating them right now." The bartender brought her beer, and Tina gulped from it. "Hey, no one likes our posts anymore. What's up?"

"Oh, we muted you guys a long time ago. I thought you knew."

"How would we know?"

Marla sucked her teeth as if she were about to break some bad news. "You never post. And with everything that was going on with you two, if you did post, it was some depressing shit. People have to consolidate their contacts once in a while, you feel me?"

"Okay, but we're in Mexico."

"You are."

"We're on vacation for the first time in years."

"Yeah."

"Can't y'all just be happy for us?"

Marla laughed inconsiderately, as she often did. "Girl, everyone's been to Mexico. You're not special."

* * *

This was how the vacation would go, Tina realized. While Chuck writhed on the cold bathroom tile, she was out and about, vacationing by herself. She took a tour of historic homes in the area. She went wine-tasting. She stumbled onto a Segway tour. Purely by chance, she was offered a little bit of weed by a bartender, too, which she saved. She'd have five to six hours of fun with complete strangers and then cobble together some food and snacks to take back to Chuck, who she was always afraid would be dead on her return.

He'd be on the couch or in bed, watching *Forrest Gump* or some other Tom Hanks movie dubbed into Spanish. This time, she'd found Twinkies and Squirt and a few cans of chicken broth and some crackers. "I still haven't seen a real grocery store. It's all quick marts."

"Just like home," Chuck said. "I'm on bread and water anyway. I've been imprisoned in a beautiful apartment. What a great vacation."

"Are you sorry we came?"

"I'm sorry I got sick." He was in bed, with the covers up to his chin, a washcloth on his forehead. He said, "Baby, I'm so hot." Then a minute later, he said, "Baby, I'm so cold." Then he just moaned.

Tina waited for the right moment to say she wanted to leave New York. Now seemed like it.

"What? And go where?"

"I don't know. Here?"

He shook his head. "You do this every time we travel. You dream of living in the place we're visiting."

"So what?"

"I get this sick, and you want to move to the place that did it? Do you just like having me on the verge of death?"

"You had bad luck. People get sick here once in a while. I talked to a white lady from Chicago who lives here. She said everything will be fine for months, but then you eat a piece of jicama that hasn't been washed, and you're shitting your face off. You get used to it. People take their stool to get tested here a lot, too, to check for parasites."

"Baby, you're not making this place seem very appealing. I gotta carry my own shit around with me? Are you listening to yourself?"

* * *

The next day, Tina strolled around, went in shops, had a drink or two and ended up smoking some of Chuck's cigarettes. Each time she opened them, the joint she'd gotten from the bartender stood like a devil in a corner of the pack. She sat down on a bench and wondered if they should leave early. She looked on her phone to see if they could rebook, but it would be an extra three hundred per ticket. She knew Mr. Fiscal Austerity wouldn't approve. She put her phone away. She went walking, working up a blister on her pinky toe with each step. She was looking for a place to get a massage when she got a call from Marla.

"Hey, girl."

"Now don't flip, but your apartment was broken into."

"Are you serious?"

"Yeah," Marla said. "When have I ever played a practical joke?"

"Was anything stolen?"

"Hard to tell. Y'all don't really have anything."

"What about Kunta? Is he okay?"

"Your door was open when I got here. He set up house in the hallway. It looks like he peed all over."

"Shit, did you clean it up?"

"Oh, no, no, no, honey. I don't do pee."

Tina looked around, feeling helpless. "How could this happen?"

"You've been posting on your vacation. When did you go public?"

"Fuck." She'd forgotten to take her last name off her profile. Shit, she even had something about her neighborhood in her bio, something goofy like "Flatbush 4 Life."

"Yeah," Marla said. "Easy to put two and two together online. Why were you posting on your vacation anyway? Everyone knows you post vacation pics after you're back."

"Well, you didn't."

"Oh, no, baby girl. Check the dates. I post as soon as the plane lands."

Tina suddenly started to cry and then stopped, a survival skill she taught herself growing up. "Well, fuck, I guess I'm not a pro like you." She could hear Kunta meowing in the background. "Please tell me my kitty's okay."

"This fat dumb cat is fine."

"Jesus." Hearing the cat made Tina break down one more time. "What is happening to my life?"

Marla just started laughing, inconsiderately again. "Girl, this is New York. Either move or stop crying."

*   *   *

Tina still got a massage and a mani-pedi that she would never tell Chuck about since it was hella expensive. She put it on her card, not their joint one. As she left she felt like she was out of things to do. It was Saturday. The town had been overrun by a million twenty-year-olds from Mexico City. They all seemed to be wealthy expats, which wasn't hard to figure out since they were so loud and drunk. Walking among them, Tina realized she still felt like a twenty-year-old a lot of the time until she was around actual twenty-year-olds. Then she was envious and repulsed. Now that she was bored and the trip was turning out to be a bust, she wasn't so sure she wanted to move here after all. She'd rather be on a coast. She wanted water and a beach. It was too rugged here.

Whenever she contemplated her latest mishap, it made her go back to her first one, getting married in the first place. She and Chuck were almost done at Columbia. They were twenty. Maybe, like all their other decisions, it had been a hasty one. What if they'd never gotten married? Would they even be the same people now? Would they be together? Sometimes, while out at their local bar Chuck would ask if she ever regretted getting married so early. She'd say no and then ask if he did. He'd say no, but they were never sure if the other one was telling the truth. But they loved each other, and here they were. Their mild doubts weren't enough to disassemble an entire life just because they were bored and getting older.

"Right?" Erica had said.

Fucking Erica, Tina thought as she looked for Chuck's cigarettes. She'd smoked all of them, but there was the joint she got from the bartender. "Okay," she said. "It's your turn." She was standing on a quiet street. She had to figure out which end of the joint to light. When the coast was clear, she took a few good drags and then saw an older Mexican couple approaching on her left. She felt lighter as she moved to her right. Whoa, she was already feeling it. It was good stuff. She hadn't smoked in so long. In her younger days, she'd liked it a little too much.

Now she wondered why she was even doing it. She thought of her mother. Tina was contemplating whether to put it out or just get rid of it, when a pack of young guys came around the corner. They took one look at her and were now saying, "Hey, mami," and "Mira, mira" in mocking American accents. "Can we get some, señorita?"

Tina took a last drag and tossed the joint at them. "Here, fuckos." It hit one of them in the chest, the ember exploding. They started to surround her. She thought of calling them other names. One kid with zigzags cut into the side of his hair picked up the joint and puffed on it, reaching out for her hand. A lighter-skinned kid with a mole on the very end of his nose grabbed her arm and said, "You're kind of fine for an older lady." Her first instinct was to slap him, which she did. The flat of her palm connected with his cheek. *Smack.* The boys gasped, and she let out a snort of laughter. Nose Mole looked back at her, slightly angry and slightly smiling. She ducked under his arm and took off running. She looked back to see if they were chasing her. They were coming around the corner, saying, "Where are you going? This weed's good. You got any more?" They sounded like kids now.

The apartment was just at an angle across the plaza. She sprinted past a mariachi band and people dancing in formation on a stage. Tina unlocked the street door and closed and locked it. She ran up the stairs and then closed the main door behind her, locking that, too. She let herself cry quietly in the foyer, bending over so her tears would fall away. When she was done, she went into the bedroom and told Chuck about the break-in. The weed was really hitting her now. She was high, and he wasn't quite awake. He sleepily asked if everything was okay. *Law & Order* dubbed into Spanish was playing on the TV. It was the end of the episode, where they got the suspect to confess to everything. She said, "Yeah, everything's fine. Go back to sleep."

"You sure?" He sniffed the air. "You smell like weed."

"Go to sleep." She suddenly loved him so much, but maybe that was the ganja talking. "You're imagining things."

He looked at her one last time as though she were a stranger, and then he closed his eyes.

* * *

Their last day, Chuck was feeling well enough to finally leave the apartment. They had a lunch reservation at an organic restaurant and farm just outside of town. It was a long, bumpy taxi ride, but they got to see what lurked in the lowland in the daylight. The Centro was eclectic and cosmopolitan, up on the hill. The lowlands were dusty and crumbling. Even the light-headedness of being up there in the Centro was gone. They felt heavy now, but oddly their minds were clearer. The lowland was where all the factories and garages and transmission shops were. People ambled along, carrying things on their heads, pushing old shopping carts full of junk. One poor man limped down one of the cracked sidewalks, and it appeared his deformed feet were not facing the right way.

The organic farm was away from all that, five miles out of town, in the middle of nowhere. It was run by British expats. The farm's small restaurant looked out over lush fields where every kind of vegetable ripened in the sun. Chuck's appetite was finally back. He ate everything in sight. He said "*Muchas gracias*" so much that Tina finally said, "They're British. They understand English just fine."

She watched him eat pasta with meat sauce and duck confit and pâté and profiteroles. She had just a salad. He was pale and depleted, looking like he'd lost weight. "But the food is so good. Maybe we should move here. Right here."

After a moment, she looked over at him and said, "You don't mean that."

"You're right." He laced his hands behind his head and sat back. One of the farm's cats jumped up on their table, and he stroked it.

* * *

Their flight the next day wasn't too early. They took their private car to the airport. They checked in and were on their plane by noon. It was the end of another vacation. They were already thinking about work and the errands they should've run before they'd left. They thought about their regular lives and reality and their bar friends. Maybe this was a good-enough life for them. New York wasn't so bad. They were broke. They would never own an apartment or a house, but at least they had culture and friends and each other.

The plane took off, and they were up in the air, leveling out. The FASTEN SEAT BELT sign was turned off.

Chuck smiled at Tina. "I had a dream that you'd been smoking weed one night. Isn't that crazy?"

She smiled and rubbed his head. "That is crazy." She made a sad face. "You were so sick. I'm sorry."

"It's okay. Did you at least have a good time?"

"Of course," she said. "It was great."

He cleared his throat and looked at her. "So, we're good, right?"

Just him asking made her have some kind of emotion. Sadness? Love? Probably both. "I think so."

They smiled at each other just as the plane shook through a few pockets of turbulence. They thought it would end, as it always did, but then there was chatter from the pilot, something like, "Sit down. Hold on." The cabin panels rattled. Their window shade dropped shut. Chuck and Tina gripped their armrests and were overcome by dread. This vacation was over. It had been a wash, and now they were going to die. They turned and looked at each other. They were just beginning to see the fear in their eyes when the ride smoothed out. Chuck lifted the shade and saw they were flying through a city of clouds, the biggest he'd ever seen. He reached for his phone to take a picture, but Tina put her hand over his. They looked out again, feeling like the only people up there in the air. And for a moment, they were mesmerized.

THIS ISN'T MUSIC

You are an asshole. Remember that when you meet Billie at the bar. She's in a booth in the back. A beer sits across from her. Every few seconds, she looks for you over her shoulder and then turns back around. You're so late you could just go home to your wife and let Billie think you're a no-show. You are a known asshole. Another person thinking so won't be the worst thing in the world. Yet, here you stand in the bar doorway, thinking, This is Billie. You have history. She already knows you're an asshole. You might as well just walk over to her.

"About time, dicko," she says.

You are a dick, so distract her. Say, "Black girl, don't you know it's bad luck to sit with your back to the door?"

"Shut up. Sit down." She fires up a fresh smoke. "I've been waiting so long I'm drunk already."

"Of course you are," you say. "You drink too much."

"So?"

"So, stop your griping. I'm here now. You can get drunk all over again."

Don't worry. She will.

Billie is an everlasting tomboy. Though you won't admit it, it's always turned you on. She lifts weights, heavy ones. She fixes old cars. She drives a truck down at the quarry. Once, she was even voted runner-up for Women's Arm Wrestler of the Year by the American Armsport Association. She nearly won the world championship, too, but she was defeated by a six-foot-five woman who many thought was on more steroids than a horse. Billie's toughness has been obvious to everyone since you were kids. It was even obvious to you, so much so that to this day you're pretty sure she can still whoop your ass.

"Where the hell were you?"

Remember, you're an asshole. Answer accordingly. Say, "I was home. Unlike you and everyone else in this bar, I actually have a life. Dreams. Aspirations."

Her tank top is stretched over her breasts like the skin of a drum. Try not to look at it. Instead, watch her make a fist out of one of her big hands and wave it at you. "Your dreams and aspirations will only get you hurt, Black boy."

She's probably right, but don't say so. Say, "As usual, Black girl knows nothing of what she speaks. Black girl has never been anywhere."

She mimics you. "'Black girl knows nothing of what she speaks.'" She waves her thick middle finger now. "How come you always sound like you're talking backward?"

"College," you say. "It does that to you."

"Hm," she grunts. "Lucky I never went."

* * *

You are at the Weigh Station. Not the actual weigh station out on Highway 13, where vehicular weights are inspected, but the bar called the Weigh Station. It's a trucker bar. Yes, you hate it. It's the kind of theme bar you find only in towns like Rock City, your hometown, population just over a thousand. No one but you can see the humor in having "city" in the name of a place so microscopic. Barely anyone in the state has even heard of it. When you went off to college eons ago, you told your two white roommates that you were from Rock City, and they thought you were talking "Black." They thought you were referring to some East Coast drug-infested metropolis. They said, "Is that Baltimore or New York City?" You said, "No, it's Rock City, as in Missouri, the state we are presently in." They nodded at each other. They could already tell you were an asshole, but at least you wouldn't steal their IBMs.

Never mind that. Marvel at the kitsch of the Weigh Station. Yes, it looks like a junkyard that's been awarded a liquor license. Rusty manifolds, carburetors, and transmissions hang by thick wire from the ceiling. The bar stools and tables are made out of old truck wheels, and there's an actual Peterbilt dumper parked on the roof. It spews exhaust out of the side pipes when the place is open.

Now check out the crowd. You grew up with everyone here, by the way. You know all their nicknames. There's Brillo and Fishin' Bait, Wrinkles and Giggles, and Herman the German because he's, well, German. They're playing foosball in the far corner as though the game is being televised. The jukebox, that crusty thing that still plays actual 45s, has the entire Kenny Rogers catalog. And wouldn't you know it? "The Gambler" is playing right now. There's a lot of flannel, a lot of chains hanging from wallets, a lot of scar-toed work boots. An old guy named Racist Randy, who actually used to be your high school shop teacher, is even sitting at the bar wearing green hip waders. It's your worst nightmare. Everyone smokes, everyone drinks, and every last one of them, including you, to your utter dismay, drives a truck down at the quarry, hauling rock and gravel out of a big hole in the ground.

* * *

Your wife? Good question. She's well aware that you're an asshole but in a lovable way. You're *her* asshole. Well, no, not literally. It's just, that's what you are to everyone, the friendly neighborhood jerk. You can be snide and opinionated to the point that people think you're compensating for something. But you're not. It's just the way every guy feels, or at least that's what you think. So, Lily, your wife, your white wife, has to put up with a lot just by being with you. At the end of the day, she's resigned herself to this simple fact: you're always going to be Captain Butthole. For example, you don't always see the gray areas, which she has a problem with. You're not a chauvinist, but sometimes you lean that way. Occasionally, it's all the woman's fault. You think all relationships are the same, all men and women are the same. You think every married man has this moment once in a while when he realizes, *Holy shit, I'm fucking married? How could I be talked into such a bad deal?*

Like when your wife reminds you every day to take off your shoes as soon as you come in the house. She doesn't say, "Can you please take off your shoes?" She just says, "Shoes." And once you get past that part of it, you're still left to think, Jesus, I can't wear shoes in my own house? It's all the rules and regulations that come with living with a woman. You think all marriages are like this, women ruining everything. This is how you relate to other assholes.

Like when she goes out of town and gives you a list of things that she wants done, as if all you're going to do while she's gone is sit in front of the TV playing with your balls. Or how when you're driving in the rain and she can't stop telling you to be careful. Or how every night before you go to bed, your wife spends an hour in the bathroom getting ready just to go to sleep. When you finally get in there to brush your teeth, to have a moment of isolation and freedom, you look down and what do you see? The limpest length of green dental floss draped over the edge of the sink. She's left it for you. You never remember to floss. Bacteria from a person's teeth can cause heart disease. She's thinking of you. She doesn't want you to die.

All you can think is, This is my life? Rock City, looking down at a piece of dental floss? Sometimes, out of spite, you don't even use it. You wet it and throw it in the trash on top of hers. But then you imagine yourself in a coffin and someone saying, "If he'd only flossed twice a day." Every married man has that kind of moment, you think. You're that kind of dude. If you could only leave, if you could only be 100 percent sure that you could survive without this person, you'd be in the wind. That's what you think every night as you get out another piece of floss, in the rare chance that she's right about the heart disease thing.

You are an asshole. You are cheating on your wife, but for fuck's sake you don't want to die.

*　*　*

Even though Billie's the only other Black person at the Weigh Station besides you, she fits right in, more than you ever will. You're a snob, but only because you're observant, hyper-observant. That's your excuse. So, watch her now. You're smart. You have a graduate degree. Study her as she sucks down half her cigarette with one pull and holds the smoke in her lungs for an ungodly amount of time. Record it in your head. Look at the black crescents of grease under each bitten fingernail on her big, hard hands.

"So?" she asks. "How's Lily?"

"You mean your competition?" God, you're an asshole.

She rolls her eyes. "Black boy, this Black woman's got no competition." Her wiry hair is tied up into a loose braid, and a few grayish strands stray from her head like bolts of electricity. She gets quiet for a moment and picks at the warning label on her Bic. "Is Lily still lily white?"

Finish your beer in two gulps and strain against the fizz threatening to bubble back up. Against your better judgment, wave at the bartender for another. "Actually, she's even whiter. She gets whiter by the hour."

"Yeah, you like your women white, don't you, OJ?"

Say, "Whiter the better. I keep her locked up in the basement so she never gets color."

This makes Billie smile. Notice the wide gap between her front teeth, that small open doorway into the darkness of her mouth.

If you haven't guessed, your little racial jokes are the only thing keeping this relationship alive. You'd have nothing to talk about otherwise. It's all left over from your time as the only two Black kids in school, when you dated simply because everyone expected you to. When you got back into town three months ago, after years of living elsewhere, and you saw Billie for the first time, you both were like, "Wow, you're married, too?" Then you both said, "Let me guess, white, right?" And she said, "Who else is there to marry in this town? What's your excuse?"

After a quiet moment, Billie now says, "I can't believe you married a white girl named Lily. It's so ironic."

Say, "It's barely an anecdote."

"Will you speak English, you freak?"

Say, "Let's not talk about it."

"No, let's," she says. "It's stupid, but stupid's good. Stupid passes the time." She holds her cigarette like a guy, pinching the filter between her thumb and forefinger. "I mean, really, did you hear the name Lily and just cream your pants, you big Blackie?"

You're supposed to be ending this. That's really the only reason you're here. You have to kill this relationship before it kills you, before your wife gets wind and kills you. You and Billie have had sex, but just the one time. You've confused yourself enough. Because of this, up the asshole quotient. Say, "What about you, Black girl? You married the one and only white guy in the world named Tyrone."

"Shows what you know," she says. "Tyrone is an Irish name. I thought you were smart."

Google it on your phone under the table. To your shock, she's sort of right. No matter. You're the one with the degrees. Confuse her with words. "That notwithstanding. Black girl, are you not self-aware? Your husband's as white as my wife."

She mimics you again. "'Black girl, are you not self-aware?' I swear, I don't know what you're talking about half the time. You're such a freak."

"If that's true, then why do I feel so out of place here?"

"Elementary, my dear Black boy. It's because you're a bigger freak than everyone else."

Again, she's right. You are kind of a freak.

* * *

Five months ago, you and Lily were living in Los Angeles, barely scraping by. For years, you both stitched together adjunct teaching jobs at five different community colleges, logging a grip of miles on the old Subaru Brat you shared, all so you could cobble together a whopping $24K a year each. You have a master's in English lit, a dissertation shy of a PhD, but you haven't quite harvested the fruits of your labor. The closest you've come is teaching composition. Rhetorical monkey work. Essays and shit. It sucked.

Eventually, you guys tried your hands at editing, freelance life, textbooks and manuals. You have an eye for detail, a knack for words and rules, but unlike her, you were too much of an asshole to really care about the work. You said goodbye to office jobs and ended up driving trucks just like your father because it was easy. You wouldn't say you're a pessimist—others would—but you always had doubts about the longevity of your academic career anyway. Even through college, you kept your CDL up to date, just in case your life somehow shit the bed, which apparently it had. It was the one thing you never told your father, that you were still driving. As far as he knew, you were a published academic, the head Negro homing in on chair of some English department. Whatever bullshit you could come up with to make him think success had somehow kissed you on the taint.

Through the lies, you wondered why you even went into academia. Why did you break your ass to earn two, almost three, degrees in something you now think is about as interesting as Parcheesi? Books. Yeah, words. You got it. You were just bored with it now. You were much more comfortable in a Peterbilt or a Mack, double-clutching, bouncing along, a full load of rock or sand or rubble steadying your course. Mr. Blue Collar but with an Education. After a while, though, even that grated on you. You thought you'd become your father. Your only soothing thought was, At least I'm in LA. Thank God it's not Rock City. And that's exactly when you were pulled back.

In April, you got a call from your father's foreman, Frosty. (His last name is Flake. You're not making that up.) He said your father had been acting funny, "forgetful and such." Your father had made a few deliveries to the wrong locations. One day, he dumped a load of riprap in the middle of Broad Street and was found wandering from his truck, muttering, "How do I get home from here?"

You flew back and drove straight to the quarry. At the town limits, you saw the WELCOME TO ROCK CITY sign, and the taste of vomit burned your throat. You hadn't seen your dad in five years, not since your mom died, and when you went into the quarry office, he was reclining on a sofa with his legs crossed, his ratty fedora covering his face. Frosty had stopped letting him drive, but your father kept showing up for work. You took him home and spent four hours trying to convince him you were his son. For some reason, he wouldn't stop smiling. "Dad, c'mon," you said. "This isn't funny." You hoped he would magically be okay so you could leave, but he kept saying, "Nah. My son doesn't look like you."

When you asked how you looked different, he gave you a grim glance, rubbing his hands together like he was cold. "Well, for one thing," he said, "you're Black."

* * *

Say, "Where's Tyrone?"

"Don't where's-Tyrone me," Billie says. "Jesus, this is the lamest affair ever. All we talk about is your wife and my husband."

"Who said we're having an affair?"

"Me," she says. "Makes it sound more exciting."

"I'm just making conversation, Black girl."

She stabs out her cigarette. "Ty's at home, dickhead, probably snoring in front of the TV. Happy?"

Hesitate. Then say, "Why the hell did you marry him?"

"Who else am I gonna marry? You?" she says. "You left before I had the chance to chase after your goofy ass."

Look away. Don't acknowledge that. Turn it around. Say, "Do you love him?"

"Enough. Do you love Lily?"

Shrug and say, "Enough."

"See, don't ask shit like that if you can barely answer yourself." She puts two fingers in her mouth and whistles to the bartender for another drink. "You know Ty hasn't gone anywhere except work for ten years. Just sits his skinny butt in that recliner all night, wakes up the next morning in the same clothes. He could get a job testing recliners he's in it so much."

"Does he eat?"

"Yeah, the recliner's got a little refrigerator built into it. He keeps snacks in there."

You want to laugh. But don't. It'll look bad. Say, "Interesting," and let it go.

You actually know Tyrone. Or, you've seen him at the yard. He drives a truck at the quarry, too. Who doesn't? He's the only guy you've ever seen who smokes cigarettes and chews tobacco at the same damn time. A little guy, kind of mopey and timid. The fact that he and Billie are married has got to be one of the wonders of the world.

"At least he's not cheating on you."

"You kidding? That TV's his girlfriend, got him pussy

whipped," she says. "We got a thousand channels, and he knows what's on every last one of them." She brings her mug to her lips, is about to take a sip but then pulls it away. "Not to mention he can't drink. One beer and he's gotta take a nap."

Something's really in her tonight, but you don't think it's the alcohol. You've seen her more smashed than this and didn't learn half as much about her marriage. Maybe she senses it's the end. You've been distant lately, shrugging off drinking with her. Don't think about it now. Say, "Is Ty religious or something?"

"No, just boring. He don't even wanna screw." She swirls the last of her beer in her mug. "His first wife died on him. I mean, like, literally. They were doing it, and something, a vein, I think, popped in her head."

"An aneurysm."

"She keeled over right on him. He's been messed up ever since."

"Jesus," you sincerely say. You aren't heartless.

A server who has just come on shift, the skinniest girl over twenty-one you've ever seen, walks over to your booth balancing a tray of beers. Her name is Tammy Faye. She has no calves. She sets Billie's refill down, and a swallow spills on the table. "Hey, girl," Billie says. "I'm not paying for that."

"It's your last anyway," Tammy says. "Musty said you're drinking us dry."

"Well, tell Musty his butt stinks."

Tammy leaves, and Billie's right back on Tyrone.

"You know, I catch him crying sometimes. I mean, slobbering on himself."

"He can't get past it, huh?"

"What do you think?"

Say, "Maybe you should just get out of here." You mean the town, the state, the country, shit, the planet, so she can see the world, get some perspective. But she thinks you just mean the bar.

"After this beer," she says. "We'll go then." She lights another cigarette off the one she's finishing. "You know what her name was?" She looks at you and smiles devilishly. "Delilah. She was white, of course."

Say, "Of course."

"But ain't that pretty? Delilah?" She says it like it's the name of her own child. "I wish my parents had named me that."

"Then you'd be dead, and he'd be crying over you."

"Yeah, but who the hell names a girl Wilhelmina anymore? Ma and Daddy really dicked me on that." She lets out one chuckle and falls into a trance. Then she wakes up as if an alarm's gone off. "Why are we talking about him?" she says. "This is the lamest affair ever."

Say, "Black girl, I think we've known this from the beginning."

* * *

For some reason, disliking your roots astonishes your wife. At dinner tonight you had one of the dumbest arguments ever. It was junk food night. That's where you are in your marriage. You name your dinners. You have fish night, chicken night, beef night, vegetarian night, Chinese night. There are so many nights, so many different combinations, that you've lost track and have to keep a calendar on the fridge.

Since it was junk food night, Lily had just brought home a take-and-bake pizza from a place called the Pizza Castle, which is inside your local gas station. You being you, you had to comment. You were already late meeting Billie, and maybe the guilt surrounding that made you a little skewed. "The words 'Pizza' and 'Castle,'" you said, "should never be paired ever. It's like naming a Mexican place the Taco Château. It doesn't make any sense." She ignored you and handed you a slice. You took a bite and had to keep talking. "This isn't even pizza. It has crushed-up Doritos on it. The Italians would spit on us for eating this."

"Who cares what the Italians think?" she said. "It's a taco pizza, and I like it. It's different. I'm sorry to say, but ever since we've been here, you've become an elitist."

"What're you talking about? I've always been an elitist. How do you think I got out of this place?"

"Stop acting like a snob. This is where you're from."

"You're lucky," you said. "You actually like where you're from. Do you know how hard I tried to lose my twang? I listened to zillions of language tapes just so I don't sound like I'm on *Hee Haw*."

Your father, whom you'd already fed, was in his room turning his electric razor on and off. Since you were little, he's played the trumpet every night after dinner, but now he confuses the trumpet with the razor, and you have to listen to Flight of the Fucking Norelco all night. He'll turn it on, let it run for a few moments, and then turn it off. He'll set it down on the bed and just stand there looking at it. Then he'll pick it up and turn it on again, the whole time mumbling, "I can't get the right tone out of this thing."

Trying your best to ignore the buzzing, you continued your manifesto. "I might as well buy an old Camaro, paint a Confederate flag on the roof, and start listening to Merle Haggard." Truth is, you're probably the only Black guy who kind of likes Merle Haggard.

"You're painting with too wide a brush, mister," she sang. It was at that point that you thought, I can't believe I'm actually married to a white woman who calls people "mister," like she's somebody's grandmother, like you're a little terrier. It's one of those things that make you stop for a second and wonder why you even married this goofball. Somehow, you fail to remember that she uprooted herself from LA to come to your hometown to help take care of your father. Maybe it's just the fact that she loves Rock City so much that bothers you. You're starting to dislike her most of the time. She loves that the town grocery store is simply a cinder block structure the size of a normal convenience store, with tiny shopping carts. "Everyone has so much character. Everyone is so real," she said. "There's no artifice."

"There's plenty of delusion, though. Why do you think the two liquor stores in town have drive-through windows?"

"Oh, Nicky," she said. "You're always your own worst enemy. You'd get more done if you didn't think about how bad everything is wherever you are."

She's right, you thought. This is your problem. You're too smart for this world, but then again, you're too much of an asshole to believe that. Really, you knew you were just being a dick.

"You're from California," you said. "This is a novelty for you. But you don't know these people." Your father clicked the razor on again. "Do you know what everyone says when they get excited around here?"

She let her head flop to one side as she chewed. "What do they say?"

"Hot dang doodle. Lawdy Lawdy Miss Clawdy. Good googily moogily."

She looked off for a moment and bit the tip of her index finger. "Hot dang doodle?" She whispered it a couple of times. She wants to be a writer and loves any new phrase that she can scribble in her Moleskine. "I might use that." She jotted down the phrase. By the way, she's already started a novel set in this place, and you're secretly afraid it's about you.

All that kind of made you lose it. "Jesus Christ!" you said.

"Nick, calm down. You're looking at everyone like they're stereotypes."

"The foundations of all stereotypes are built on fact." You don't even know why you said that.

"Not a rigorous argument."

You pushed your pizza away. "Fine, then. Look at us. The big Black man with his white wife."

"Stop it," she said.

"You think we're not a stereotype? We're one of the biggest ones." You kept talking, even as you saw her face redden. You said something about you being her Mandingo. You pounded your chest. But it wasn't until you referred to her as "pink toes" that she finally exploded.

"Fuck you," she said and then froze. Your wife is so regulated, so in control, that she can't even curse without scaring herself. It's the same reason she only ever wanted to have sex in the missionary position. You told her this, like an idiot, and what did she call you? You guessed it.

You wanted to tell her that she forgot to call you "Mr. Asshole," but your father clicked his razor on again. You and Lily looked to his bedroom. You stood up from your chair so fast it fell back and clacked against the floor. You ran in there and snatched the razor from him. "Give me this fucking thing!" It took you half a minute to turn it off. "It's not a trumpet, god-dammit. It doesn't play music."

You watched your father tremble like a startled child. He could barely look up at you. "Boy, please don't take my things."

As you told him to stop calling you boy, the razor turned back on. "Boy is not my name. I am Nick. My name is Nick." You couldn't believe you were introducing yourself to your own father. "Why can't you remember my fucking name?" You knew why, of course, but you've been over the edge since you've been back. The fact that he still doesn't believe you're his son might have something to do with it. You hate how he always looks at you with a smirk, as if he thinks you're an imposter and it's so funny to see how far you're taking this charade.

You looked down at him as he held his hands out like some-one receiving communion.

"Nick?" He looked up hesitantly, as though he wasn't sure he was saying the correct name. "Can I please have my instru-ment back?"

The razor still buzzed. You turned it off. You set it in his palm and wrapped his fingers around it.

* * *

Billie hits you on the arm. There will be a bruise there tomor-row. "You better be treating Lily right," she says. "Or I'll kick your ass, Black boy."

Rub your arm but try not to show that it hurts. "What're you talking about, you Amazon?"

"You better not be mean to her."

"I'm not. But what business is it of yours?"

"Us women gotta look out for each other."

"Do I have to remind you that I'm here right now with you instead of her?"

"Hey, don't blame your wickedness on me. I'm not telling you to stay. Go home to your lily-white Lily."

Say, "You've drunk at least a keg so far by yourself. Let's get out of here."

She tilts her beer mug from side to side. It's mostly suds. "After the next one how about." She starts to stand up and falls back into her seat and laughs. She stands up again and waits a moment to maintain her balance before coming over to your side of the booth, flumping down next to you.

She scoots over, and your legs bump. "You know what would be fun later?" She's having a hard time keeping her eyes still. She rubs them to get them to focus. "Let's go for a swim," she says. "Down at the quarry."

You've had only three beers, but your eyes are burning, too. Lily is probably on the phone with her friend Linda in San Diego, the one she talks to about you. "I don't know, Black girl. It's getting a little late." Check your watch. Show her that it's ten thirty already.

She grabs your arm and raises it up and down like a well pump. "C'mon, you pussy. You can go for a swim." She taps her cigarette out in the ashtray and looks at you as seriously as you've seen her. "Remember?" She raises one eyebrow and then squints the opposite eye. It's as seductive a look as she can muster.

You two went swimming there not long after you got back to town. This was when you had sex. "Once was enough," you say, but it comes out wrong. It sounds like you're talking about a prostate exam.

She turns away and swallows. You're not sure if she's fighting back vomit or rejection.

Say, "Don't you remember how bad that water used to smell, how bad we would smell when we got out?" Try to make her laugh. "We smelled like a deer's ass."

"So what? It was still fun, getting out of the water, all that rock dust drying on us. We looked like ghosts, right?"

"Maybe."

"Well, I wanna be a ghost tonight, goddammit!" She slaps the table with the flat of her hand, and a saltshaker falls over on its side.

You want to look at her, but you can't. You'll probably say yes just to get her to shut up.

"We're going," she says. "That's final."

"Bullshit. Black girl doesn't know what she's talking about."

"We're going after I finish my next beer."

"They're not gonna serve you anymore," you say. "Black girl is already drunk."

* * *

Maybe it's just you, but why does it seem like every wife confiscates her husband's sex life at some point, without consulting him at all? It's another one of your tired arguments, but in your case, sadly, it's true. You and Lily haven't been intimate in quite some time, since before you left LA. Naturally, this plays on your mind. You're only in your early thirties. You and Lily have been together for six years. You should be getting plenty, but you don't. Even before your dry spell, your sex life had already fallen into a once-a-month, don't-even-think-about-foreplay chore. And that was if you were lucky. Now you get nothing, and all you can think about is when you first met, when you fucked like hamsters. Up against the wall, upside down. Naked yoga with a side of rumpy-pumpy. Is it your fault it isn't like that anymore? Admit it, you have put on some pounds. You do like beer and french fries a little too much. Maybe she doesn't want to die of asphyxiation under your big old belly.

How could things have changed? They were so good in the beginning. She was on the pill. You were spoiled with sex. Neither of you wanted kids. It was paradise. But only a few years later, she decided she didn't want chemicals running through her body. Prescription drugs were suddenly killing people. One day, eggs and aspirin were good for you. The next, they gave you herpes. But it didn't end there. She got health conscious. No more smoking. No more drinking. She started doing Pilates every day with DVDs in your living room, wearing the tightest spandex outfits you'd ever seen. You'd be sitting there feeling all pubescent, sex on the brain, while she was gyrating and sticking her ass in the air like she had stripper tryouts in the morning. It was torture.

How could she abandon you? Without the pill, you had to try every condom on the market—latex, polyurethane, lambskin, glow in the dark—thinking one of them would make sex seem bearable. Once, you brought home Magnums for shits and giggles, but they were just too embarrassing to use. You haven't bought condoms on a regular basis since college, and now, because of your low frequency, you order them one at a time from an online condom store so you don't have to see a pack of expired ones every time you open your dresser drawer. And still your lovemaking, or the idea of it since you still ain't getting any, is the same. Nada.

Maybe it's just you, but why does it seem like you can't touch her anymore without her taking it the wrong way? A hug and a kiss and suddenly she thinks you want to do anal. Has your sexual life simply run its course? Has your marriage devolved into just companionship, something only old people want? You have so many questions. Doesn't every relationship need something physically pleasurable, dare you say it, an expression of your love for each other, to keep the thing going, so you can forget the times when they make you want to pack a bag late at night and slink out of their lives the first moment they aren't looking?

Then again, maybe it is just you.

*   *   *

Okay. Don't be alarmed. You've had five, maybe seven or eight, beers. You might feel like you're hammered, but really, you're not that bad. You've been here before. Besides, Billie is worse off. You wouldn't know it by looking at her, but she's trashed. Obliterated. You're pretty sure of it. So, be a gentleman. Steer her toward the bar door. Walk straight. Tell her not to worry about the cheer she gets when she leaves. When Musty says, "Don't let the door hit ya where the good Lord split ya," it sounds racial to your ears. You tell Billie to be cool, but she doesn't even hear you. She just waves and says, "See you degenerates tomorrow."

Don't be surprised or even a little confused when everyone waves back happily. "See ya, Billie."

Walk her to your father's pickup, which is now your pickup. Though it's true, try not to think about it like that. Fumble with your keys. Then, of course, drop them. Don't trip about it. People drop their keys all the time. Even sober people. You stoop over to pick them up. Billie pushes you out of the way and snags them before you can. She unlocks the passenger door and gets in. You walk to the driver's side, and she acts like she's going to unlock your door, but she just crosses her arms and smiles at you.

"Is Black girl having fun?"

"Yep. And she wants to have more."

"No, Billie," you say. "No." Your center of gravity is only slightly off, but you just want to go home and sleep.

"Yes, oh, yes, oh, yes." She laughs at you, and you know what she wants. She slides over and cranks down the window. "It's swim time, you big nigga."

There's no talking her out of it. Fine. Pull up your door lock and get in. Let her have this last moment. She puts the keys in the ignition and starts the truck for you. "Vroom, vroom," she says. Close the door. Back up the truck. For God's sake, don't hit any cars. That pole you just backed into, that just took out your taillight? That doesn't count. Pull out onto the road. Get this heap of a truck going, put it through its paces. Forget first. Jump straight into second, air the puppy out.

Just so you know, Granite Road will take you to Highway 13. Follow that for a few miles. Roll your window back down so Billie can smoke. Listen to her comment on the mechanical state of the truck. The clutch slipping. The carb needing a rebuild. Stuff you already know.

"I can fix that for you."

"It's okay. I'll take it to a shop."

"No, we're gonna do it. Wouldn't take but a few hours. Lily can watch."

You suddenly don't like her saying your wife's name. Say, "I don't work on things anymore. I pay people to do it."

"Oh, that's right," she says. "I forgot. You don't like to get your hands dirty anymore." She jabs you in the ribs, tries to goose you. Nudge her away.

Luckily, the quarry is coming up on your left. Slow to take the turn into the secret entrance only truckers know about. Follow it as it hugs the rim of the mile-wide pit. Slow to go over that big bump that you two used to jump with your little Mazda in high school. Billie sticks her head out the window and tells you to jump it. "C'mon." She sticks her arm out and slaps her door. You say no and go over it easy. She calls you a pussy. Never you mind. Just descend, coast down the switchbacks. Watch that loose gravel.

By the way, you're having déjà vu now. The night you two had sex, this was exactly how it happened. You were both shithoused, drunk as skunks. After you'd gone skinny-dipping, you got back in your father's pickup. You were wet and gritty. It was only then that you could see each other's bodies. She kept looking down and then back up at you, shyly, as she cradled her breasts in her arms. Without a word, she turned around and faced her ass toward you. The light in the distance played off the curve of her spine. She peeked back as you moved in close. You could smell all her scents, see her pores go to goose bumps. You read the small range of pimples on the round of her buttocks with your fingertips like braille. She flicked her long, thick braid, and it landed right in front of you. "Grab it," she said. "Pull it. Fuck me." You wrapped it around your hand. You felt like a bull rider. Her back bowed. The truck rocked. She said, "Pull harder," and you wondered how many men she'd done this with since you'd been gone. Maybe none. You realized right then, as you came, as you hoped she was also coming, that out of everyone in the world you were the only person who understood her. She was the only person who really understood you. Because of this, and because you are what you are, you thought it would never work. That window had closed.

But try not to think about that now. Let her down easy. Skulk out of this as smoothly as you skulked in. Everyone has been a coward at some point. Fret not. Just park and don't say anything at first. Take in the sights. Let her get the drift. You're in the center of the pit, terraced rock walls half a mile in every direction. You haven't been down here after dark in a while, not since that night. You are 286 feet below the surface, in the bowels of a man-made crater, a big-ass hole. Surrounding you are piles of aggregate, and way over there, cranes and work lights that look like large sleeping insects.

Billie lights another smoke and slides over to you. She leans against your arm, puts her head on your shoulder. "What're you thinking about, Black boy?"

She wants you to say her. Look at your watch, but don't be obvious about it. "Just stuff."

She rubs her cigarette out in the perfectly clean ashtray. She sits up and looks at you, grabs you by the collar. You flinch as she kisses you so hard your lips almost split.

Your eyes are still open. You don't part your lips, though you want to. You don't care that she smells like beer and ash, that she smells like a man. You want her again, but it'd be a bad move.

She senses your reluctance and opens her eyes. She sees yours have never closed. She wiggles her tongue, going for a frenchie, but you don't budge. Her eyes go to anger. "Well, fuck it, then." She pushes you away.

Say, "I'm sorry, Billie." Say, "We shouldn't be doing this."

She slides to the passenger side and says, "I don't know about you, but I'm going for a swim." She peels off her tank top and throws it out the window. Her magnificent breasts are right there, perky and large. You could reach out and cup them, lean over and kiss one. For a split second, you really, really want to. You remember how you were scared to touch them when you were sixteen. She had to put your hands on them for you. "You know, you really are a sucker," she says now. "I had you going this whole time." She gets out of the truck, forcing a laugh.

Watch her slam the door. The dome light goes off. The cabin goes black. She disappears in the darkness and then there she is, lit up in the beams of your headlights. She kicks off her Red Wings. She unbuttons her jeans and wiggles out of them. There are her broad hips, her muscular legs. If you gave her the chance, if you let her wrap them around you, like you wish you could, she would break you like a twig. Watch her twirl her jeans over her head by one of the pant legs. There are no pools where you are. She sees this and decides to just dance around. She whoops and hollers, ignoring you.

Stick your head out the window and say, "Billie, get in the truck."

She tells you to fuck off.

Say, "C'mon, girl, it's a school night. We've got work in the morning."

She lets out a ridiculing laugh. "Fuck work. Fuck school. You sound like you're sixteen, you punk." She's right. It's something you used to say when you were kids. She never wanted to leave this hole. You had to beg her. Her laugh turns into a scream. She's screaming at you now. Asshole. Deal with it. You deserve it anyhow. She throws her jeans, and they land somewhere in front of the truck. She looks around for something else to throw. Her boot. She picks it up, reels back, and hurls it. You realize she wishes she could hit you in the face. The boot tumbles through the air, goes out of view. Then it lands on your hood with a thwap, perfectly upright, as if she's walked up and placed it there. She calls you an asshole again.

Say, "I know." Say, "I'm sorry about that. Seriously."

"If you know you're an asshole, then why do you still do asshole things?"

Tell her the truth. Say, "I don't know why." Say, "I still love you, Black girl." You could say so much more. You could get poetic, apologizing for your lives diverging, for leaving her behind, for never thinking of her. But you leave it there because you're beginning to see how much of an asshole you really are.

She stands there in her underwear, a small American flag on the back. LOVE IT OR LEAVE IT is written under it. She looks off, away from you. She searches the dark horizon, as if for an answer. Slowly, she looks down at her clothes scattered everywhere. She gathers them up and gets dressed, climbs back into the truck.

You want to say something to make her feel better, to smooth all this over. You open your mouth, and she says, "Don't say a fucking thing."

So, you sit here as she finishes getting dressed.

"Start the truck," she says. "Take me home."

You head toward the haul road. You climb back up the switchbacks. In a matter of minutes, you're cresting the surface. That big hole is behind you, receding. You rumble slowly down the access road. You don't know what to say. You keep looking over at her. You just want her to understand, but then you realize she already does. This is it. The end of everything. You don't know what to do. You want to say, "No. We can make this work. We can still be friends. Come over. We'll fix up this stupid truck. Me and you. Lily and my father can watch. Bring Tyrone. We'll make a day of it." But the suggestion would just make things worse.

You bounce along. Up ahead, you see the big bump. It's coming. Billie finally looks at you, but doesn't say anything. She still thinks you're a jerk. So, speed up. Don't say a word. Feel the torque throw you both into the seat. Now look at her. You swear you see her smile, even for a second.

In high school, you two ruined your Mazda's suspension jumping the little hill over and over, taking turns, seeing who could fly farther. It was all the entertainment you had. A bump. A bump to jump, you used to say. Bumps are hard to come by here, since it's so flat. You both loved the launch, that moment of flight. It was better than drugs, better than sex. You're an asshole, but there are still some things you can appreciate. Going too fast in an old pickup. The wall of blackberry bushes sweeping by on your right. The pulsing chirp of a million crickets singing at once.

Floor it. Do forty. Do fifty. Watch the speedometer climb. Look in your rearview at that trail of dust. Know this: No matter how much you hate it, this is your life. It isn't a mistake. It isn't a joke. Watch out. The bump is coming.

Look at Billie. Reach out for her hand. Hold it until this is over.

THE LIFE AND LOVES OF MELVIN J. PLUMP, ESQ.

We were near the end of another boring therapy session when out of nowhere Dr. Neblitt said I should go on a cruise, a themed one. I shouldn't have been surprised. She was a liberal after all, a lefty. I thought only a lefty would think a themed cruise would bring anyone inner peace, especially me, but for once I was wrong. Evidently, in Therapy Land, quacks of all kinds now considered themed cruises a new approach in healing. You didn't have to go on a regular cruise anymore. It could be one involving your specific interest or affliction—AA cruises, NASCAR cruises, even Democrat cruises, an affliction if there was one.

"O-kay," I said. "So, what cruise should I go on, then? One for the—*disturbed?*" Even though this was court-ordered therapy, I, for damn sure, wasn't crazy. That being said, I did speak in a spooky voice sometimes just to get on Neblitt's nerves.

"Melvin," she said, "no one thinks you're—'disturbed.'" She made air quotes. "And no one thinks you're all that funny either. No, this particular cruise is for people known as—unseen souls."

"Right," I said. "Of course. Unseen souls." I was reclining

on her chaise, my shoes off, my head back. Believe it or not, given the year I'd had, I was actually comfortable. Whenever she started with all the mumbo jumbo, though, it set me off. "What in the holy hell are unseen souls?"

"People who are shunned by society because of their physical appearance. It's just like how it sounds. Unseen souls, Melvin."

"Huh. I didn't know that's what we're calling them now. Whatever happened to 'freaks' and 'cripples'?"

Neblitt cringed noticeably. "Those terms are outdated because they're, you know, really offensive. This new one, however, is trending in the lexicon quite nicely."

"Great," I said. "What else is it doing? Farting? Fucking? Opening a 401(k)?" I sat up, ready to say something else about her liberal foolishness, but Neblitt brought me down with a slow, soothing, "Melvin?"

Truth be told, I was already keyed up. We'd just conducted a postmortem of my marriages, and for some reason I was stuck on my fifth ex, my most recent ex, Deb the Democrat. She was an unruly pill popper, a left-wing loony, but I couldn't stop thinking about her and her heart-shaped derriere, the perfect dimple above each buttock, as though two fingers, my fingers, were gently pressing her waist.

"In literal terms," Neblitt said, "it's a cruise for people like you, people with—conditions." She held out the brochure, which I took only to humor her. The cover displayed a collage of pictures: a cruise ship on Caribbean water, a wheelchair-bound Latino man shooting craps in a casino, a one-armed white woman being spit down a waterslide.

"Tell me again why I should go on this." I tossed the brochure onto her coffee table. "I don't look like any of those people."

"No," Neblitt said, "but you do have a unique physical condition. Meeting other unique people with whom you can commiserate might allow you to grow."

I glanced over at the brochure again and bit my lip. "You are aware there will be cruise people there. I've spent my whole life avoiding those people."

Neblitt deflated with one of her nose-whistling sighs. "And just what kind of people are they?"

"You know, sun visors and fanny packs, socks and sandals. The true soul of America." I laughed because it was so true. Why I thought she, a pinko, would laugh, I don't know. When I looked up, there she was, an old dreadlocked hippie, frowning at me like I was a senior citizen who'd just shit himself again.

"You know," she said, "maybe you should stop avoiding people you think will make you uncomfortable." After a moment, she added, "Maybe you should stop calling other people 'those people' all the time, too."

I nodded and shifted on her chaise. I gazed out her window at the Manhattan sky. "I see. So, you're saying I do that a lot, then."

Neblitt winced, clearly embarrassed for me. "Um. Yeah, Melvin. I'm afraid you do."

* * *

It was the spring of my fifty-first year, the spring I, Melvin J. Plump, noted Black conservative, suddenly turned white. The condition, vitiligo, a pigmentation disorder, had taken hold over just a few months, record speed. Day by day, moment by moment, the melanin in my skin vanished in patches shaped like states and congressional districts until the only color left on me—save for a few spots—was the stark pinkish hue of an albino. My face, my arms, my legs. Even my little friend down there. I was the most uniformly white, or pink, Black person my doctors had ever seen, and nothing except makeup on my face and spray tan on my hands could make me presentable to the world. Quite a ridiculous situation for anyone, especially a person of color, but despite what others may have thought, I was taking this dilemma in stride, especially given my recent past.

Two months earlier, my employers had made the colossal blunder of firing me. I'd been tasked by the party to master-mind the reelection of Tennessee governor Ronnie Givens, vacuous retired quarterback and well-known sex freak; i.e., a white guy. Despite all that, I engineered, quite deftly, I might add, the Givens image, sweeping under the rug a nasty string of extramarital affairs complete with YouTube footage. We were well on our way to defeating an up-and-coming Black Democrat when everyone abruptly severed ties with me. Some said it was my skin condition. Before it had even taken hold, people could barely look my way. Others said it was my dirty tactics. I may have manufactured an old gangbanger past to illustrate—the press said sully—the character of our oppo-nent, but that's neither here nor there.

Bottom line, I was let go, the coup de grâce a bouquet of lilies sent by the governor to my home, as though someone had died. The small card read,

Mel,
From one creep to another, I hope you
understand.
        Ronnie.

And the weird thing was a degree of understanding did come over me. I, Melvin, who'd once fired a woman because she had a rather bulbous, hairy mole on her forehead. I, Melvin, who'd fired a man because he tended to have saloon door boogers constantly lurking in his nostrils. Oh. The irony. Unfortunately for me, the degree of understanding I had over my own dismissal wasn't high enough to keep me from calling Givens for a few weeks straight to detail the various ways I would exact my revenge, many of which may have involved a pair of dildos and a blowtorch. Was it stress? Maybe. A fault of character? Perhaps. Whatever the case, it should be noted that I corrected my behavior days, weeks, in fact, before Givens and his new advisers actually pressed charges.

No one, not even the judge, seemed to remember that.

* * *

On the day of departure, a Saturday, I waited inside Terminal 21 at Port Everglades, standing ass to elbow with my fellow passengers. I saw my suspicions were correct, as they usually are. "Unseen souls" was just a liberal's way of saying the afflicted, of which I was apparently a card-carrying member. I was an otherwise healthy individual. I didn't smoke. I barely drank. I'd never done a single drug. Yet here I was, about to ascend a gangway with the hobbling and limbless, the misshapen and genetically unfortunate, four thousand of them. I took in the terminal's DMV-on-crack ambiance, inhaled the fusty air-conditioning, and suddenly found myself getting a bit miffed. Neblitt, I thought, you Rastafarian fruitcake. What the hell did your New Age ass get me into? Not only had she somehow convinced me, in her own passive-aggressive way, to go on this eight-day voyage, she'd also arranged, of all things, a chaperone for me. Another one of her clients, a veteran of this particular cruise, was also in attendance, and ostensibly we were supposed to chum it up for the entire week, which to me sounded about as appealing as eating at a fast-food restaurant.

Whatever. I tried to forget about it as I wound my way through the passport-check line. In front of me was a balding muscle-bound man with no legs, much less a torso, who sort of scooted himself along by way of his veiny bodybuilder arms. In front of him was a man with a hump on his back so large that even the hump had a hump. I glanced around, adjusting to my surroundings, and I slowly realized very few of these people covered their conditions. There were people with eyes missing, jaws missing, ears, noses, half of their heads. And those without any visible situations had a generally broken comportment that suggested there was something under their clothes that wasn't good.

Other than me, the only person I saw who truly hid herself was a woman a few yards ahead. She was wearing a large veiled hat and a long dress, both of which made her look as though she should've been running through a field, chasing butterflies with a net.

"Ah," someone said. "Scoping out the ladies already, huh?"

I looked around and then down and found the man with no legs smiling up at me. "No, I'm just assessing." I looked away for a moment. "This is my first cruise."

I looked back, and he was nodding slyly, not believing a word. "Sure. Incognito. I see what you're doing." Before I could respond, he said, "You wait. There's gonna be all kinds of tail on this boat."

"Tail," I said.

"Yeah, man. Booty, ass, cushion for the pushin'. You should've seen it last year. Girls galore. I made out like a bandit." He nodded and smiled, recalling it all.

I looked away again, trying to avoid his gaze. When I looked back, I found him still regarding me, as though he knew all my secrets. I leaned over to get a better look at him, and he pulled my ticket from the front pocket of my blazer. He examined it for a moment before I snatched it back.

"Don't freak out," he said. "It just looks like we're gonna be deck twins, bro."

He showed me his pass, and it appeared our cabins were right next to each other. I wondered if I should say something enthusiastic about this turn of events, but, alas, I drew a blank.

"I knew I had a feeling about you."

I gave him a funny look.

"No, not that kind of feeling." He looked around and then beckoned me close. "I could already tell, you and me, we're gonna be like this." He intertwined the middle and index fingers of his right hand and smiled again.

I focused on his perfectly clipped nails, his thick digits, and I couldn't help but wonder which finger was supposed to be him and which was supposed to be me. It was then that I finally looked at Neblitt's note describing her other client. It said, "Double amputee with muscles! Tommy Defarillo, but just call him Tommy D." And I thought, Wonderful. This crass, legless little Italian gigolo was going to be my traveling partner.

* * *

Evidently, as a cruise novice, I'd been operating under the false assumption that cruise liners were just a means of transport, schlepping cruise goers from one poor Caribbean island to another. It turned out the onboard activities were as much an attraction as the ports of call. The ship contained twenty decks, ten lounges, six casinos, fourteen restaurants, seven bars, fifty shops, four comedy clubs, six movie theaters, ten fitness centers, an amusement park, a nine-hole golf course, a driving range, a shooting range, and four Olympic-size swimming pools, not to mention the hundreds and hundreds of cabins. The vessel was Vegas and the Mall of America but with a rudder and lifeboats. And I kept wondering how the behemoth didn't sink.

It had been christened the *Ocean Wanderer*, which to me didn't sound as though it would instill much confidence in its passengers. It might as well have been called the *Ocean Nomad* or the *Ocean Vagrant*. We could end up anywhere and not at all on time. Before this trip, I did my usual googling, being the fact-whore that I am. I found out the ship was brand new, the first of what was called "mammoth ships," one step up from the long line of megaships that were now considered small potatoes. I told all this to Tommy, my new short friend, who seemed genuinely enthralled.

"Wow, man," he said. "You really are a Republican."

He was a former welder from the Bronx and a Democrat, but I thought it'd be unkind to hold those facts against him so early in our relationship.

After we found our cabins, I went through my six-times-a-day ritual of reapplying my makeup where it always seemed to rub off around my neck and ears. Ten minutes later, Tommy pawed past my cracked cabin door, rotten with cologne, and now in a red Hawaiian shirt, the bottom of which was knotted under his torso. With his massive arms and nothing else, he looked like a man waist deep in quicksand. "So, are you ready to get some booty? Or are you ready to get some booty?" He stood there on his hands looking up at me, waiting. "C'mon, you're supposed to say you're ready to get some booty."

"Please, God," I said. "Tell me there's a third option."

He palmed into my cabin, all arms like a gorilla, and paced back and forth in front of my closet mirror. He checked his teeth and his hair, of which there wasn't much remaining. "Man, I'm gonna tell you right now," he said. "We can't hang together if you're gonna be a downer."

"Hang together? Hey, I don't know what Neblitt told you, but I plan on spending my time on this cruise entirely unfettered. I'm a bit of a dick like that."

A fidgety little bastard, he turned around, smoothing what used to be his hair. "Yeah, she said you were a dick. But that's cool. We can still have a good time. Most of my friends are dicks." He pulled out my desk chair and leapt up onto it like a frog. He labored himself back around to face me. "So, what's your story anyhow? You don't look like there's anything wrong with you. Are you a mental or something?"

"A mental?" I said. "No, I see everything quite clearly. I'm a—"

"Republican," he said. "Yeah, we determined that." He jumped off the chair as easily as he'd jumped up and came scooting past me. "Politics aside, you're not used to this at all, are you? You haven't been one of us for very long."

"Less than a year." I felt compelled to unbutton my collar and show him my chest, where I hadn't applied any of my makeup. It was the first time I'd shown anyone other than a doctor.

"Gotcha," he said. "You're all splotchy and—pink!"

"A skin condition," I said. "A pretty rare one."

He nodded more as he studied me. His amazement grew. Of course, then it just went away. "Well, you don't see that every day. A Black Republican with skin the color of bubblegum. Amazing." He contemplated it for a moment. Then he turned and pawed coolly toward the door. "So? Are you coming or not?"

"Coming where?" I said. "To do—what?"

"Everything." He stopped and looked back at me. "That's kind of what you do on a cruise. Time to hit the fun button, my friend. Follow me."

* * *

For some reason, call it old-fashioned conservative courtesy, I let him talk me into going to one of the ship's watering holes, the Bar Ye Matey. We sat at a cocktail table under the shadow of a large blow-up pirate, drinking mai tais out of glass boots. The *Ocean Wanderer* had just departed, like a giant white slug, and inched out to sea. That slightly unmoored feeling of being on a large ocean vessel was actually quite apparent in my shorts. I could feel it and the almost imperceptibly low rumble of the engine as I watched passengers stream into the bar.

Bored already, I said, "Did you know—cruise ships like this one have often been called 'floating cities'?"

Tommy was watching the crowd expectantly, as though waiting for someone. "Nope," he said. "Did not know that."

"Yeah, the volume of waste they produce is unimaginable. Sewage, wastewater from sinks, showers, and galleys, otherwise known as gray water, hazardous waste, solid waste, oily bilge water, ballast water." I then segued into the air pollution issue and global warming and the questionable liberal agenda concerning the two. But as expected, it all went over his head, literally. He sat there stirring his drink and scanning the other patrons, not paying me any attention.

"Who exactly are you looking for?"

"Who do you think?" he said. "A lady."

I nodded. "One you know from the last cruise, I gather."

"Not necessarily. Just one who wouldn't mind a pickle tickle, if you know what I mean."

He went back on the hunt, and I looked down the bar. The woman I'd seen in the passport line had come in, the veiled hat lady. Mary Poppins. I wondered if she was British. She was sitting at the far end of the bar annihilating a book of crosswords. Every now and then, when she got stuck, which wasn't often, she'd press her pen to her lips. Her veil would move, and I could see a vague outline of her face. I turned back to Tommy, who was lost in thought, staring at a buxom middle-aged woman with no arms.

"What do you think?" he said. "She's hot, right?" The woman was sitting alone at a table by the door, half a martini sweating in front of her. Armless and big-boobed, she wore a tight T-shirt that said MAIN ATTRACTIONS across the front. So, there was that. But she was also barefoot and in bell-bottoms, her left leg crossed over the right in the male manner. As I got a better look at her, wondering how she was actually drinking that martini—it didn't have a straw—she smoothly lifted her left foot, pinched the glass by its stem between her big and second toe, and brought the glass to her mouth. She even swirled it like a snifter, which, all afflictions aside, was impressive.

"Hot," Tommy said. "Am I right?" He kept eying her, mentally tapping one of his phantom feet. "Bro, I'm gonna talk to her."

"Suit yourself," I said. "But you'll probably just embarrass yourself."

He dismounted his stool and whinnied. "You kidding? I embarrass myself all the time. Maybe you should give it a try. You look like you haven't had your silver polished in, like, forever."

Outside the bar entrance, as she was leaving, he said something to her, something I hoped was crude enough to elicit a slap across his face with her foot. Remarkably, though, she blushed. They conversed for a moment and then walked away with each other, but not before he gave me a sly thumbs-up and mimed his index finger pumping in and out of his fist. I turned back to my mai tai, glad the runt had scooted away.

Aside from Neblitt, the last few months of my life had been unmarred by people. I happily spent days on end inside my Central Park West apartment, ordering in food and groceries, streaming films in my pajamas, dusting. I still put on my makeup, but I didn't need to see anyone. It was glorious. Neblitt foolishly thought I was becoming a hermit, but I'd always enjoyed my own company inside my own apartment, oblivious to the world. Admittedly, before I started wearing makeup, children did wail at my appearance, say, on the street or on an elevator. That could turn anyone into a hermit. But children were usually afraid of me, even before I'd gotten my disease.

This may have been percolating in me as I bellied up to the bar for another drink. To my right, veiled hat lady, whatever, the butterfly hunter, was perched on a bar stool, blasting through a crossword puzzle in two minutes easy.

I watched her finish one and then move on to another without missing a beat. When she finished that one, I leaned in and said, "You must be a pro."

"A pro what?" She didn't look up.

"I don't know," I said. "A professional crossword puzzle—person. I don't know what you call them."

"Solvers," she said, her voice low and slow, every syllable precisely pronounced. I gave her a quick look-see and could tell she was obviously bookish but then again obviously not. There was something else there, a variety of roughness I couldn't place. Perhaps she was a reformed thug with a knack for words. Whatever it was, it made her interesting. She was tall, possibly well proportioned if you squinted a little. There was a certain dignity in the way she could disregard people, even me. She was diligent. Her pen kept moving a mile a minute and then she flipped to the next puzzle.

I plucked a toothpick from the dispenser on the bar and unsheathed it from its wrapper. "Anyway," I said, "you're fast, and you're using a pen!"

"I am," she said, "and you're bothering me."

She went back to her puzzle, and I tried to remember why I thought it was a good idea to talk to her in the first place. I scanned the packed bar, trying to get the bartender's attention, and for some reason a little Caucasian man off in a corner caught my eye. He was making out with a little Asian woman in a dimly lit booth, both of them slobbering all over each other like teenagers. That was exactly when my surroundings came into focus, and I realized an interesting fact: I was standing in the middle of an orgy. Over the speakers, Marvin Gaye was singing "Let's Get It On," and all I saw were sloppy kisses and dirty gropes being traded in the bar. My fellow passengers were profoundly horny, probably the horniest people on earth. With reason. Starved for attention and now among their own, they were virtually acting out a scene from *Caligula*. And this woman wanted no part of it.

I turned back around. "I'm Melvin, by the way."

She'd finished yet another puzzle and now glanced up at me, as if to say, "You're still here?" Through the veil, I could see her face was long and sharp featured, serious, but the right side, the side away from me, which she appeared to hide, seemed to droop in an odd way.

"Your name?" I said.

She hesitated as though she had a stutter. "Zz— Zarrella."

I asked if the name was a South American derivation. Peruvian? Chilean?

"Neither." She hesitated again. "My mother made it up. I'm from Cleveland."

I offered my condolences about being from Cleveland, but I said I liked her name. I repeated it a few times even, playing with the r's and the l's a little bit till she said, "Really. That's enough."

I thought I'd broken through one of her layers so I offered my hand. I wasn't sure she saw it, though. I held it out there for quite a while before she extended hers. It was long fingered and short nailed, wiry and ringless. I beheld it. Then I took it in mine. As soon as I did that, I could tell she didn't like it very much. I could feel an almost undetectable tug in her direction. But her skin, it was strangely textured. It had the appearance of melted wax, swirly in spots yet wrinkled as a raisin in others, the result of serious burns. Curious, I tested the surface of her skin with my thumb. Two quick rubs, and she immediately snatched her hand back and slid off her stool.

"Oh, great," I said. "You're leaving? Why?"

"Because," she said. "You are a stranger. And I prefer strangers to remain strange." With that, she shrugged, as if to say, "Tough shit," and walked out of the bar grumpily, like one of my ex-wives.

Fed up with the whole experience, I left, too, and wandered into one of the ship's internet cafés. Homesick for my usual routine, I found solace in my daily dinking around on the RNC site, the obligatory glance at TMZ. When I checked my email, my comfort level fell. A message from Neblitt glowed in my inbox, the subject line simply, "Havin' Fun Yet?" Apparently, the hippie couldn't leave me alone for even a week. Suddenly peeved, I clicked Reply and found myself typing out an assessment of her skills, detailing, perhaps viciously, every instance of her incompetence, including convincing me to go on this idiotic cruise. When I was done, after I'd perused my work, I had to admit it was a long, and possibly baggy, appraisal. Around paragraph eight or nine, I may have even accused her of terrorism. I stopped.

For whatever reason, lambasting her just didn't feel right. Maybe empathy for her liberal foolishness washed over me. I don't know. I closed the message. I started a new one, but I had no clue what to write. I stared at the screen. I drummed my fingers on the keys. Trying to write something, anything, that fit in Neblitt's cheery parlance was pointless for someone like me. So, just to be done with it, I typed the first thing that popped into my head—"I think I've met a woman."

* * *

On Monday, in Cozumel, the *Ocean Wanderer* roamed into port at sunrise. Being an early riser, I just happened to be up already, standing at the deck 12 railing, watching the entire docking procedure: the flurry of crewmen, the massive anchor dropping from the ship's belly button, the honking of the earth-shattering horn. It was almost as ridiculous as the sleep I'd gotten the night before. I was still a little groggy, still a little weirded out since I'd spent most of our day at sea in my cabin. So, I dosed myself with caffeine, had an unimpressive breakfast, and at ten, found myself standing in front of the jumbotron that displayed the shore excursions. Tommy and his new companion, Deirdre, were at my side, not that they noticed.

They'd stoked their romantic fires so efficiently our first night at sea that through our shared wall they sounded like two chimps moving furniture into the wee hours. They still couldn't keep their hands, and feet, off each other, both of them so ener-gized I wondered if they'd smuggled contraband aboard. They were "rarin' to," as Deirdre, an apparent Texan, kept saying. Rarin' to do everything: snorkel at Chankanaab, ride a cata-maran or some Jet Skis, and, if they had time, eventually have a "dolphin encounter," which Tommy said as though it were a sex act.

I had other plans. I pointed at the excursion to San Lazaro, an old leper colony, and said, "That sounds like fun to me." They both gave slow, polite nods, as though they didn't want to betray the fact that they thought it was maybe a bit morbid. Being of strong mind, I could tolerate gloom as long as it had a point to it. I had a feeling they, like the rest of their progressive ilk, were more content to have their picture taken holding an iguana that was dressed like Captain Ahab. We parted ways.

I strolled out of the port terminal toward Punta Norte and quickly located the pier where my excursion was to begin. Un-surprisingly, San Lazaro was not a well-liked attraction. There was no one in sight, a fact the shriveled curmudgeon of a boat captain seemed rather pissed about. I sensed he'd somehow been saddled with this unpopular charter and wanted to make as many runs to and from San Lazaro as humanly possible. "*Rápido,*" he said, "*vamanos,*" as though we were making an escape. He fired up the outboard motors tout de suite and was settling inside the cockpit when, from ashore, a woman's voice pleaded for him to wait. I turned and saw it was Zarrella jogging hastily toward us. I waved. When she saw me, however, she stopped and immediately looked ashore as though she'd left something important behind.

"Oh," she said, inching toward the boat. "It's—you."

"That's right," I said. "The stranger. Try not to sound too excited."

She approached but seemed indecisive. She straddled the pier and the boat for a moment, giving me a displeased look.

"Well?" I said. "Are you coming? Or are you just going to keep looking at me like I stink?"

With that, she boldly stepped aboard and sat across from me on the starboard side, as though she wasn't going to let my presence ruin this for her. The captain, who I sensed had a hatred of tourists, wasn't in any better mood with a second passenger. He floored it, smacking the outboard controls all the way to the console. The force sent me and Zarrella sliding back toward the stern as the bow rose and cut through the water like a Ginsu. We reached top speed pretty quickly. The ride smoothed out from a stomach-churning romp to a nice, pacifying bounce. With the wind in my face, I peered over the port side and watched the water fly by, clear as an aquarium. I could see schools of spear-shaped fish and big dumb turtles gliding near the surface as well as other nasty things on the ocean floor.

Every now and then, when I dared, I even looked at Zarrella, who didn't seem that interested in looking at the water or me. When we were hit with a gust or spray, her only reaction was to smooth her dress, a strapless red flower print this time, her bare shoulders beaded with water. She was wearing a different hat, too, something dressier. It was red and white with a small white veil that barely covered her nose. She held it clamped on her head with her other hand, the veil pointless in all that wind. After a particularly strong blast hit us, I got an unobstructed view of the burned side of her face. The damage stretched from her right temple down her cheek and neck. The corner of her right eye was burned slightly shut. She must've sensed me looking. She tilted her hat and turned her head, showing me her good side. Then we both just faced forward like it never happened.

That was when San Lazaro, a speck out there in the ocean, appeared before us. It was one of the lush atolls the cruise ship had negotiated before we'd eased into port. As we approached it now, the captain swooped around the right and circled the overgrown islet, giving us full view of the ruins before docking. I must say, it was not a sandy paradise like the others. It was not brochure material. It was, for lack of a better phrase, ugly as a motherfucker. The entire isle, from base to peak, was a rocky fortress, a jail, really, with shrubs and trees growing up through any opening they could find. Even its point of entry was ominous, simply a tall, wide stone staircase that started right at the water's edge.

The captain glided up to it and docked, and Zarrella and I

disembarked, me climbing a few steps ahead of her. At the top, we were greeted by a weedy courtyard and two giant wooden doors that opened into the ruins. We strolled around wordlessly but together, both of us probably thinking the same thing: Is this it? The place was a sty. There were no gift shops or guides, no historical markers. I hated to admit it, but it *was* morbid, like touring an old, burned-down house. I felt like the whole place was just going to fall on us.

"I hate to be the bearer of bad news, but I think this is what's called a bullshit excursion. We've been suckered."

She produced a parasol, opened it, and twirled it as she looked around. "Gee, how did I know you were going to say that?"

"Because, you obviously have a nose for certain kinds of people: complainers and assholes."

After more walking, she said, "You're right. You definitely seem like both."

I took this as a good sign. Though she was younger than me, she'd apparently dealt with my people before. Maybe that's why I got her to agree so easily about San Lazaro. So far, it sucking was the general consensus. We tried to make the best of our depressing milieu and strolled more, hoping there was actually something to see. We walked through a short, dingy tunnel, and amazingly when we emerged, we stumbled onto a sunlit courtyard with a few gnarled fruit trees. Zarrella went over and plucked a petite apple from a branch. She wiped it on her dress and bit into it. Her pleased reaction said it was sweet. I picked one, was about to take a bite, but then, from behind the stem, a girthy worm wriggled into view. I tossed the fruit like a hot coal.

"According to the guidebook," Zarrella said, "the island is known for cliff diving. But the gusts are probably too strong today."

"I don't know," I said, testing the wind. "Seeing people splatter themselves on the rocks might make this place more interesting. Right now, I feel like I'm at a landfill." I found a clean spot on a rickety stone wall and sat in the shade of a big dead bush. She investigated a cluster of colorful plants that I was pretty sure were just weeds. Still, I watched her smell each and every bloom.

"It's good no one's here," she said. "It's peaceful."

"Yeah," I said. "People tend to just ruin things, don't they? I mean, look around."

She lit a long, skinny cigarette and fogged me like a roach. "A bit of a misanthrope, are you? I never would've guessed."

I moved over so she could sit. "It's what my pothead therapist says."

She said hers, too.

I took my blazer off. "Well, what do you know? It's kismet. We're finally getting somewhere, aren't we?"

"Slow your roll," she said. "We're not."

Instead of spelunking into the island's deeper cavities, after a while we went up another long set of steps to the next level of boringness, sending sunning lizards skittering out of our way.

I asked if her therapist had made her come on this trip, too.

She shook her head no. "He suggested it, but he doesn't know I'm here. No one does."

"Ah," I said.

"Do you think that's peculiar?"

"No. I didn't tell anyone I'm on this trip either. They'd think I'm a nut."

She gave me a look but didn't respond. At the next little courtyard, she headed right for one of the crumbling stone buildings, as if to change the subject. She went through a doorway with a crooked iron gate without any hesitation and vanished into the darkness.

"I wouldn't go in there if I were you. You might—I don't know—die." I stood outside, waiting. Just when I thought she'd never return, she came breezing by me.

"It's a good thing you aren't me, then, isn't it?"

She strolled away, and I looked inside the doorway. There was nothing but a pile of rusty junk: old children's tricycles from who knows when, metal doors, and collapsed bedframes. Somewhere in the mangled mess, I even saw large chains and medieval-style cuffs. "Jesus," I said. "This place really is a bummer."

As we walked up yet more steps to the top of the island, toward some sort of watchtower, she said, "Did you know, since 1995 an average of twelve people vanish from cruise ships every year? Gone, never heard from again."

"Interesting. That one of your crossword clues?"

"No." She thought to explain, but then she said, "It's just trivia."

"Well, I'll try to remember that the next time I want to ruin someone's day." We walked and climbed for a few more minutes, stopping at a little overlook. When I thought she was off investigating something, I turned my back, removed my compact, and checked my makeup. I was worried the boat ride had thinned my foundation, that I was getting pinkish. This was my plight. Luckily, my face wasn't bad. A few pats of powder were all I needed. I turned back around.

"Everything okay?"

"Just rosy," I said. "Why?"

"You looked a little worried about your makeup."

I stopped for a second. "I don't know what you're talking about."

She watched me. "Maybe go easy on the powder next time. It makes you look a little—chalky."

With my back to her, I fondled my compact and then slipped it into my pocket. "Maybe you should mind your own business." I walked over to a stone archway. I stood in its shade, fanning myself. After a moment, I said, "Is it me or is it hotter than a whorehouse on nickel night?"

She walked up. "It's hot. That's why there's such a thing as cruise wear. But that's not quite your style, is it?" She finished her cigarette and flicked the butt away.

"Damn right. I don't want to look like everyone else on board."

"Because dressing like you're at a presidential debate makes you better than them."

"Hey, if you look like a million bucks, you attract a million bucks. When you look like them, all you attract is a buffet. Who wants that? Besides, you're the last person who should be saying anything about how anyone else is dressed. With that hat on, you look like Mary Poppins at the Kentucky Derby."

I laughed, maybe too much. I may have even cackled. But she'd gotten personal with me. How could she not expect some reciprocation? Then again, how would I even know? Five dead marriages, and I still had trouble telling when I'd struck a nerve with a woman. I knew I'd done something the way Zarrella puckered her brow, though. She stood in front of me, as if ready to plant her foot in my crotch. She peeled off her hat and for a long moment just glared at me. With her hair matted and damp, she made a show of turning the burned side of her face toward mine. "Take a gander." Up close, it was a raw swirl of pink and red, the healed skin still somewhat fresh. It looked like Hollywood makeup, enough to make anyone wince, but the way her right eye looked out defiantly through the burns made her intriguing.

That being said, I still looked away. I had a feeling that was what she wanted.

"Ugly, isn't it?"

"No." It took some will to look her in the eyes. "Not really."

After a moment, she lifted her hand, dragged her index finger down the side of my cheek, and looked at the brown makeup on her fingertip.

"Ridiculous, isn't it?" I said.

She shook her head no and rubbed her thumb and finger together, wiping the makeup off. I could make out the streaky burns on her temple, cheek, and neck. I could smell her musky fragrance. It pulled me toward her.

"You're kind of interesting, aren't you?"

It was apparently another wrong thing to say. "Kind of messed up is more like it. I think we both are."

"Yeah, well, I hate to break it to you, but my ex-wives already came to that conclusion long ago."

After each divorce, my lost loves all said I needed serious, serious help. It made perfect sense. Every last one of them hated me when we first met. The way it starts is the way it ends.

Greta, my first ex, said being with me was like reading a bad novel: the beginning was okay, the middle stank, and it wasn't worth getting to the end. Mimi, my second, a marine biologist, often called me her little sea urchin, her little uni, most happy in my thorny shell. Tatyana the Russian, my fourth ex, agreed in her own Russian way. She said my love was like a plastic bag used to pick up dog shit: turned inside out so I didn't have to touch anything. "Yet you fall in love at the drop of a hat," she said. "Explain this, Melvin." I couldn't. It just was. I was a romantic. On that gloomy island with Zarrella, though, I was realistic enough to know my exes were right. I had interpersonal problems I had yet to correct. But at least I was on this cruise. I thought I was trying.

I followed Zarrella to the tippy-top of the island, to an iron staircase whose integrity I checked thoroughly before we ascended. We emerged atop the watchtower, in the blinding sun, where two crumbling turrets looked out over the perimeter of the island. Zarrella went over to the east-facing one. I investigated the west-facing and quickly realized this was where the cliff diving took place. Each turret was plastered with Mexican graffiti that translated to "Dive to Live. Live to Dive" and "Gringo, don't hit your head."

I looked over the edge and down. The crashing waves tried to lull you off the cliff, so I made sure to stay far from it. Instead, I looked farther out to sea, at the vast emptiness. Though I'd never been much of a nature lover, the quietude up there did slurp out any thoughts orbiting my brain. Of course, after only a few minutes, me being me, I reached my threshold. I was bored. I turned toward Zarrella and found her standing in her turret, close to the edge. She was looking down at the water so long I thought she'd fling herself into it.

"Be careful. One good gust, and you're a goner."

But she just told me to mind my business. She put her arms out like a cliff diver. I thought she was about to jump for sure. But, weirdly, she just took off her hat and started to undress.

"Whoa. What're you doing?"

"Sunning myself, you weirdo. Calm down."

She was wearing a bathing suit under her dress. Still, I turned my attention back to the sea. I hadn't been in the company of a relatively bare woman in a few years. Yet I couldn't help looking back. The spectacle was too strong: her olive skin, her arms in a crucifix pose, most of her body goosefleshed and continented with burns. The ocean kicked up, and a wave of mist cascaded over her. Her body tightened for a second. Then she relaxed, ready for more.

"So, in addition to being a misanthrope, you're a goddamn nudist. You aren't a Democrat, are you?"

She shook her head, the wind taking hold of her kinky brown hair. "I'm a fierce Independent."

I actually laughed. "You think you're funny, don't you?"

She shook her head. "Believe me. I'm the least amusing person you're ever going to meet."

* * *

We had dinner that night at Bionic, the ship's space-themed bistro. It seemed like a fitting backdrop for people like us. The place was cold and precise, glass and stainless steel. Actual robots tai chi'ed their way around the restaurant, bringing us precisely made tapas, perfectly cooked prawns. They even uncorked the two bottles of fruit bomb Cab we quaffed in the process. At first, it all seemed natural. We got snockered quickly, the crappy vino bringing out our vulnerable sides. Eventually, we got all therapy on each other, swapping tales of mental hygiene. Like me, she'd been married a few times. She'd loved and lost. It was apparent she had more wounds than just her burns. It was probably apparent that I had way more wrong with me than my skin. Yet, even drunk, we still didn't want to get too close. We didn't know each other. We were like a couple of pie-eyed mimes trapped in our invisible boxes.

That was why it seemed a bit shocking when we reached the sediment of our last bottle and she asked if I'd like to go back to her cabin for a nightcap. We smuggled out another bottle of fruit bomb and sat next to each other on the end of her bed sipping the vino, not saying a word. A few minutes into it, I said, "You know what I like about you? You don't suffer fools."

"That's funny," she said, mildly slurring. "I feel like that's all I do."

I said, "Me, too. Fools everywhere. Fools aplenty. Ships of fools." It was the best I could do.

There was a long, uncomfortable silence, both of us nodding really at nothing. Then it just sort of happened: She looked at me. I looked at her. Like two horny cats, we pounced on each other and proceeded to ineptly hump with the lights on, even the bathroom light, at her insistence. "Tell me if it's too bright," she said.

I was a little occupied at the moment, but I did say it was kind of like a hospital room in there. "Can we turn them down a little?"

She dimmed the overheads. "I just want to show myself." I stopped and looked at her, was almost flattered, but then she added, "Oh, not to you exactly. Just to prove I can do it. It's for me." She shoved my face into her cleavage, smearing my makeup over her surprisingly smooth chest.

"Right," I said, between gasps. "I get it." I peeled off my pants over my shoes and asked if showing herself was part of her therapy.

"Sort of," she said. "My therapist said if I went on this trip, I should at least get laid. It would be a milestone for me. Hope you don't mind."

"Your therapist sounds like a very wise person. You should get me a referral."

The sex barely lasted a few minutes, but even in that short time we mapped the geographies of each other's skin. We surveyed each other's wounds or blotches like children comparing scabs. Some of hers were as tough as leather. Others were so soft and on the surface that they looked as though I could peel them off like stickers.

Though I'd been successful in life, I understood wounds. Racism, no father, endless ex-wives hating me. Like anyone, I had injuries only I could appreciate. It was probably why people thought I was a creep. It was probably why she had trouble connecting. I hoped we were realizing this about each other as we entered the second minute of our escapade. We turned over, and she climbed on top. She moved her pelvis back and forth. She gyrated and then climaxed without any help from me. As she shuttered above me like a defective droid, I realized I'd stumbled onto a version of the opposite sex I'd never encountered before: the damaged woman. Given some of our similarities, I wondered if I was a damaged man. Who knew? Maybe she was thinking the exact same thing about me and was doing all this because she pitied me. Who cared? I was fine with us being malcontents taking from each other what we needed at the time. With the contention we'd had earlier that day, it was a miracle she was fine with it, too.

* * *

We saw each other every day after that, a fact that amused Tommy. The next morning, while he and I were pumping iron in fitness room 6 and Zarrella and Deirdre were on the ellipticals across the gym, Tommy started dancing around, singing a song whose childish lyrics were "Melvin got some booty. Melvin got some booty."

Naturally, I looked at my watch and asked when he'd grow up.

"I don't know," he said. "How about a quarter past never?" He lay back on an incline bench and pressed two 150-pound dumbbells for so many reps I lost count. When he was done, he tossed the weights to the rubber floor and sat up, breathing easy. "So, how's it feel to be part of the club?"

"Which one is that?" I lay back on the bench and started my set with 30-pound dumbbells.

"The coochie club." He snickered and stood on his hands beside me, correcting my form.

"It just happened," I said. "I don't know how anything feels." I was only on my second rep, struggling already.

He looked across the room at Zarrella and Deirdre for a moment. "What's to know?" he said. "She likes you."

"Maybe."

"Man, there ain't no maybe about it. I can tell." Tommy looked at them again and then slowly at me. His face softened into one of those Neblitt looks. "What do you say we don't mess this one up, okay?"

I told him to shut up and give me a spot.

Since losing my job and my color, since I'd awakened that day, I'd begun to realize I'd been transitioning. As impossible as it sounded, I may have even been a bit unstable without knowing it. Throw a woman into all that, and I was at sea, figuratively and literally. I kept reminding myself that we both had lives before the cruise, that this was just a fluke. It wouldn't go anywhere. So, don't even think about getting attached. I was self-aware enough to know that probably wouldn't happen.

As we sailed on toward Belize, for some reason she was the one who got serious. She actually said, "I want to unpack my marriage history for you. Would that be okay?"

"Unpack?" I said. "Um, okay." It was midnight, and we'd sneaked over to the Southstar right off deck 12. It was one of the amusements, a large crane-like arm hanging off the ship with a jewel-shaped capsule at the end. We were in the capsule, just the two of us, hanging thirty feet off the port side, three hundred feet over the water, drinking G&Ts under the stars.

It really didn't take any prying from me. She rattled off the starting lineup of her deadbeat husbands as if she'd been waiting all day to tell me. Her first one, Larry, was, according to her, "an ultimate prick." He knocked her around, cheated on her, the whole enchilada. Though she didn't hold back on the details, I wished she had. It was outside my realm, but I listened for once, especially when the word "abortion" was mentioned a few times. It turned out her therapist believed she had paternal issues. I asked why, and she said, "Well, every one of my exes looked exactly like my father," which sounded like a whole other ball of wax. It didn't stop there. Larry the Prick died, appropriately, and she got with Butch, another prick, who did the same thing. Her third prick, "who shall remain nameless," she said, "He was—" and then she stopped there. I didn't ask, suspecting that was where the injuries came from. How? I don't know. Why? I didn't want to imagine. She'd been through hell, with the burns to prove it.

"What do you think of all that?" It was such a depressing story that she rightly viewed overcoming it as a triumph.

I stirred the lime in my drink. My exes, all of them high-profile successes, had always put a hurting on the world, not the other way around. Thoroughly out of my element, all I could think to say was, "Sounds like Cleveland's a crazy place."

She looked away, disappointed. The gin had brought out a brooding side. "I'm serious," she said. "Say something that means something."

I thought of the things that broke up my marriages, how they were so unimportant, so entitled, on both sides. "Your relationships make mine sound like nursery rhymes. And I've been married more times. I don't know who's luckier."

She shook her head. "That still didn't mean anything. All you do is crack jokes."

The Southstar capsule was in a reclined position, which made me feel like a baby in a crib. The sky was a big black dome salted with stars. Zarrella looked away at a cluster of long-dead constellations to her right. After a lengthy hush, I said I was sorry.

"For what exactly?"

"For everything that happened to you."

She looked at me but didn't say anything, which was no help.

She was seeking compassion and understanding. Though we'd been intimate, I didn't feel confident putting my arm around her just then. It wasn't like that with our kind. I did peer down at her hand, her scarred one. I thought of taking it in mine, but I don't think she wanted to give me the satisfaction. She hid it in her pocket before I could make a move. Then she slowly turned back to the stars, and so did I.

*　*　*

Wednesday, in Belize, we spoke of none of it. We spent the day investigating a massive cemetery, and on the way back to the ship, we toured the markets. The previous night, and its accompanying hangover, were behind us. We breezed around effortlessly, the locals not batting an eye at the multitude of unseen souls who had just flooded Belize City. Since I wasn't that far removed from the land of "normal people," I was sure they'd think the freaks had escaped the asylum. But the Belizeans were unmoved. Zarrella and I fondled trinkets and weird vegetables at the markets, dodged the odd pickpocket. At lunch, we dined on ceviche, and after, I bought her a carved rain stick that she didn't really want but graciously took anyway. Occasionally, I caught myself wondering what it would be like to actually live with a woman again. I was feeling unusually open and spread out, maybe a bit upside down. We'd been sampling exotic liquors and home brews all day. By the time we were sitting outside a café that served beer and rum, I began taking stock of my life, my makeup, my blackballing Party, my being pink. None of it seemed that bad.

Zarrella was there. We were getting along, satisfied with each other's presence. Though I'd never been much of an animal lover, I even petted a three-legged dog that was using our table for shade. The dog was missing its front left leg and had to pogo around on his front right, but the animal was still young and agile. It had adapted. I stroked the mangy pooch, lit on Belikin and Travellers. I mentioned how funny it was that deformities in animals were seen as endearing. "But in humans," I said, "they're disgusting."

Zarrella nodded, giving me a pat but kind of grim smile. "Just now figuring that out, eh?"

I sensed some sarcasm in her tone and asked if everything was all right.

"Sure." She took off her hat and her shawl, her burns there for everyone to see. She weaved her hair into a french braid and let the end curl over her shoulder like a snake. I thought she'd put her hat back on. She seemed to think about it, but then she gave me a funny look. As if out of spite, she just left the hat where it was. She suddenly had the air of a nicotine addict who'd finally quit the butts. Distracted by that, I patted the dog's rump so much the beast gave a displeased groan and limped away.

I looked up at Zarrella as she stared off. I watched her blink a few times and then asked if she was happy.

She swigged her beer and shrugged, as though it wasn't a question she wanted to answer. "I guess," she said. "You?"

With some trepidation, I said, "You kidding? I'm always happy."

* * *

She was cooling on me. I was fairly certain. After we boarded the ship that evening, she was different. She walked around hatless and unencumbered, which was a little unnerving. Not her burns. I'd seen enough of them in the few days I'd known her to accept them. For me, they were becoming invisible, but for other passengers, even those who had way more hideous shit wrong with them, they still triggered a double take. Zarrella suddenly couldn't care less. Whereas before she was shy and misanthropic, covering herself up, now she was proudly defiant. She was exposing herself in a way I couldn't. To say all that kicked it up a tick on the weirdometer would've been accurate. And that was saying a lot, since all of it, the entire cruise, was just weird anyway.

On a trip for people with "conditions," you inevitably got to know how your fellow passengers came to be that way. Some, like me, were born with their problems, but others suffered from accidents. Tommy, a master welder, was fusing beams on a skyscraper one day and took quite a fall. Deirdre, a former farmworker, had a very unfortunate incident with a wood chipper and never saw her hands again. Dave, a passenger who sat with all of us at dinner that night, was missing both legs and arms. He whizzed around in a state-of-the-art voice-controlled wheelchair. He said he'd been run over in quick succession by a car, a bus, and then a trash truck.

When someone asked what had happened to Zarrella, she said, "A domestic accident, a few of them," in such a dark, discomfited way that it was like someone farted. Nobody said a word.

With those terrible histories, I was sure my ailment and the fact that I covered it up seemed a bit cheesedick to them, even Zarrella. When Dave's wife, Rita, who accompanied him, cutting up his food and feeding it to him, doing other dirty work, I was sure, responded to my condition with "But you look so normal," Zarrella said, "It's the makeup. He wears it on his face."

I looked at her. She looked away. Everyone looked at me and gave piteous nods, as though I were someone's slow child. Everyone except Dave, who compensated for not having limbs by being a prodigious asshole.

"Makeup?" He giggled like a villain. "Well, lucky you. Because let me tell you, there ain't no makeup for all this shit." He gestured over his limbless body with his chin. "Mascara can't cover up not being able to wipe your ass, tie your shoe, and oh yeah, have arms and fucking legs." Rita stuffed a piece of food in his mouth to quiet him.

Of course, just as we were having this conversation, another Black man with vitiligo, who didn't wear makeup, happened to pass our table. Granted, unlike me, he was in the early stages. Barefaced, I looked a bit like a raccoon, since the color around my eyes hadn't left me yet. His face was still pretty well splattered with his original brown. He nodded politely and said, "How y'all doing?" in a viscous southern drawl. The entire table smiled back, watching him go. Then they all looked back at me.

* * *

That night, as Zarrella showed me some makeup tips, I asked what she thought about our dinner conversation.

"What exactly?"

"The fact that I wear makeup and no one else can."

"You mean the fact that you can cover your condition while others can't?"

"Yeah, sure," I said. "Whatever."

We were in my cabin, sitting at my vanity. We still hadn't

done anything else sexwise, but the possibility was in the air. I was at least trying not to mess it up. She was putting the final touches on my brow area. My eyes were closed. This was the third attempt that night, and she wanted to get it perfect. I almost wondered if she'd taken on my makeup project in some vicarious way since, short of plastic surgery, her skin was irrevocably changed.

"I don't know," she said. "Do what you want. You're not hurting anyone, so who cares?"

"Yeah, but would you wear makeup if you could? If it made you look normal?"

I heard her fumbling with makeup containers and brushes. She was deliberating. "I don't believe in normal," she said. "Makeup would never make me look how I used to look anyhow. There's no point."

"But if it did?"

There was another silence. She took so long to answer that I did it for her. "You wouldn't. That's why you outed me tonight." I opened my eyes. She was looking down at her lap. "You didn't even wear any of your garb."

"What's your point?"

"You're moving on," I said. "I have a sense for these things."

"I don't think you do. We just met. You don't know me." She motioned toward the mirror. "Take a look."

I didn't. I wanted to keep talking. "You've bought into all this, haven't you? You're one of them now. You've been converted."

She stopped for a moment. "Have you ever thought that instead of suffering fools, maybe we've been suffering ourselves? Maybe I'm just tired of being angry and cut off from everything."

"Therapy talk," I said. "You're an Independent. I should've known you'd say that."

She snorted, but it was hard to tell what it meant. "And you're a conservative who's lost his mind. Big surprise. Now look."

I waited for a sign that she was still into me, that she really wanted to be there. It didn't come. She was humoring me. I was sure of it as I turned my head toward the mirror. Unbelievably, my old face was staring back. Unlike me, Zarrella at least had a clue with makeup. I moved closer to the mirror and turned my face side to side, up and down. I brought my hand up to touch it, but I didn't want to ruin it.

She'd gotten the tone right, the foundation and concealer just so. I didn't look like I'd been rolling around in Nestlé Quik. For the first time in six months, I looked like me. But as soon as I saw myself, I had a terrible realization: I could never reproduce it. Like a brick on the head, it hit me, what I'd secretly felt but couldn't admit: I was wearing a mask. I had been since I'd started with the makeup. If I indulged the fantasy any longer, it probably wouldn't be good for my brain. I'd be like some denial-ridden toupee wearer who couldn't let go of his rug, no matter how ridiculous it looked.

"What do you think?" she said.

I didn't want to think about any of it right then. I said it was great and touched her hand. Boldly, I leaned in to give her a kiss, but she moved away.

"Sorry." She wiped her lap and put all the makeup away.

"I guess I shouldn't have done that."

"It's okay."

"So, our night together was a one-time thing, I take it."

She kind of nodded but kind of didn't.

I slowly began to wonder if her change in attitude was due to me. Maybe she recognized a part of herself in me and was so frightened by it that she forced a change in her outlook. I felt something catch in my throat. I took a long time clearing it away. Eventually, she said we could still hang out for the rest of the cruise. I said, "Sure." She let herself out, and I sat at the vanity, looking at myself in the mirror one last time, my old life somewhere in that face. I took out my wipes and rubbed them over my cheeks until they turned from white to brown, until my face turned from brown to pink. I dropped the towelettes into the vacuum toilet and watched the suction pull them away.

* * *

I'd fallen for women too hard before. I'd turned many a woman off, too. I was a habitual divorcé. I'd been renounced many times. With Zarrella, it wasn't a total bombshell. I could detect the signs the way an animal could detect an impending earthquake. Bringing all that up, though, would've just caused problems. I had no idea what was going through her head, and I knew for sure I didn't want a repeat of my embarrassing breakup with Deb.

Not long before our divorce, she'd been on a tear through the DNC, ascending like a launched rocket. In the RNC, I was descending like a wounded duck, my influence waning. I began to feel as though her success would compel her to forsake me. I falsely accused her of more things than I cared to remember. I even dared her to leave. She said I better be careful. "Keep saying it, and I'm gonna believe it. Or I'm just going to leave so

I don't have to hear it anymore." Ultimately, she was right. She left for both reasons.

As Zarrella and I sailed on, I didn't say peep, knowing I'd just get myself in trouble. Thursday, in Roatán, I tried to focus on the island's flora and fauna. We zip-lined through a botanical garden, visited an iguana farm, and birded toucans and parrots and other freaky flying creatures. The whole time I felt like a heroin addict in full withdrawal. I had to act like nothing was wrong.

"Aren't you having fun?" she kept saying. "Don't you just love this?"

"Sure," I lied. "Birds, lizards, plants. It's all just so— satisfactory!"

Her sudden attitude adjustment made a brief annoyance toward her bubble in me. Still, I tried not to obsess, about her cooling on me at least. I avoided any thoughts about our inevitable parting at the end of the cruise. Oddly, by avoiding it, I had plenty of time to review all the time we'd spent together up to that point. Like a detective, I examined every conversation, every look, with a different lens. In doing so, I tripped over something I hadn't noticed before: She was on the run from something. The bad marriages, the ex-husbands, the domestic accidents. It took me a day or so to lock it in, but I knew I was on to something. I found a way to work it into a conversation on Friday night in Costa Maya. We'd just reboarded the ship after an uneventful day ATVing through Mahahual with Tommy and Deirdre. Zarrella and I were at the Ice Bar, our butts stuck to the frozen bar stools. Frosty daiquiris breathed cold mist in front of us. The absurdity of the entire trip was, at least for me, now becoming less comedy and more errors.

Maybe the hunch was all luck, but I'd learned that if you obsess long enough, you'll discover a whole bunch of shit purely by accident. I even googled Cleveland and her first name—I didn't actually know her last name—hoping I'd find solid internet evidence, but nothing came up. When I asked her about it, however, her reaction confirmed my suspicions: I'd excavated a secret. She couldn't maintain eye contact. It was so obvious that I almost pointed at her and yelled, "Aha!"

"Who would I be running from?" She lit a cigarette and took a puff. Then the bartender said she couldn't smoke.

"Who said anything about who?" I said.

The bartender brought over a shot glass. She stabbed her cigarette out in it. "I meant what."

"Well, you have been married a few times to pricks. How about them?"

"So have you."

"True," I said. "But in my marriages, I was the prick. I know how pricks think."

She took out another cigarette but didn't light it. She just tapped it on the bar. "Not these pricks."

"What about your last husband, who shall remain nameless?"

She snorted, which was starting to get on my nerves. "You don't know what you're talking about."

"That's probably true," I said. "I don't really know you, but it's never stopped me before." I did some more delving. "Is he after you? Are you in hiding or something?"

"Hiding?"

I touched her arm, covering one of her burns with my hand. "He's the one who did this to you, isn't he? Maybe he's some psycho obsessed with you. There are a lot of crazies out there that can't be happy unless their exes are—I don't know—"

"Dead?"

I nodded, but the way she bit her lip made me think I'd overstepped.

"Whatever mind you previously had, I think you've finally lost it."

"Maybe," I said. "But I'm on to something. My break-throughs usually come on the verge of breakdowns anyway."

"You're not insane. You're just a cynic."

"Well, who was it that said the cynical man is the one with all the facts?"

"William Burroughs," she said. "And it's the paranoid man, not the cynical one."

I asked if that was one of her crossword clues, but I hadn't accurately gauged her annoyance level. She'd already eased off her stool and walked away by then.

I don't know. Maybe I was paranoid. Aboard, if I wasn't thinking about Zarrella, I was thinking about the other Black guy with vitiligo, whom I couldn't stop running into accidentally—at the Serenity Deck as I tried to catch up on my reading, at the Wave Rider surf simulator, at the glass-canopied solarium. The guy was more than just my doppelgänger. He was my nemesis. I began to curse him whenever he came my way, all the happiness in the world somehow beaming from his pearly whites. He just seemed so good, so wholesome. His southern drawl even sounded sinister. I almost wondered if he'd been planted by someone just to torment me. Then I wondered if I was losing my mind. As I walked back to my cabin, I thought, Thanks, Neblitt. For a cruise that's supposed to heal me, make me more harmonious with my peers, it's sure doing a shit job.

* * *

Saturday, as the *Ocean Wanderer* performed a U-turn and we began our journey back to Port Everglades from Costa Maya, the crew informed everyone that a hurricane had formed in the Gulf of Mexico. Hurricane Joaquin, fittingly. It was slated to move out to the Atlantic but not before it tore tail through the Florida Straits at the exact time we'd be crossing. The *Ocean Wanderer* would have to spend a last night, an extra night, in Cozumel to wait it out. This would've bothered me normally, but I needed more time to figure things out. There was something going on with Zarrella, and me. It sounded ridiculous, since we'd just met, but I felt—I don't know—something. I needed some certainty before the trip was over, though I was pretty sure I wouldn't get it. When she found out we'd be in Cozumel again, her mood changed even more. Maybe all my investigating her past had a negative effect. She started avoiding me.

That day, at sea, I left my cabin and knocked on her door. When she didn't answer, I walked around the ship aimlessly, looking for her. It took almost the whole day. Bored at one point, with no leads, I sat in a lounge chair on deck 3 and watched a man with one arm hit golf balls at the driving range. After that, I watched a little family play doubles on a tennis court. By two or three, I was barhopping around the ship— the Commodore, the Crown Lounge, the Funky Whistle. I thought if this Unseen Soul thing didn't work out, I could try alcoholism. I was turning into a pretty good drunk.

As I continued looking for Zarrella, I happened to see the other Black guy again, before he saw me first, thank God. I had to be cautious. He was the gregarious type. There'd been a few close calls already. He seemed like he wanted to meet everyone on board. One time, he'd even spied me and headed my way, looking to make a friend. Naturally, I ran the opposite direction. I hid behind a column and let him go by this time. I headed bow-ward and saw Tommy in the RipChute, the glass-walled skydiving simulator. I stuck my head in, and he and Deirdre were whooping and hollering as giant fans kept them hovering twenty feet in the air. I shouted up, asking if they'd seen Zarrella. They said no. Tommy did a few somersaults and twirls and then he righted himself, belly down, his face distorted by the wind. He shouted, "Bro, come on in. It's a blast."

I looked around the tall glass silo, the vertical wind tunnel that was the RipChute, and shook my head. "None of this is real," I shouted. "Don't you see? It's all a simulation. I'm not sure any of this is really happening."

They suddenly looked concerned. They said, "Hey, are you okay?"

I looked at them suspended up there like phantasms. "No," I said. "I'm drunk."

They said, "Oh," and I waved goodbye. I stumbled back to my cabin to take a nap.

* * *

My timing for getting blotto couldn't have been worse. Though the cruise technically had another day left, the captain's ball was that night. Before I left my cabin, a little absentminded, maybe still a little off from the barhopping, I almost didn't touch up my makeup. I almost didn't care. During any kind of breakup, I tended to go unhinged.

At dinner, I told Zarrella I'd been looking for her all day, and somewhat flippantly, she said she'd been at Vim and Vigor, the ship's full-service spa.

"All day?"

"Beauty takes time." She was oddly happy for someone who was so messed up.

"What's going on with you?" I said. "I'm not imagining this. You're freaking me out."

We were sitting at a table alone. It was black tie so I was in a tux. Zarrella was in a black evening gown. I looked down and realized I'd forgotten to put on socks.

She stirred her Manhattan for quite a long time. "I'm sorry."

"For what?"

"I shouldn't have started with you."

Her candor stopped me. "Well, that's a nice thing to say." I wasn't crazy, though I would've preferred that option over her not wanting me anymore. "What the hell's that mean?"

"This was supposed to be simple," she said. "Now, somehow, it's complicated."

"What're you talking about? We can make this work. Believe me, I'm the least complicated person you're ever going to meet."

She didn't believe me. Neither did I.

I said we could still see each other. Maybe I could move near her. But she didn't seem enthused with that option. "See," she said, "complicated."

I'd been dropped before, but something about this was different. I didn't think I'd done anything wrong.

"He'll just find me, find us."

"Your ex. So he *is* looking for you."

I looked around the festooned ballroom. I told her I had money, lots of it. We could go anywhere. Stupidly, I said I could hire security.

But she didn't bite on that either.

"Not part of the plan."

"Well, what is the plan? Maybe I can help."

She didn't respond.

We sat there just looking at each other while everyone else partied. Finally, I said, "You know, maybe you're right. This is complicated. And, for once, it's not me."

She seemed to concede the fact, a tear in her eye.

Feeling ornery, I broke away from her after dinner and started mingling. I got to drinking, again. I lost count of my consumption pretty quickly. I had a few bouts of conversation with a string of people I would never remember, even with their conditions. I ended enough of those conversations with "I'll probably never see you again" that people started looking at me funny. Tommy, at one point, even came over, tugged on my coat-tail, and said, "Easy, killer." I told him to mind his business.

All the while, I kept Zarrella in the corner of my eye. I checked who she was talking to, how she was acting. People were weirdly coming up to her as if she was some kind of celebrity. They congratulated her on shedding her shell. Maybe that did something to her. She appeared to be getting a little stinko herself. I saw her drunkenly kick a few chair legs as she socialized. Outside the ballroom, I saw her light the filter end of her cigarette. She even spilled a drink or two. I did as well. By the time I started wobbling, I'd had enough. I headed for my cabin.

I took one of the escalators up to deck 12, hoping to get there before I had to ralph. When I looked back, Zarrella was behind me steps below.

At the top, I said, "First, you're done with me. Now you're following me. What other mixed messages do you got?"

"I'm just going back to my cabin, you putz," she said. "I had to get out of there."

"Being weird takes a lot out of a person."

"You tell me."

Though she obviously didn't want me to follow her, I trailed her all the way to her cabin. She looked back at me every few steps. As she swiped her keycard and opened her door, she said, "What're you doing?"

I didn't know. I peeked in and saw all her stuff was packed. She couldn't wait to be rid of me and this trip.

She said, "This was supposed to be our last day."

I couldn't tell if that was an explanation for her stuff being packed or if she was saying I'd ruined our last day together. "I guess you're ready to go, then." I looked at her and realized she was way drunker than I thought. There was an inconsolable sadness in her eyes. Her face just hung there on her skull. I realized an awful truth: I didn't know her well enough to have a clue as to what she was feeling. I didn't know what her past was pushing onto her present. For once, I recognized a feeling that all my exes described as selfishness. Desire had brought too many assumptions out of me. Now she hated me. The way it starts is the way it ends.

She stood in the doorway, her foot holding the spring-loaded door open. "I'm sorry," she said, "for getting you mixed up with me." She looked guilt ridden.

"I'm confused," I said. "I don't know who's the crazy one. It's usually me."

"It's both of us." She moved her foot, and the door slowly closed. As she went out of view, she said, "Just let me go. Okay?"

* * *

Sunday, in Cozumel, that's exactly what I did. I didn't knock on her door in the morning, didn't try to accidentally run into her. I sunned on a different deck just so I wouldn't see her. I even shot some hoops, which I hadn't done since I rode the bench at Yale. As I toweled off, an announcement came over the ship's speakers. The hurricane had torn through the Florida Straits faster than expected. Instead of staying in port all night, we would set sail after reboarding. This gave me hope and a little concern. I thought maybe Zarrella would snap out of her mood now that we were going back earlier. Then I thought maybe that would just speed up the inevitable. This was confirmed when I came back to my cabin, and the rain stick I'd bought for her was sitting on my doormat. I picked it up and turned it over a few times, listening to the beans inside make their sound. I went to her cabin and found the door cracked. I pushed it open, expecting to see her, but it was just housekeeping cleaning the room. Zarrella's suitcases were there, but I sensed there was stuff missing.

The housekeeper stopped and looked up at me. "I'll be done in a moment."

"It's not my room," I said. "It's my friend's."

"Oh, well, it looks like they're gone."

"It's a she." I looked at the bed and imagined Zarrella sleeping on it, me next to her.

The housekeeper started changing a pillowcase. "She's more than a friend, isn't she?"

I said, "I don't know." Then I said, "I guess."

"How's it going?"

"Terribly."

"It happens on these cruises. People get too close sometimes. You should see the singles' cruises. Love and heartbreak in a matter of hours." After a moment, she said, "Who knows? Maybe you and"—she looked at her clipboard—"Susan aren't meant to be."

"Hold up," I said. "Susan?"

"That's what it says here." She lifted her clipboard and read it. "Susan Pasternak."

Baffled, I said thanks and left. I disembarked, and one of the stewards said I had only an hour before the ship left. I wandered down over to Punta Norte, to the San Lazaro pier, but the boat was gone. I roamed the port area, looking around, hoping I'd spot her. The *Ocean Wanderer*'s horn began to blare. I boarded, but I felt as though I'd jump right off if I saw her. I made my way back up to deck 12. Before I knew it, the ship was slowly inching out to sea. I stood at the railing, watching Cozumel leave my view. I ran everything I knew about Zarrella through my head, wondering what was fact and what was fiction. Finally, I remembered: *Since 1995, an average of twelve people vanish from cruise ships every year. Gone, never heard from again.* I stood there, bathing in the shock, as the ship moved farther out to sea. We moved by the same tiny atolls we had our first time in Cozumel. As San Lazaro appeared on my left, I could see the cliff divers out on the turrets, jumping gracefully off, one after another. Some went headfirst, some feetfirst, but all of them were

tanned men in Speedos. They pulled themselves up onto a small
speedboat and made their way back to the front of the island to
climb back up and do it again.

As the ship moved past the island, I walked back, sternward,
by other people on deck. I thought I made out a last figure
standing there in one of the turrets. The person was tall and
pale, lissome, a woman. I didn't know if she could even see me,
but I lifted my hand anyway. It brought back something Neblitt had once mentioned, how one good gesture could build on
another until the entire being was built back up brick by brick,
gesture by gesture, tranquil and healed. It'd always sounded like
yoga babble to me, but at that moment, I was compelled to try it.
I reached the end of the deck, the end of the boat, bumping into
the stern railing. I could feel the distance between us growing. I
lifted my hand higher and gave a long side-to-side wave. Zarrella
lifted her hand. She could see it was me. She knew I'd figured
it out. Off the turret she sprang, her arms out at her sides. She
sailed toward the water like a bombing bird, her arms out in front
of her now. She dropped into the water like a knife. There wasn't
a splash. There wasn't anything. She didn't even come up for air.
It was like it never happened. Zarrella, Susan, whoever she was.

* * *

The brochures don't tell you how sobering it is to come back
to your departure port. It's been such a long trip. You've done
so many things. You've met so many people. You love the sight
of Port Everglades, and you hate it. Compared with the places
you've seen, it's ugly as hell. Yet you can't wait to kiss the gum-
dotted asphalt, and you can't wait to leave again. It's America.
It's Florida. It's not your home, but you'll take it.

As I stood in the disembarkation line with Tommy and Deirdre on Monday, I thought they'd look at me funny. They took note of me, but they didn't stare. Tommy said, "Hey, buddy," as I waited behind them, my bags in tow. I watched him fondle Deirdre's leg. I watched her rub his bald spot with one of her stumps. It was as close to holding hands as they would get. When they asked where Zarrella was, I told them she had an early flight. She'd already disembarked.

"Lucky her," they said.

No one mentioned my makeup, or lack thereof. Not Dave or Rita behind me. None of the stewards. No one mentioned my raccoon face. I was thankful. It would be bad enough back in New York. People would look at me, ridicule me. People would point and move away. I still had yet to confront many things. I turned my phone back on, and it buzzed nonstop with texts and emails. I deleted all of them. The line moved inch by inch toward customs. I thought I'd get a new phone, a new number. Start over. When I first got my disease, I'd hated how people said it could be a new beginning, that I could be a brand-new Melvin, as though the Melvin I'd been my entire life had been the wrong one all along. Now I wasn't so sure.

I was so occupied with those thoughts that I didn't see the other Black guy coming down the disembarkation line until it was too late. He was wheeling his suitcase behind him, happy as can be. Like a politician, he gave people high fives. He shook their hands. He kissed their babies. His name evidently was Ronald. People kept saying, "See you next year, Ronald." "Had a ball, Ronald. You're the best."

As he approached me, my first thought was to hide, to look the other way, but he'd already spied me. To ignore him would've been mean, stuck-up, things I usually had no problem with. In good faith, I waited for him. When he came into view, I looked him right in the eye. He stopped for a moment. His smile changed to wonder. Like long-lost twins, we studied each other's faces. I offered my hand, and he shook it firmly, slowly. "Right on, brother." Summoning something dormant deep inside, I said, "Right on," too. I meant to add "brother" to that. It was only right that I reciprocate. But Ronald had already moved past me, down the line. He was smiling, shaking hands, kissing cheeks. He was so happy to have one last moment with all those people.

GIVE MY LOVE
TO THE SAVAGES

It was spring break, the riots had broken out, and I'd just flown into LA to visit my father. He picked me up from the airport in a new Porsche drop-top, and before I could even get my seat belt on, he was yelling, "Status report, Junie," right in my ear. No "Hi, Junie," "I missed you, Junie," "Hey, how you been, Junie boy?" I hadn't seen him in a year. All I got was, "That crackerjack jury just let the cops off. It's a goddamn uprising."

We were ripping east down the 105 by then, breaking away from traffic, and we could barely hear a thing. Pop refused to ride with the top up on any of his convertibles—it was California, for shit's sake—so whenever we got on the freeway we had to shout just to be heard over the wind.

He leaned in close, as he always did, and said, "Hey, dummy? You hear me?"

I leaned in close and said, "Yes, dummy. I heard you."

"Good. Because it's a goddamn rebellion, Junie. It's a fucking revolt."

I was twenty-one at the time and admittedly kind of a turd. When I was around my father, sarcasm was my mother tongue. "Really?" I said. "A revolt? You sure someone's not just having a really big barbecue, Pop?" I grinned at him, pleased with myself, but he never took kindly to my mouth. He looked at me like I was a mental patient. His face shriveled into a scowl. "No one likes a smart-ass, smart-ass. Watch yourself."

As we curled onto the 405 interchange and a new tangle of cars appeared up ahead, I told him to save the riot talk. The flight attendants had told everyone on the plane before we landed. But he didn't want to hear it. He was still in a mood. A few of his businesses had screwed the pooch earlier that year, and he'd nearly lost his ass. The possibility of losing more in a riot probably had his sphincter knotted up good. He kept making the same face as when he'd broken his ankle two years before, when the painkillers he was on made him ferociously constipated.

"So, the flight attendants told you about the riots, did they? Well, that's just fucking awesome. Did they tell you what it's really like down here, too? People looting and setting fires and shit?"

"No," I shouted. "But isn't that what people usually do when they riot, Pop? Loot and set fires and shit?"

He turned his head slowly and gave me the look, the icy gaze of ill intent he reserved just for me. He shouted, "Hey, smart-ass? What did I just tell you about being a smart-ass?" Naturally, when I opened my mouth to answer, he lifted his hand and said, "Shut it."

* * *

He'd called me right before spring break, talking like a loan shark, as usual. Just under the wind, through the crackling connection of his car phone, I could barely hear him say, "You owe me a visit, Junie," "owe" being the operative word. Pop always liked his favors returned to him one way or another, and clearly, he thought he'd done me a solid by "bumping pelvises" with my mother in the first place. I spent every spring break working as cheap labor at one of his car dealerships: answering phones, changing toner in the Xerox, and generally acting like I was working without actually doing any work, which, at that point in my life, was a talent of mine. He was always quick to remind me that he, not my mother, was paying for my East Coast education. In his mind, I had to repay him with the only valuable thing I had at the time: the best days of my youth.

Though I hadn't seen him in a year, much less talked to him, I didn't see any change in him whatsoever. He didn't look any older. He didn't look any wiser. He didn't look any less tan. If anything, he looked more like himself than he ever had. His hair was still long, bound into a glistening ponytail. He still preferred mercury-colored suits and white dress shirts open at the collar. And his jewelry—a pinky ring, a left earring, and a single gold chain—all sparkled as blindingly as ever, even in the haze-choked sun.

The only thing different about this visit was what Pop was now calling "the mutiny." It'd started around three that afternoon, a Wednesday, while I was flying somewhere over the Southwest. From the air, during my plane's descent, LA didn't look any different. It was the same sprawling mess I'd always known, the motherboard of downtown barely visible through the clouds. Everything seemed fine until we pierced the smog. I could see packs of tiny fire trucks and police cars in the streets, the odd blaze just beginning to grow. Something wasn't quite right, even for LA. And of course, now Pop's sneaky ass was driving us right into it without any explanation.

* * *

He rocketed us onto the 405 North, zipping us in and out of traffic, cutting off practically every car on the highway. After the interchange, though, he miscalculated and got us stuck behind a bus of schoolkids. He cursed, swerved out onto the shoulder to MacGyver around them. Then he got neck and neck with the driver and gave him the finger. Pop saluted the guy so long the kids on the bus laughed and waved their middle fingers back at us. He flipped them off, too.

At the Manchester Avenue exit near Inglewood, he aimed the Porsche to the right, saying, "Get ready," but mostly to himself.

Naturally, I asked what for.

He reached under his seat for his Walther PPK, checking the clip and then popping it back in. "Assailants," he said. "And before you ask, this is so they'll think twice about fucking with us."

I nodded, since getting fucked with in Inglewood was always a possibility, even without a riot going on.

We shot off the freeway and turned onto Manchester and ran straight into a wild mob. Every car in front of us immediately tried to pull a U-ey and get back on the freeway, but all they did was clog the street like cattle in a chute. "Geniuses," Pop said, as he kamikazed us into oncoming lanes. At Inglewood Avenue, we were met by an even bigger hive of people.

Everyone was pissed off and confused, an odd mix of anger and exhilaration hot on their faces. Some ran from one side of the street to the other and then decided they didn't like it there and ran back. Some held bricks and rocks in their hands, just waiting for a worthy target, like us. As we weaved through, their white-people radar must've gone off, because they all stopped rioting, turned around, and watched Pop and me like we had horns growing out of our heads. I wanted to tell them we were the good guys, or at least that I was. Something like, "Hey, my mother's Black. Like, really Black. I'm one of you."

But Pop took a different approach. "You don't have bumpers on your Black asses. Get out of the street, numbnuts."

I elbowed him and said that probably wasn't the best thing to say right then.

"Yeah? Why not?"

"Because your ass isn't Black. If your ass isn't Black, you can't call their asses Black. That's kind of the rule."

Pop shook his head as we threaded through another gang of looters. He laid on the horn, parting the crowd, and one of the harder-looking guys smiled at us. "Damn, white man. You got some nuts on you, you know that? Don't you know where you are?"

"Yeah," Pop said. "I'm in America. Where are you?"

"Hell!" someone shouted.

Given our present surroundings, right then seemed like a good time to ask what the fuck we were doing there.

"Oh, I don't know," Pop said. "How about driving around this town making sure none of my dealerships have been torched yet. Fine with you?"

After he picked me up from the airport each spring, he usually took me to a bar or, if I was lucky, a strip club. By one or two in the morning, we'd end up at his house in Malibu, drunk and stewing away in his Jacuzzi. At that moment, however, flying down the road, I was in no position to complain, because, really,

I never was. He was liable to say, "You want some cheese with that whine?" and then leave me there on the side of the road. He'd done it before.

* * *

At the Inglewood car lot, we were greeted by Pop's fleshy face. It was pasted on a large billboard over a double-wide that served as the dealership office. His image was so gargantuan that his pores were as large as divots, his nose the size of a car door. Like most of his other lots, this one spanned an entire block, nothing but an asphalt parcel of clunkers, a neon price tag plastered on each windshield. Most of the inventory had been in accidents, fires, floods, or other cataclysmic events. Knowing Pop, there was always at least one that'd been sheared in half in a wreck and then welded back together.

We pulled inside the gates, and on the office roof, Burger, one of Pop's guys, was doing the cabbage patch to a soul song blasting from a boom box. Behind his lumbering silhouette, a helix of smoke twined in the air. "Look at him," Pop said. "The roof's on fire, and he's dancing up there like a circus bear."

The roof wasn't on fire. Burger was just grilling, albeit in an odd place. I pointed out the grill and the bag of charcoal, the pair of tongs in Burger's hand, but Pop still sprang out of the car like someone tossed a tarantula in his lap. "Hey, I'm paying you to make sure the place doesn't catch fire, not help it along."

"What you mean?" Burger said.

"Grilling on the roof doesn't seem like a fire hazard to you?"

"Maybe." Burger considered the situation now, apparently for the first time. "But everybody's on their roofs. Plus, I got hungry."

I checked the surrounding buildings, and, sure enough, there was a person atop each one, armed with a gun or a fire hose or both. Across a side street, a young Korean man patrolled the front of a small grocery with a pistol, while another watched from the roof like a tower guard, an AK-47 cradled in one arm and what was big enough to be a rocket launcher in the other.

"We're turning bad rioters into good ones. Ain't that right?" Burger raised his fist in solidarity. The Koreans gave a salute and then returned to duty. "Y'all wanna get your stink on while you're here?" Burger held up two cans of Schlitz.

"Of course," I said. "When have I ever turned down a beer?"

He pointed at Pop with his tongs. "What about you, ballerina?"

Pop was still pissed, but he took one, too. He'd never turned down a beer either.

We went back a long way with Burger, Pop's longest-serving employee. He was one of those Black guys who always seemed at ease with his place in the world, even if deep down he really wasn't. I admired him for it. As a kid, when Pop wasn't around, I used to tell people that Burger was my real father. It was our little game. But for some reason, no one ever believed me.

"Goddamn, youngblood," Burger said. "You sure picked a hell of a time to visit."

I cracked my beer. "Hey, I was cursed with bad timing and a rotten father. What am I gonna do?" I smiled at Pop as he guzzled his beer. In return, he gave me the finger.

"Well, what've you been up to?"

"No good," Pop chimed in. "What do you think he's been up to? This is Junie you're talking to."

"Shit, I guess that makes two of us," Burger said. "I just got out of jail."

I asked what he was in for, and he gave his usual answer: "Various things."

Pop took a long pull and finished his beer, his eyes darting around as though he expected the lot to spontaneously combust. "Enough chitchat. Burger, tell me nothing's happened yet."

"Nothing's happened yet."

"Nobody's tried to steal or burn anything down?"

Burger removed a revolver from his waistline and sat on the edge of the roof. He balanced the gun next to him and let his legs dangle as if he were sitting at the end of a dock. "Hell no. Ain't no niggas messing with this place. I told you. With me here, you can count on that." He shouted the last part loud enough for the gangbangers on Manchester to hear. They were my age, maybe a little younger, and veterans at mean-mugging. As I watched them, a light-skinned Blood with a red bandanna around his neck waved at me. I nodded at him, and he mouthed, "Fuck you, white boy."

I envisioned walking over there and telling him I was only half-white. But then I envisioned him kicking my ass. I slowly turned back to Pop.

"We're counting on you, big man."

"I know," Burger said.

"Only shoot if you're absolutely threatened. You hear me? Absolutely." Pop always put extra emphasis on "absolutely." According to him, ex-cons couldn't understand instructions without this word, and ex-cons made up the majority of his workforce.

"Only if I'm absolutely threatened," Burger said. "I got it."

That was it. I told Burger to stay out of trouble. He said, "Ditto." Pop and I got back in the Porsche and sped off like criminals making a getaway.

* * *

I was used to this. I'd been dividing time between Pop in LA and my mother in Boston since I was ten, when my parents went splitsville for good. I spent every spring break of my childhood with Pop, running endless errands around LA and the surrounding counties. Whatever he did, I did: lounging at the bar of Sam's Hofbrau while he flirted with dancers who fawned over me. Shooting at the LA Gun Club with my own Browning Hi-Power 9mm. Smoking Humboldt because Pop thought I should choke on the good stuff with him in a controlled environment. How I hadn't been maimed or killed yet was beyond me.

From what I could glean as a child, my parents met during the height of their checkered pasts. Pop had connections to some crooked characters in Boston, owners of an establishment that my mother worked at called the Peephole. What her work actually entailed I never wanted to know. Regardless, my parents became a couple almost instantly. My white father had, at the time of meeting my mother, an exclusive thing for nonwhite women. My Black mother, conversely, could never shake her attraction to moneyed men of the pale-faced variety. That being their only criteria for love, it was a wonder the marriage lasted long enough to produce light-skinned, curly-haired, bony-assed me.

For as long as I could remember, every time my mother packed me off for my cross-country jaunts, she'd say, "You can't change the fact that you got some white in you, Junie, but it doesn't mean you gotta act like your father's white ass."

Sadly, up to that point in my life, I'd failed her.

Back at school, everyone called me June the Goon. Like my father, I'd cultivated a reputation as one of *those guys*. I was fairly smart, but I tended to do fairly dumb things. Not quite a troublemaker. Not quite a fuckup. That fall and winter, though, I'd found myself sinking into trouble, having barely avoided jail time for an unfortunate incident. I was starting to look a lot like Pop, who'd found himself in the clink once or twice around my age. I knew if I kept it up, I'd quit school in a year, start selling cars, and, like him, date a series of shady women. I'd grow a ridiculous ponytail and start driving a Porsche. It was my biggest fear, one that produced a recurring nightmare: me not living my life but reliving his. Afterward, I'd always wake up in a sweat and reach for the jug of antacids I kept by my bed, crunching them as I tried to fall back asleep.

* * *

By eight p.m., the entire proceedings were, in Pop's scholarly opinion, a shit circus. We were back on the 405, heading north again, and in the distance, more plumes of smoke snaked above the skyline. Even though the freeways, each an orgy of brake lights, were as still as paintings, Pop didn't let it stop us. He used every piece of pavement he could find—shoulders, medians, off-ramps—to zip us around the city. We'd checked on three more dealerships by then, Carson, Long Beach, and East LA. Each lot was being guarded by new hires, guys I'd never met before. All three were Black. All three had Jheri curls. And all three were named, oddly enough, Doozie. At each lot, it was the same as with Burger. Pop made sure they were armed. They were keeping the gates locked. Everything was tip-top. We moved on.

At the Huntington Park exit, he dumped us off the freeway, and we trolled down Pacific Boulevard. I asked where we were going, and he just patted his potbelly and grunted, "Food." I said, "Who gets hungry at a time like this?" But we both knew it was a stupid question. Pop's appetites could be described only as gluttonous. We passed a few restaurants, and they all seemed to be closing or getting plundered. So we skated a little farther down Pacific until we stumbled on an open but deserted In-N-Out. We pulled up to the drive-through, and they took our order as if it were any old day. When we pulled around to pay, though, the Latina cashier didn't take our money. She just tossed the food at us, locked the window, and immediately put up the CLOSED sign. We pulled around and parked by a dumpster. Behind us, all the employees burst out of the restaurant like someone had tossed a bomb into the place. Pop looked back, softly biting a Swisher Sweet with his teeth. "Well, that sure was interesting." Then he just stabbed a straw into his drink and started to eat.

We were the only bystanders out there, pushing our luck in a new Porsche among all that lawlessness. But relatively speaking, things didn't seem that bad yet. No one was bothering us. No one even noticed us. Across the street, a Payless shoe store was being ransacked, the parking lot littered with empty shoeboxes. Down the sidewalk, an interracial couple steered a new leather sofa dollied on two skateboards. Even some guy clutching an armful of bathrobes rambled by, touting, "Robe. Robe here," as though peddling peanuts at a Dodgers game. Who knew what would happen next?

On our left, a Humvee rumbled past Dick's Donuts. Not far behind, six National Guardsmen on horseback clopped by. A Black dude who'd somehow climbed on top of Dick's and was now sitting inside the large donut on the roof yelled, "Hey, GI Joe. You hungry?" as he pelted them with donut holes. I turned back to Pop, but he was lost in thought, studying the smoke churning over downtown and feeding his face. He'd ordered two double-doubles animal style and had already dispatched both in ten flat. He was stuffing handfuls of fries into his mouth while I only nibbled at my burger. I hadn't had an appetite for months. I didn't even bother with the bread, just ate the meat, which I was trying to choke down when Pop said, "You know why those flight attendants couldn't tell you nothing, Junie?"

"No, but I'm sure you're gonna tell me."

"Because they don't know nothing. I do. Cops in this town think their shit don't stink. But that don't make it cool for every Black mope and his fat mother to turn the city into a goddamn ashtray, know what I'm saying?"

I just shook my head. "Black mope? Fat mother?"

"You see any white people out here other than us?"

"You mean other than you?" I scanned the street and spotted a scruffy white guy in two seconds. He maneuvered a shopping cart full of Budweiser with a perverse glee. "What about him?"

Pop blinked at him and then glanced at me. "An anomaly," he said.

"I'm just saying, Pop. You sound kind of Aryan right now."

"Do I? Well, I guess beating up a bunch of Pakistanis makes you Martin Luther King."

My belly gurgled. I was pretty sure I had the beginnings of

an ulcer. "It wasn't a bunch," I said. "Just one. And I didn't beat him up. I was only there."

He looked at me out of the side of his eye. "Only there, huh?"

I nodded and tried to take another bite of my burger but couldn't stomach it. I lobbed it into the nearest trash can, took my pack of antacids from my duffel bag, and chewed a few.

"There or not, you're lucky I got you that lawyer. Otherwise, you'd be doing time right now."

"That lawyer was a horrible person."

"I know. Why do you think I hired him?"

"He made me sound like a sociopath."

"Yeah? What if you are one?"

I looked at him, wondering if he actually thought that. When he cracked a smile, I told him to eat me, and he slapped my thigh and laughed.

"Who cares what he said? You're free, aren't you?"

I was just about to say I shouldn't be when he turned to me with an indignant sneer.

"And how can you call *me* a racist? I married your mother, let's not forget. She's as Black as they come."

I studied him for a moment. If I disagreed, he'd be mad at me for the rest of the night and probably punish me for it. I just said, "Yeah, you married her. And you had me."

He said, "Yeah, I did," as though that proved his point.

We sat there a little longer, being father and son in our own dysfunctional way, and for some reason everything stilled around us. The sirens ceased. The crashing glass and bleeping alarms stopped, too. Looters froze midstep and searched the sky curiously. Maybe it was over. In the distance, two helicopters clapped toward us from the south, their spotlights scanning

Compton. I heard what sounded like a string of fireworks blocks away and watched as the helicopters split off from each other. One of them seemed to teeter, as if it would suddenly drop from the sky. Then, as if nothing happened, it righted itself, and the two of them moved back into formation. They quickly banked east in tandem, and I realized it'd been an evasive maneuver. Someone had shot at them from the ground.

"Damn. You see that?"

Pop swiveled his head, oblivious as always. "See what?"

Everything started back up, the sirens, the looting, the alarms, like a crazy merry-go-round cranking back to life.

"Nothing," I said. "Can we go now?"

He smirked and tossed his soda overboard. "Stop whining. We're going." He backed the car up and got us on the road. He pounded the Porsche into high gear. The whistling turbocharger went up an octave. The tires broke loose a bit.

"Where are we going now?"

He smiled. "You'll see."

* * *

That school year, I'd moved in with some white guys I barely knew. We shared a crumbling Victorian near the UMass Boston campus, where our academic careers hung by a thread. Their families all had a lot more going for them than mine, but we'd all been given the same opportunities in life, good schools, summer camps, money. So, all of us living together didn't seem like such a bad idea. We were spoiled and took things for granted. We operated under the assumption that no matter what dumb shit we did, everything would somehow work out, the usual attitude of people who were high most of the time. We had so many pills and herbs and mind-altering powders in our house we didn't know what we were taking half the time. Speed or Ritalin for studying, K and E for screwing off. We were so out of hand that at parties we'd leave stray tablets of Correctol around and then make bets on which guest would be the first to mistakenly take one, hoping it was a Valium or benzo, and get the squirts for a day and a half.

Our time would end badly. It was obvious. But stopping that freight train would've taken more willpower and sense than I had at the time. At the trial for the thing with the Pakistani kid, I thought our guilt was pretty apparent. We'd be going away for a while. But not everyone thought so. Our families had money and lawyers. Young men like us couldn't have done such a thing. My mother blamed the white boys for it. They corrupted me, she said. Anyone would end up in court after hanging around white kids named Tyler, Tucker, and Chase. They sounded like a law firm.

Her support was unquestioning at first, but once the trial started and our pictures were in the *Globe* every other day, she could barely look at me. She'd sit in the back of the courtroom, if she was there at all, wearing a wide-brimmed hat. When reporters rushed us as we left each day, she lowered her head, putting a gloved hand out at the sight of photographers. A couple weeks of that, and she stopped going altogether. From then on, I sat at the defense table, trying not to look over my shoulder every two seconds to see if she was there.

I couldn't blame her. The lawyer Pop hired painted me as some racially confused kid with neglectful parents. He even used an expert witness, a psychologist who testified to the emotional effects of being of mixed race in this country, how it led to "antisocial behavior in the desperate quest to fit in." During the cross-examination, I turned to my lawyer and whispered, "You're making me sound like a freak." He said, "That's because you are a freak. This country made you that way. It's not your fault."

He insisted I believe it if I wanted to stay out of jail. In the end, he was right. I came home from sentencing and found my mother in her bedroom, whiling away her evening as she always did, at her vanity, nursing a glass of red wine and a roach clip. She didn't look at all surprised when she saw me there. "And?"

I loosened my tie. "Probation. Three months."

She took a sip of wine, set her glass down, and then turned away as though the sight of me burned her eyes. "And your friends? What about them?" She'd never called them my friends before.

"A year of jail time each."

She grunted as though it served them right. Then she got up and closed her door on me. I retreated to my room and hid there, chewing antacids till they stole all the moisture from my mouth.

* * *

By nightfall, Pop and I had to stick to the freeways, the 5, the 10, the 405, the 710. Driving the surface streets was no longer advised. Radio reports said whites traveling through Black areas were being pulled from their cars and beaten. On Florence and Normandie, a white truck driver had been dragged from his semi and smashed in the head with a brick. At the same intersection, a Latino man, mistaken for Korean, had been wrenched from his car, stripped of his clothes, and spray-painted. And of course, we were in a new Porsche, a fact Pop now regretted. "I should have my head examined for taking this car out on a day like this. Should've driven the Jeep. I finally had the bulletproof windows installed. I ever tell you that?"

"Why would you need bulletproof windows?"

He looked at me like I was stupid. "Because, Junie, this is LA."

There was no way we were going back to Malibu to switch cars. We just made do, ripping along, stopping to check on this dealership or that, Pop's mood gradually changing. He was back to his old self again and kept going on and on about the cops and the verdict and what he would've done had he been an elected official. None of it made sense. He took us down freeways and off-ramps so fast I could barely hear him over the wind, but I was trying to listen as best I could. I didn't know what he'd get me into.

We'd checked on all his dealerships but the one in Koreatown. Pop was still talking a mile a minute, and I caught only a word or two. We slowed to take the 110 North exit, the wind dying down as we curved around the ramp, and I finally heard him clearly. "So, I'm afraid I have to put you to work earlier than usual, Junie." His preface to any sort of bad news. "So, I'm afraid your mother kicked me out, Junie. We're getting a divorce." "So, I'm afraid you're going to rehab, Junie—again, you little shit" would come later in my life.

"Hey." He snapped his fingers. "You hear me?"

I nodded but didn't say anything. I looked farther up the highway at a white sheet draped over a fenced overpass. On

it NO JUSTICE 4 RODNEY was painted in a bloody maroon. I
wanted to raise my fist in solidarity at the Black kids standing
next to the sign. But then I thought it might look weird coming
from me: a mixed kid riding next to his white father in a new
white Porsche.

Pop snapped his fingers again. "Hey, I asked you a question."

I rubbed my eyes. "Put me to work doing what?"

He actually grinned and patted my thigh again, his ponytail
lashing his headrest. "Oh, you know. The usual."

I popped an antacid into my mouth.

"Keep eating those things, and you'll get kidney stones."

I waved him off and grabbed his pack of Swishers from the
console. There was only one cigarillo left, hiding in the corner
of the pack. I took it just to spite him. "Don't change the subject,
dummy. You're getting me into some shit. Just say so."

He reached over and lit the cigarillo for me with his butane,
a sly look on his face. "Don't doubt your pop." He gave me one of
his special winks, the kind he used on ladies next to him at red
lights. "Believe me, it won't be bad." He waited a moment, calcu-
lating as ever, and said, "Really," as though there were a chance
of me believing him.

* * *

The Koreatown lot was the dealership I'd worked at the most,
and also the shittiest. Pop, the shrewd businessman, positioned
his dealerships in some of LA's sketchier areas, places you'd see
a good number of walls tattooed with graffiti, crackheads trying
to sell you a broken VCR, or maybe a few women on the stroll.
Whether he'd admit it or not, Pop capitalized on the low re-
sources of the poor. Immigrants and Black single mothers didn't

have the money to sue if the hooptie they just bought took a crap a month later. It was how he made his money, how he buttered his bread, all of it owed to the inequity of the world. One day, my riches would be owed to it, too, as long as he didn't blow it all before he croaked.

As we exited the freeway, Pop took out the PPK again and held it in his lap. We crossed Venice and Olympic Boulevards, coasted down South Western Avenue. The surroundings worsened street by street. The tang of burning wood and rubber was heavy in the air. Crowds roared and security alarms sounded in the close distance. On Wilshire, hordes of people blocked the intersection, pushing each other around and throwing bricks at passing cars. A Toyota a block ahead got all its windows broken out. The glass had barely hit the ground, and looters were already reaching inside. The driver sped off with a couple of them hanging on for dear life.

We wove through the loose crowds as we approached Wilshire, Pop honking the horn for people to move. With the sun down and the fires more intense, Koreatown glowed a dangerous orange. I could feel the heat as we passed blazing storefronts. The ones that weren't on fire had looters gushing out of the shattered windows like water through a breached dam. They carried every kind of merchandise imaginable, random things like hair dryers and lamps and packs of lightbulbs. As we approached the mob, a small pocket of space opened, and Pop told me to hold on. He mashed the throttle, raised his gun, and waved it around like a wild man, parting the crowd.

We turned onto West Sixth and pulled up in front of the car lot. He gave me a ring of keys, and I got out and unlocked the gate. I got back in the Porsche as fast as I could, even though

West Sixth was quiet and seemed to be untouched. Unlike Pop's other lots, this one was a small affair, a stamp of asphalt with a ten-foot fence surrounding it, only about fifteen clunkers on the premises. Once we'd pulled in and parked, I looked up at the roof to see if anyone was standing guard, but there was only Pop's huge face on the billboard. WE FINANCE in big block letters jumped out of his mouth.

"No one's here."

"I know." He scratched his nose.

"No fucking way."

He nodded. "We're gonna watch it till all this blows over." He shut off the engine and unlatched his seat belt. He opened his door halfway, and then he turned and looked back at me. "C'mon."

Without thinking, I got out of the car and closed my door. When I looked back, he was still behind the wheel. "Sorry to have to do this to you," he said, sitting back.

"You're not sorry. You're never sorry."

"Junie," he said. "Take it like a man. I need you here tonight. I got guys watching the other dealerships."

I hesitated and then asked if he was crazy. It seemed like an appropriate question.

"No," he said. "I'm as sane as ever."

"C'mon, Pop."

He crossed his arms over his chest. "What? This'll all blow over by tomorrow. You'll forget all about this."

Sometimes, this was true. I could be bought off with drinks and a good time in the right context. It was how our relationship worked. He'd do something to piss me off, and then he'd buy me something or take me wherever I wanted. There'd be women and weed, and we'd be friends again.

"C'mon." I tried to climb back in, but his eyes went black.

"No, no, no." He took the gun from the dash and just held it. He chewed his lip and considered me for a long moment. Finally, he leaned over the seat. I thought he was going to let me back in. But his hand went to the glove box instead. He pulled out a PPK identical to his and held it out for me. "Here." When I refused, he shook the thing at me and then forced it into my hand. "And don't start whining. I'm tired of it. You sound like those bastards you call friends."

I was about to say they weren't my friends when he said, "Junie, don't kid yourself. You wanted to be just like those kids."

"I'm not like anyone."

"Sure you're not. You're unique." He fluttered his hands in the air. "A pretty little baby. That's what your mother wants you to believe."

As soon as he said it, something lit me up. I stood back and kicked the passenger door. "Say something else about my mother, motherfucker."

His eyes went blacker. "I swear, if you do that again, Junie—"

That was all it took. I kicked the door again. "Look, I even took some paint this time."

A tense few seconds passed, and then a pack of looters ran near the lot. Some were silent and ashamed, the rest desperate and mechanical. They left quickly, and another small gang stopped at the entrance, at least ten deep. They were teenagers, Black and Latino, in T-shirts or wifebeaters. They'd apparently never noticed the dealership before and now thought it suddenly looked like a good place to steal shit from.

Pop waved his gun. "Keep it moving, people." They didn't move, so he aimed his gun and added, "Unless you feel like catching one in the ass." The pack paused for another second and then did as he said, shouting epithets as they left. Pop just rolled his eyes and waved, as if he knew them. "Yes, and give my love to the savages."

"Your mama's a savage," they said.

He opened the car's console and removed a fresh pack of Swishers. "I don't care, Junie. Kick the car till your foot breaks. I can get another. You know how many insurance claims there are gonna be after all this?" He lit one of the cigarillos and sent smoke out his nostrils. For a long minute, he watched me, the smoke slithering up around his eyes.

"What?" I said. "The guilt finally getting to you?"

"No, not really." He slid the lighter into his breast pocket and put the car in reverse. "I don't have time for this. If I don't get off the streets now, that'll be the end of me."

"Yeah, that would be really unfortunate, wouldn't it, Pop?"

He looked at me and sighed. "Junie, it makes more sense for you to be here. No telling what they'd do to me, but you— they'll think you're one of them."

I shook my head, astonished at his stupidity. "How are you my father?"

He sighed again. "How are you my son?"

Both questions hung in the air. He'd been doing this to me since I was ten, leaving me places or with strangers, saying he'd be right back, and then not showing up for hours. Once, he tried to leave me at his girlfriend's house when I was eleven. As he left, I beaned him in the face with a rock, splitting both his lips. He put me right on a plane back to Boston and didn't talk to me for a year.

I gripped the PPK. I hadn't held a gun in a few years, but I raised it and homed in on his tires as he pulled away. The PPK felt heavy, its trigger tight. It took a bit of finger power to pull it, but when it finally gave, the gun released a puny click.

Pop stopped the car and looked back at me with a smirk. "I knew you were gonna do that."

I tried to rack the slide to chamber a round, but I couldn't get it.

"You really are out of practice, aren't you?" After another moment, he pointed at the side of the gun. "It won't fire with the safety on, genius."

I unlocked it, and he sped off. I chased him into the street just to scare him, but he was already in third gear, heading down Sixth. I lowered the gun and reached into my pocket for my antacids. There weren't any left.

* * *

Most nights, after my probation was up, I hid in my room with a towel under the door, smoking a bud or two I'd pinched from my mother's stash. I'd been forced to transfer to community college and was still just skating by. Somehow, I found myself back in my mother's good graces. My instructors were bigots, she said. They'd heard about my troubles and were punishing me for it. I'd look at the newspaper clippings I kept from the trial, studying that boy's name, Amarpreet, and his face, round and doughy, dark around the eyes. When I couldn't look at him anymore, I'd sneak out of our Back Bay condo and ride the T around the city. Some nights, I'd ride until they kicked me off. Other nights, I'd get off in Roxbury or Mattapan and wander the pitch-black streets, hoping I'd get shot or robbed or beaten within an inch of my life. It only seemed fair.

The night everything happened, my roommates and I were making one last drug run for the night. We were trying to cop some coke from some Black guys in the projects. As soon as they saw the money, they promptly robbed us, laughing as they pointed a gun in the car. I thought it was a sign we should go home, but my roommates wanted to hit a couple more spots. Every dealer was dry so we drove around, pissed off and drunk, passing around another bottle. One of the twins, Tyler or Tucker, said they felt like beating the shit out of someone. I thought it was just talk.

We'd never gone looking for fights. We weren't even that tough, but because we had numbers, the feeling gained momentum. Pretty soon, they were assessing people we drove by, looking for someone alone. I said, "Hold on, hold on," but they told me not to be a pussy. When I saw Amarpreet, I knew they were going to pick him, even before Tucker said, "Towelhead, twelve o'clock." With a screech, we parked. They jumped out of the car like a SWAT team, stopping the boy under a streetlight. When he looked up, he actually smiled. He couldn't have been more than eighteen, a chubby kid with pointy breasts pushing at the front of a Sox jersey, a tan turban around his head.

From the back seat I thought, Okay, a couple punches, a bloody nose, fine. They'll get it out of their systems. The kid could go home to his dorm room and cry himself to sleep. But after some pushing and shoving it was clear they weren't going easy on him. Tucker knocked him down with a brutal right. Amarpreet tried to get up and run, but Tyler promptly dropped him with an identical right. Chase grabbed him by the neck and unraveled the turban from his head like a bandage. They stood him up, the boy crying now, whimpering. They pushed him against a wall. His hair cascaded over his face, black and shiny and stretching to his knees. It freaked them out enough to knock him down again and start kicking.

I didn't get out of the car. I just watched, the whole time wondering who that kid was. Someone's good son, an only child, a late arrival? Maybe his parents, older and gentler, were tirelessly devoted to him, blessed to be given a child at all. Maybe they kissed him on the cheek every morning at breakfast, a small ritual they performed all the way up to the morning he left for a far-off school. Even now, he would remember to call them before bed, knowing the time difference would make it morning back home. They'd tell him not to call, to save his money, to buy himself something special, but he still called every night. Not just for them but for him. So he would feel like nothing had changed. He wasn't a lonely boy in a foreign country. He was there, next to them, at home, like a family. Because that was how most families worked.

When Chase said, "Junie, don't you want a piece of this little fucker?" I thought of all that, jealous of that poor kid. I almost got out of the car. A part of me wanted to hurt him, but I decided to stay put. Chase punched him and then looked back at me, laughing. "You sure?"

"Yeah," I said. "I think I'm good."

* * *

It was well past one o'clock in the morning, and I hadn't heard anything from Pop. I called my mother, but the line just rang, so I wandered out to the parking lot and stood there, looking around. The rioting had quieted down for the night. Alarms were still going off, but I couldn't hear the crowds on Wilshire anymore, only an occasional whoop or shout. West Sixth was still empty, except for the Koreans who owned the convenience store across the street. Though there was no danger in sight, a younger Korean man barricaded the store by stacking metal shopping carts in front of the store's glass windows while an older man held a shotgun and patrolled the street. I watched them for a few minutes and realized they were father and son. Every now and then, the father would walk over and pat the son on the back, saying something encouraging in Korean. I looked over my shoulder, and there was Pop's billboard on the dealership's roof, his cartoon face smiling down at me. I aimed the gun at him, imagined a clean bullet hole in his head, but I couldn't pull the trigger.

I went inside the office and left the PPK on one of the desks. I rummaged through the lockbox till I found the keys for the sturdiest vehicle on the lot, a Chevy Suburban. Outside, I unlocked the gates and pulled the monster out into the street.

I left down Sixth and turned onto Wilshire, passing buildings that had once stood three stories and now were charred rubble. Outside the buildings that still raged, people stood mesmerized by each fire. One man in particular tried to quench twenty-foot flames with a garden hose. Down alleys, I saw guys rocking cars that were lying on their sides. But I couldn't tell if the guys were trying to put them back on their wheels or flip them onto their roofs. Every block was like that. Glass glittered the pavement, the specks glinting under the lights like a million tiny diamonds.

Traffic lights still worked. Abandoned cars still idled at intersections. I drove aimlessly, hoping I'd find someone to rescue, but no one needed my help. I navigated the streets, venturing deep into Compton and Watts, driving past shadowy figures gathered on porches and in yards. Occasionally, as I'd pass, a rock would hit the side of the truck, and I'd hear them yelling for me to leave. I didn't know what I was looking for. I turned down dark streets, one after another. I honked the horn to let people know I was there.

* * *

It wasn't until I went down a residential street near Slauson that I saw them: four Black guys standing in the street next to an eighties Impala. They were leaning against the car, talking as if on their lunch break. Above them, a streetlight shone down in such a way that they looked like actors on a stage. I killed the Suburban's lights and rolled to a stop a half block away. I put the truck in park across the street from them and ended up sitting there for a few minutes before they noticed me. They wore loose khakis, no shirts, and were passing around a couple forties of Olde English.

When I rolled down my window, one of them pointed me out to the others, and the tallest of the four stared at me, wary. He kept looking around and then squinting at me as if he thought I'd pull a drive-by. Finally, he walked over. An armor of muscles covered his body. His Jheri curl glimmered in the light. He came up near my window and looked at me for a minute before shouting, "What you doing?"

I didn't know, but I knew I couldn't say that. "Just driving around."

This didn't please him. "The fuck for? You crazy?" Even from five feet away, I could smell the liquor on his breath. He walked closer. "I asked you a question, white boy."

I must have smirked, because he was suddenly ready to kill me.

"I'm funny to you?" He looked back at his friends, who'd lost all interest in us.

"You called me 'white boy.'"

"Yeah, I know. That's because you're white." He checked his friends again, but they were shooting dice on the hood of the car, which upset him. His attitude seemed to be for their benefit. He yelled, "I know you ain't trying to cop some dope."

I shook my head.

"What you want, then?"

I wanted to tell him to just hit me, to beat me into a coma, but I couldn't get the words out.

He spat on the truck and then started back to his friends. That's when I got out. I closed the door as hard as I could. He turned around, fists up. I needed to make it worth his while, so I took a clumsy swing from too far away. He sidestepped it and threw a punch that hit me on the chin. I saw a flash of white and then found myself on the ground.

"That all you came here for?" He seemed honestly disappointed.

Blood trickled from my mouth.

He kicked me in the side, and now I was lying face up. "You want some more?" He looked back at his friends, but they just shook their heads as though this kind of thing happened all the time. "You're crazy." He glanced at his friends. "He's crazy. Look at him." He started to walk off, but I grabbed his ankle.

"C'mon."

He pulled his leg away and looked at me again, puzzled. He crouched down and stuck his face closer to mine. With his hot, beery breath on my skin, it felt as though we were sharing a moment. We could both see all the dumb things we'd ever done, all the dumb things we were ever going to do.

"I'm right here," I said.

He blinked and swallowed, and I realized just how young he was. He could've been my little brother. He could've been my little cousin. And in my mind, I said, You understand, don't you?

His hard look softened as he scanned my face. He seemed to hear me.

Sorry. I'm wrong to make you do this. I just need your help. I looked into his dark eyes and thought I could hear his voice now, gentler this time.

It's okay, white boy. I can help. But just this once.

I'm really not a bad guy.

Neither am I.

I just did some fucked-up shit.

Hey, I've been there. He looked at his friends and then back at me. You sure about this, though? You know it won't feel good, right?

I know.

Those boys over there will probably join in.

The more the merrier.

All right. He shrugged and took a step back. As long as you're sure.

Positive. I looked up at him. Thanks, by the way.

He chuckled. Don't thank me yet. And don't go thinking this is a fair trade for what you did.

I said I wouldn't.

Our eyes locked. Our hearts beat as one. Somehow, through it all, we even managed to smile.

Ready whenever you are.

Good. He cocked his fist. You better be.

ACKNOWLEDGMENTS

Thank you to my editor, Tracy Sherrod, and my agent, Dan Mandel, for believing in and shaping this book. To Amistad, HarperCollins, and Sanford J. Greenburger Associates. To my love, Lisa, especially. To my parents, Doris and Jerry; my brothers, Kerry, Michael, and Darren; and my nephew, Victor. To my best bro forever, Gabriel Louis. To all my other homies, readers, teachers, and mentors: Mat Johnson, Victor Lavalle, Tayari Jones, Matthew Klam, Elizabeth McCracken, Richard Bausch, Alan Cheuse (RIP), Stephen Goodwin, Susan Shreve, William Miller, Keith Clark, Barbara Pierce, Bernie Cabral, Roger Skillings (RIP), Lamar Peterson, Salvatore Scibona, Justin Tussing, Nam Le, Kate and Kevin Clark, Christy Zink, Christine Lee, Andrew Boryga, Andrew C. Gottlieb, Matt Wilemski, J. M. Holmes, Annell Lopez, and Chris Terry. To the organizations that supported me: George Mason University's MFA program in creative writing and the class of 2001; the Fine Arts Work Center in Provincetown and the fellows of 2001–2002 and 2006–2007; the Callaloo Creative Writing Workshop 2007 and its fellows; and Literary Arts. Finally, to the editors and readers at the *American Literary Review*, *Bennington Review*, *Callaloo*, *Meridian*, *Natural Bridge*, *StoryQuarterly*, and The Pushcart Prize Anthology XLV. Thank you.

CREDITS AND PERMISSIONS

"And Then We Were The Norrises," *American Literary Review*
"Cowboys," *Callaloo*
"Every Time They Call You Nigger," *Meridian*
"Give My Love to the Savages," *Bennington Review* and The
    Pushcart Prize Anthology XLV
"This Isn't Music," *Natural Bridge*
"How to Be a Dick in the Twenty-First Century," *StoryQuarterly*